HANNAH
WEAVER OF LIFE

E. Ruth Harder

Blessings, Ruth Harder

A Russian Hill Press Book
United States • United Kingdom • Australia

Russian Hill Press

The publisher is not responsible for websites (or their content) that are not owned by the publisher.

Cover and Book Designer: Coleen VanMeter

LCCN: 2015943527

ISBN: 978-0-9911937-7-8

Dedicated in memory of my dear husband Chuck Harder who encouraged me to pursue my passion for writing.

ACKNOWLEDGEMENTS

Many people made it possible for me to create and publish *Hannah ~ Weaver of Life.*

I am grateful to all family who encouraged me: my parents, who told me I could do anything I set my mind to do as long as I was willing to work hard; my wonderful children, Debby and Rod Turner, Coleen Van Meter, Chip and Christy Harder who helped keep me on course with this writing; and my four sisters, Lillian, Jean, Margaret and Linda who knew I could write and publish this book.

My dear Holy Cross Book Club friends eagerly read the story in its infancy and wanted to know when I would publish: Kathy Brooks, Mona Furnberg, Jo Johnson, Audrey Sato, and Julice Winters. Pastor John Bost. My friends Jo Alexander, Sondra McGee, and Stevie Westberg, who told me that Hannah could tell the story more clearly in first person than in third.

The California Writers Club, Tri-Valley Branch, especially the critique groups, the STEM Group, and later a novel group gave valuable insights and suggestions to improve. Hector Timourian who gave me information about Bedouin shepherd life; Pat Coyle who kept everyone on task; Karen Nuelle, Kara Wilde, and George Cramer who spent time reading and making constructive comments.

Beta readers Christina Harder and Mary Heaton helped me hone the manuscript. Line editor, Violet Moore, gave me valuable input to put the final polish on my text.

A very special thanks goes to graphic artist, Coleen VanMeter who designed the beautiful cover and worked the interior design.

I am forever grateful to Paula Chinick and Russian Hill Press for keeping me on track throughout the entire process of publishing this book.

Thanks to God for giving me the words to write. Without His guidance I could not have accomplished it.

HANNAH

WEAVER OF LIFE

CHAPTER ONE

The sun swept away the dark web of night and bestowed upon the earth a warm balm. How could it be, on what dawned as a sunshine blessed day like every other, I would experience something that would influence and shape the rest of my life? I live in a shepherd encampment with the tribe of Dan in the tent of Moshe and Lydia. They pitied and took me as their own child when they found me alone, starving and crying. More than anything else, I want to be a woman people admire and remember. People say I am a wild girl because my behavior is unlike the other young women who are meek. I am curious about everything I see from bugs to stars. They say I ask too many questions. Gathering up the hem of my tunic in my hand and running as fast as I can is my favorite thing to do.

"Hannah, my girl, I have I told you time after time you are too old to be playing with the boys and running foot races." Mother Lydia pointed to our heavy brown earthen jug, and I knew before her words were spoken she wanted me to go draw water from the well on the northwest part of Nazareth near where we camped.

"You cheated," Benjamin bar Cleodan yelled, pouting.

"I won fairly by two donkey tails," I called back to him.

"You are a simple girl and I will beat you next time." Benjamin raised a fist in the air.

"No, I will win," I said. Mother Lydia waited silently for me, and I ignored the rest of his ranting.

With the jug on my shoulder and skin bucket in my hand, I joined the other girls and women on the trail to draw water from the well. The sun near the horizon made the shadows of the people on the trail have the appearance of shepherd staffs. I laughed. I became engrossed with the sand puffs I created scuffing my feet, and I failed to watch my step and bumped into a girl. We went down in a heap of swirling garments the same creamy colors of the dust, and our jugs rolled down the incline next to the trail. Giggling noises of the other girls filled the warm air. Women were lined up at the well, chatting and calling to the children who played nearby.

"It is my fault," I said, expecting the girl with the sweetly rounded face to give me a cold stare or scream at me. Instead her doe brown eyes expressed warm concern. "I am Mary," she said. "Are you hurt?"

"No, I am not hurt at all. My name is Hannah." I brushed at the dust on my woven wool tunic. "I am sorry I ran into you. I failed to watch my steps. Oh, and are you all right? Is your jug cracked?" My words came out in a quick tumble. Being from a nomadic tribe, I knew several dialects, and I spoke to her in the local tongue.

"I have seen you on this trail before, but never up this close. You must be with the tribe of Dan who herds sheep and goats outside the village this season." Mary moved back onto the trail, wasting no time while she spoke.

"Yes, I am." I felt grateful to Mary for her kindness to me. My shepherd friends would have shoved me in turn, and teased me about being blind or dumb. Near the well I said, "Let me fill your jug for you. I want to make up for running into you."

"There is no need for atonement." Mary smiled. "I have already forgiven you. Neither one of us intended harm."

"You have kind words." I drew up the water bucket and poured from it into the two jugs. I lowered it and brought it up again quickly. My brown arms shone with water droplets as my sleeves dropped back when I handled the ropes. I dipped into the bucket with my goatskin waist bag. "Have a sip of cool water."

"Thank you," Mary said, between swallows of water. We moved away from the well because others were waiting.

As we walked, the sun beamed even warmer than usual. "Where do you live in the village?"

"Not far. It is the second lane from the grove of olives we passed before we had our fall. How far do you walk?"

"Oh, you know where the camp is outside your village? We live in goat hair tents, and Father Moshe and Mother Lydia raised me. Father Moshe has sheep and goats he shears, and milks the she-goats. My mother makes goat cheese."

"Forgive me for asking, but what happened to your true mother and father?"

"That is unknown to me, and Mother Lydia told me I have been with them from babyhood. My friends tease me, saying someone found me under a rock. Do you live with your own parents?"

"Yes, I have brothers and a sister, too. We live a short way from this trail." Mary pointed toward the lane to our right.

"So you live in a real house made of stone and wood. It must be very nice. You are safe at night from wild animals."

"It must be a pleasure to live in a tent where you can see the night sky filled with stars instead of the inside of the house."

"Pleasing, yes, if you like sand in your bed, sand in your shoes, and in your food. It is a pleasure if the smell of wool and goat dung in your nostrils brings a smile to your lips. If you are fond of living with a bunch of travelers who are coarse in language and tough in dealing with each other, or if you are satisfied to stay in one place for a season and then move on to new pastures, then it can be a pleasure. As you said, it can be a good life if you are pleased marveling at the night sky and wondering about all the stars." I stopped, almost embarrassed. "The life I describe is all I know, and it is good enough." I shrugged my left shoulder.

"I am happy we met today, but I must hurry home."

"I must go back as well. Will I see you again?"

"I always come on Friday, but earlier than today. I come almost every day, except Sabbath. Once in awhile my cousin, Abram takes my jug along with his, but soon he will not be allowed in the company of women who go for water, because he will be twelve." She waved her hand. "I will see you on Friday."

"I will be coming for water and will see you then." I waved, and I hurried across the sand.

That evening, a light came into my life with my new friend. We saw each other a few more times, and learned we were almost the same age. We stood next to each other and some of the women thought we were sisters. We even talked about trading tunics, but never did. Then the grazing season for our flocks came to an end and our shepherd tribe had to move.

The next year we were encamped outside of Nazareth when the grass grew green on the hillsides. A beautiful day dawned the first Friday we were back. Mother Lydia could save her words, because I eagerly expected to go draw water and see my friend Mary again.

At first I wondered if I had come too early. My eyes searched among the women. Suddenly from behind me I heard, "Hannah, wait for me."

We quickly set down our jugs and kissed cheeks. Her smile beamed as bright as a lovely rose flower. Had I been away for a few days instead of seasons? We were friends forever.

Up ahead, a tall man walked beside a donkey laden with bundles of wood. He crossed the trail on which we walked. Although Mary wore a light veil, she quickly covered her face with her shawl, but kept her eyes visible. I covered my face because we both were supposed to cover our heads in the presence of men. I hated wearing the thick covering Mother Lydia had provided for me. I seldom used it. After the man left from our sight, I tore the black cloth from my face and put it back inside my waist pack. "Why did you cover up so hastily? Does he steal beautiful young women?"

"No, he is an honorable man." Mary laughed. "My father has made arrangements for Joseph, the carpenter, to become my husband." She removed the shawl wrap from her blushing face. "It is disgraceful for my betrothed to see my face before we are married."

"Good blessings for you." I felt surprised. "He appears as one who is old, at least thirty."

"I suppose so, but he has a house, and is a well-known and respected carpenter. Are you betrothed?"

"No. Maybe I will be given to a king to become one of his courtesans. Maybe I will find an agreeable old shepherd who wants a wife."

"You will find a husband yourself?" Mary's frowning face expressed disbelief. "I believe the responsibility belongs to your father?"

"If you remember, he is my father who cared for a forgotten baby." I thought about the way my clan treated me. I wanted for no necessities of life, but at times the women shunned me because of my uncertain birth mother. They whispered that I was a gypsy child.

"Oh, sorry," Mary flustered. "I thought your Father Moshe would…"

"Well, he has not. I cannot simply go and remind him of how old I have become. I have tried to talk with Mother, but she is too busy. When I started my, you know, the way it is with women thing, she told me how to keep myself clean and brought me to the tent of uncleanness for women. It is where we are to go when we have our issue of blood. She would allow no mention of it. Unclean? I am very upset with it all." I felt self-conscious. "Let us stop speaking of this."

"Yes, you and I must not talk about it." Mary sat beside her jug, patting the sand next to her in the scant shade of an olive tree. She smiled. "We can talk about whatever else you want. I think it would be good to see each other more often."

"Me too." I sat next to her.

"I wonder how it would be to have a baby. I have heard my sister cry out in pain when she gave birth." Her voice dropped to a confidential whisper.

"Mother goats bleat awfully when they bear their young. Serena, our healer, told me the first child is the worst, and then it gets easier. I think I shall never want to bear children. The blood issue is bad enough." I relaxed and kicked my legs out wide in the warm sand. My tunic flapped up to my knees. I shook my dark black hair and tried to imagine how it would be for others to see it cascading freely on my shoulders. "I suppose we must rise and go fetch our water."

Mary smiled. "Can we be best friends?"

"I think we already are." I stood and offered her my hand.

"I have a secret." Mary got to her feet. "I have been learning from the *Torah*."

"No, girls are not taught lessons. Who teaches you? I learn weaving, spinning, and milking." I lifted my jug to my left shoulder. "And Mother Lydia has let me spend time with Serena, the healer. Serena puts this pungent smelling mint leaf oil in a cloth and people sniff it when their heads are stuffed."

"That is very interesting. It is important to take care of the body as well as the soul, I suppose." Mary's jug rested on her left shoulder and she steadied it with her right hand.

"Serena also wraps bodies in spices for burial."

"Oh, will you learn burial practices?" Mary frowned.

"No. Dead bodies have a foul odor, and fear of it makes my arms prickle."

"Maybe, but it surely must be done by someone."

"Truly, but I want to learn more about healing. Serena has dried herbs and spices lined up in wrappings along with flasks of olive oil in her tent. Leaves of plants, tied with leather thongs, are hung to dry. It smells very strongly. She stays with women when they give birth. Do you think it would be awful, I mean to watch the pain, the blood and all?"

"Childbirth might be painful, but to have a baby would be wonderful. Joseph and I will have children."

"When you have your firstborn, I will take care of you during and after the birth." Enthralled to have Mary as my best friend, I thought we would be close forever.

"You would?" Mary had a faraway look in her eyes.

"Oh, who is teaching you the Torah?" She had boasted earlier and I wanted to know.

"My cousin Abram. We have always been play friends, but he is a few years younger. He recites for me what he has memorized. Maybe I am not truly learning it all. He does it to help himself study, I think. I also like to go to the place of prayer in the corner of our upper room on our roof. I am fascinated by the prophecies Abram is learning."

"We ought to go draw our water."

"You are right." Mary smiled. "The sun is going toward the hills."

We walked in silence until we got to the well and filled our jugs. We met more days and talked companionably. I had never before had such a good friend. Time went by quickly and the few remaining grass blades turned a golden brown.

One day when our jugs were full, and we were going back home, I said, "Well, here is where I turn off. The others have gone ahead and I will be scolded for being late." The outline of a few women and the silhouette of goat hair tents appeared as a fuzzy mirage in the distance.

"Oh, you always have a long way to go. See where the trail curves up ahead? You have watched me on other days so you already know I go to my right past there. Then I am on the lane where I live."

"I will see you next time." Talking the way we had on these walks we had taken together, I thought I knew almost as much about Mary as I did those in my community. We kissed cheeks, and I walked a short way, turned and waved to her. She neared her lane, and watched me as she waved. I neared the encampment and saw everyone busy working and packing rugs, tents, and food onto the donkeys and onto their own backs. Male goats, the size of young donkeys, were being pressed into service to carry light loads. The camp prepared to move on to greener pastures for the flocks and herds. The regretful thought that I might never see my friend again put wild ideas in my head. I wanted to rush back to the village and tell her I would be unable to see her the next day. Mother Lydia had already spotted me coming down the trail.

"Come on, hurry, my girl. You were gone longer than usual. Did you have trouble?"

"No, I am fine." I patted the jug and I set it down beside another. "When are we leaving?"

"Moshe says a storm is on its way and the grass is

almost gone. We must leave at dawn. Come, my girl, roll up these rugs for me." An array of woven mats appeared to be a dusty fallen rainbow in the sand.

Dejected, I thought I might never see Mary again, but I knew better than to ask to stay in Nazareth. I rolled the rugs to pack for travel, folded my loom and secured the yarn. Mother Lydia poured most of the water into goatskin bags, and then strapped the water jugs on one side of a donkey and the olive oil jugs to the other to even out the load. Our family donkey and others would be leaving soon with a group of men who would set up the next camp ahead of us.

People were excited about moving on, and men sang while they worked. A general din of noise floated around. Mothers called to children and men yelled good-naturedly back and forth as they organized the group. Sheep and goats bleated on the hillside, and their shuffling feet created a dust ball against the fading sunset. Men were already moving them ahead of the shepherd caravan. All the familiar sounds produced a chorus of comfort, yet disappointment brought unrest to my spirit.

Life was terribly unfair. No longer too busy to think, I lay down on my sleeping mat and gazed at the blue-black skies, and listened to the regular snoring sounds of Mother Lydia. Stars were beginning to twinkle brightly in the heavens, and I wished I could touch them. I wondered how I could love Yahweh with all my heart as Father Moshe taught me. Where did God dwell? He might be one of those bright stars, or the moon? I suppose

Yahweh always watched people, as Father Moshe told me. Would the foretold Messiah come soon? Sleep deserted me, because I disliked leaving without telling my friend. Would she worry? Moonlight streamed a path before me. Mary had given general directions to the lane on which she lived. I breathed a prayer. "Yahweh, please let me see Mary again." I rose from my straw mat, determined to go. I usually slept between my parents, but Father Moshe had left to travel with the sheep and goats. Mother Lydia snored in slumber. I crept outside, afraid of what I might come upon alone in the dark.

Only burly Ham the watchman sat beside his tent.

CHAPTER TWO

Ham saw me. "Hannah, I have been watching your wanton ways. You are a wild and pretty girl. Do you come to me now?"

"No, no, I am going to...to." My skin prickled as if in a thorny patch of weeds. I cowered, and felt ashamed. I pointed toward the place we went to relieve ourselves.

"Oh, come, come. Everyone is asleep. We can have pleasure together. I will show you how to please me." He beckoned with his hand, yet his form stayed as a boulder in the shadow of his tent.

I froze at first. My knees wanted to collapse, spilling me into the dirt, but I started walking as fast as I could in silence. I did not look back, hoping he meant to tease me. Ham, a strong man with a thick bushy beard and hair, had a wife and two sons. Being a butcher, he bled animal flesh to make it suitable to eat. If he wanted to frighten me, he certainly had. For the first time in my life I felt a sickening terror. Even in the darkness, I could sense his leering eyes on me. I tried to hold my breath until I reached the outskirts of our camp. My stomach did flips and my heart pounded furiously. I worried what would happen when I came back later.

Afraid, I ran fast even though I heard no footsteps. My robe flapped around my legs and my toes kicked up tiny dirt devils. Finally, I bade my terrified eyes to look back, and saw the dark night, with highlighted tufts of dry grass. The moon showed half of a face, and guided me on my path as I found the trail, I breathed a sigh of relief as I turned down the lane where Mary had told me she lived.

The sand-colored houses before me were all dark, and I wondered if I had been foolish to come here. For a moment I envied the cozy families who lived on the road where the modest homes were built neatly around a common courtyard. These people were surely all in bed. I walked with silent mouse steps trying to imagine which house would belong to her family. My bare feet skimmed over the path that was smooth and clean from its nightly sweeping. I wished I had asked Mary for more directions. A short time ago I had been on the trail with my dear friend. Still weak-kneed from the encounter with Ham, I sank down to the ground to think. A figure moved in the shadows of nearby bushes. My arms prickled. Perhaps a thief lurked. Well, I had nothing for him to steal. In my haste to leave I had not even brought a tallow candle.

"Psst," the shadowy form, no taller than me, whispered hoarsely. "Mary?"

"No, I am Hannah." I hoped it was a neighbor who knew her. "But I hope to see Mary."

"In the dark it is hard to tell." The shadow came closer and I saw a young boy. "You know Mary?"

"She is my friend, and she told me her home is on this street. I want to talk with her tonight. Who are you?" My knees shook when I stood.

"I am her cousin Abram, that is, if we speak of the same Mary, the only one by that name who lives on this street." His long dark hair dangled loosely across his shoulders in the customary way for a Nazarene. "How did you meet Mary?" He demanded. "What do you want with her?"

"I am pleased to meet you, Abram-her-cousin. You sure ask a lot of questions. I ran into her when we were both on the trail to draw water." I giggled. "I mean, I did run into her the first time we met. Now I have to leave, because our whole camp is moving again. Can you please tell me which house is Mary's?"

"The one over there with the white doorposts is it." He pointed to a simple limestone and clay home similar to those around it.

"And does she often meet you at night?" Could he be the cousin who recited his lessons for her?

"Not for a time, but we once did meet often." His voice became sad. "We were play friends until Pia, my nursemaid, said I could no longer be her playmate because she has been promised to Joseph. We used to gaze at the stars together."

"And when you saw me sitting here you thought ..."

"I hoped to see her."

"Can we catch her attention without disturbing the whole household? You know, did you have a private signal when you were children?"

Abram gave a low whistle that sounded like a night bird. He repeated it three times. The evening remained quiet, as we hearkened our ears for a word from her in the dimly moonlit darkness. I held my breath. I feared being caught and sent away by her father before I had a chance to tell her I would leave in the morning. My heart beat so loudly if anyone were near they would think they heard a drummer. Again, Abram whistled the night bird sounds three times.

"She is ignoring me, or maybe she is already asleep," he whispered. No sooner had he spoken than a figure appeared at an open window well off the ground. Abram went and stood beneath it and let her climb onto his shoulders. First a thud barely echoed as he helped her, and then footsteps neared.

"Mary," I whispered, so happy I had found her.

They walked toward me in the shadows of the house and the low bushes until the three of us stood in a circle. We looked at each other nervously at first, and then started to giggle.

"I heard the night bird and I did not know whether to come out or ignore you." Mary stepped back, laughed, and cuffed Abram on the arm. "We played in the dark long ago, cousin."

"Play as you wish." I was jealous of their close friendship.

"I am so sorry. Abram, have you met my dear friend Hannah?"

"We are old friends," Abram said. "I have known her for about five minutes."

"I have known her much longer. We met more than two seasons ago." Mary laughed. "I am delighted to see you, but whatever brought you here at this hour?"

"I am leaving with everyone at dawn and I wanted to tell you." I controlled my voice despite the sob that threatened to swallow my words.

"Oh, I wish it were not so." Mary grasped my hand firmly. "Do you know which direction you will travel?"

"I forgot to ask. I think we will follow the river Jordan until we find the next green pasture." An awkward silence prevailed until Abram spoke.

"Well, let us all go and lie on our backs and find shapes in the stars the way we did when we were children."

We linked arms and walked on the trail behind the houses until we stopped at a patch of dry barley. I felt an instant acceptance and a bond like none I had ever felt before.

"I am very happy you came, Hannah. It is a beautifully clear night and we can see a heaven full of stars," Mary said.

As we walked, I realized the village was smaller than

I had first thought. Houses were built on the side of a Galilean hill. I had heard Moshe say its residents grew gardens, fig trees, and date palms. Wheat and barley fields filled the valley. We three went toward the nearby valley where my people had been encamped this season. Abram sprawled out on his back and folded his hands behind his head. It took awhile for Mary and me to find a comfortable spot. We smoothed out our cloaks and lay on top of them to soften the scratchiness of the dry grass stubble.

"This is a good place, at least I like it," Abram said.

"I suppose it will do," Mary said.

Abram pointed. "See, to the west is Mount Carmel, and to the east and south Tabor and Gilboa loom in the distance. I hope one day I will travel far."

"I have traveled more places than I care to tell," I sighed.

"When I am grown I will travel," he said. "Right now I go far enough to take our milk goats out to graze, and no farther."

"Do you hate the thought of being grown up?" I asked.

"Sometimes," said Abram, "Problem is…" He paused for a long time, and then said, "Mary already is grown up."

"I am not." Mary frowned.

"You are betrothed," Abram argued.

"It is customary for a girl my age to be promised to a man. I had nothing to do with it, except my parents did ask for my opinion."

"So you like Joseph." Abram grinned while he teased her.

"He is a fine man." Mary's chin jutted out as she spoke. "His father is from the lineage of King David."

"He has a royal lineage. I am from a few people which broke away from the seafaring tribe of Dan and became nomads."

"Mary and I are from the tribe of Judah," Abram boasted.

"Mary is very blessed to have Joseph. I have no one. Tonight when I came here the watchman wanted to…" I stopped speaking, because fear constricted my throat as I thought about the dreadful Ham. "…wanted me to go back home, as girls are forbidden to be out alone at night, but I pretended to make a necessary walk before bedtime."

"Do be careful, Hannah." Mary sounded motherly. "You could be in danger walking alone at night. You have no staff in your hand to fend off wild beasts."

Abram grabbed a round stone and pitched it. "Shepherds have a long history among our people. King David was a shepherd and wrote psalms about them. The one I have in my head is one in which David speaks of the Lord as his shepherd, which means he views himself as a lamb in want of protection. I will try to remember all the words for you."

"Please do." I wanted to learn from him.

Abram chanted, "The Lord is my shepherd, I shall not want. He makes me to lie down in green pastures. He leads me beside still waters. He restores my soul. He leads me in the paths of righteousness for the sake of

His name. Even when I walk through the valley of the shadow of death I will fear no evil."

"Did you finish it? I think last time you recited it you ended with being in the temple of the Lord for all your days." Mary tossed a piece of dry grass stubble at him, but it fell short.

"Mary, I am tired of reciting lessons. I want only to lie here and be still."

"I suppose a person could think of themselves as wanting the protection of the Lord, yet I think a king would take care of himself. I am one who cares for sheep, which proves I am brave."

"Yes you are." Abram tossed a dry grass blade at me.

"I am glad we came here, and tonight we are children." I threw it back and laughed.

"Look, a dipper," Abram said. "Is that a good sign?"

"It may be. Oh, I see it. I see a lion, I think. No, maybe it is something else." I pointed to the heavens.

"It is a lamb. But, we are not supposed to find omens in stars. It is a pastime of the heathens." Mary propped herself up on one elbow to shake her finger at him.

"Tonight we three are heathens." Abram laughed. "My lessons have created such weariness in my brain it can hold no more. Soon I will be twelve. I will then have more important things to do and will go often to the temple in Jerusalem. We have no proper synagogue in Nazareth. Father and I must travel to Sephora to attend."

"You already do go to Jerusalem along with all of us for *Passover* and for the *Festival of Booths.*"

Mary settled flat on her back. "See the star racing across the heavens."

"Yes, I saw it. At times, signs in the heavens give men knowledge of things that will occur," Abram said. "When Moses led the people across the desert, they used the stars to help guide the way. A flame and a cloud stayed with them, too."

"Our old men may use the stars to travel by night when they seek a new grazing area, or to know the seasons. They have come about this wisdom in ways I have never learned. I would like to gain knowledge about such things. Do you ever want to learn about it?"

"Yes, I would. Wise men know about signs in the sky. I think it would be wonderful to gain information from stars, weather, and seasons. There must be reasons for everything, do you think?" Abram raised his hand up. "Ah, a storm is coming," he intoned, deepening his voice.

"Wise old Abram," Mary teased.

"Not truly wise. I have to age quite a lot to be like Rabbi Eli in Sephora, or my father. I hate to think of things seriously. I see amusing things and I laugh. When I do, I endure a smart whack across my shoulders. If I even hint at smiling while I am repeating my lessons, they berate me. I have never seen them enjoy themselves. Playing *Mancala* is even serious business. Do I have to stop playing when I am twelve?"

"Um-huh." I was very drowsy and safe next to these friends. I saw clouds gathering on the horizon, hiding a few of the stars.

"We must not tarry," Mary roused us. "It is time we were all home in bed, or our parents will find out we are gone and worry."

"I am sad," I said.

"I feel sad, too. I have an older cousin named Elizabeth who has no children, but it is a full day's walk to go see her. I had hoped, dear Hannah, you would stay here, be my best friend, and come with me to visit her."

"Maybe someday." My eyes became moist. We held both hands, and lightly kissed wet cheeks. She stepped back.

Abram cleared his throat. "God be with you." He touched my shoulder, quickly kissed both cheeks and turned away. I stood and watched as they walked slowly toward Nazareth. Mary turned and waved one last time. I waved back. I was alone.

I strolled to our tent in the cool stillness of the impending storm where not even birds chirped. I looked back once. Mary and Abram became two dots in the dim moonlight and disappeared. Nobody stirred about in camp, including Ham who snored at his post. Mother Lydia slept. I heard the first drops of rain. Sleep deserted me, and I pondered many things as I often do late at night. Today I had experienced my greatest fear when Ham threatened me. I found a deeper sense of purpose and faith because of my friendship with Mary.

"Oh, You whose name I cannot say, please give me, no, I mean show me..." I paused, at a loss for words to express my thoughts. I knew a long day lay ahead of me in the morning, and I had failed to ask what direction we would be going. I prayed for faith. Mary, would I ever see Mary again?

More thoughts were in my mind while I lay on my soft mat to sleep. I had been learning to weave on a simple lap loom, and Serena had given me the Egyptian cotton yarn to make a swaddling cloth. Her kindness to me gave me feelings of worth. Other women whispered bad things about me, but Serena never spoke ill of me. I decided to speak directly with her about learning to be a midwife.

I hoped Father Moshe would agree to let me study with Serena. Maybe I could convince them it would help to tame what people called my wild ways. I was jealous of Mary who would wed a nice man in about a year. Father Moshe had not ever mentioned a betrothal for me. I decided I would become a healer, a weaver too, and never marry.

To my mind, my future plans were all made that night. After stirring my thoughts awhile, I slept peacefully, and spoke with Serena the next day when we all traveled together. Father Moshe agreed to allow me to learn healing.

Once we set up our encampment by the new grazing area, I tried to be the obedient daughter Mother Lydia desired. I set up my loom outside the tent near her. She smiled encouragement and helped me. "My girl, you must take care how you set the *warp*, and be mindful of the *weft* or the weaving will be too loose." Sitting at my loom to create mats soon became the one chore I loved the most, and I resolved to learn to make fine cloth.

One day revolved into the next while we wandered about Galilee, and grazed our flocks. In truth, each encampment had a similar appearance as every other one.

Existence is somewhat like a weaving. I set the warp end to end. That is like the foundation Mother Lydia and Father Moshe give me with their love and guidance. Then the weft is how I spend each day creating the fabric of my life. Life is good. But, of course, one can never rely on things to remain the same.

CHAPTER THREE

Mother Lydia called me. "Hannah, come."

I left my weaving loom where I hopelessly tangled gray woolen threads again, as I attempted to set the warp perfectly on the pegs, and wondered if I would ever master the art. Was I in trouble for being bad, or had I wronged them in any way? Naturally, although I had done no wrong, I braced myself for a lecture. When I sat down in the sunshine on the straw mat beside Mother Lydia and Father Moshe, and saw the knowing smile on her face and the stern expression on his face, I knew they were about to say something important. The air felt all too stifling and still.

"We have come from Naliah's and Cleodan's tent." Father Moshe did not look at me. Mother smiled expectantly.

"My girl, we have such good news. We have…"

"We have made arrangements for your betrothal." Father Moshe spoke quickly, with calm authority. "We have the necessary promise of sheep and goats for you."

"Who?" They had one eligible son. "Judah bar Cleodan?" My neck suddenly dampened with perspiration.

"Yes, he is to be your husband." Mother Lydia smiled at me.

"Oh." How should I respond? Judah was the skinniest young man in the entire clan. He kept to himself a lot. Besides, he had a crooked nose. I wanted to protest, but how could I without being disrespectful?

"But he is shy." I politely avoided pointing out his ugliness.

"We think it will be a good match, my girl." Mother Lydia patted my arm.

I watched the footraces of the young boys and longed for the bygone days when I had been part of the game. I still wanted to be young and play.

Seeing my lack of enthusiasm, Mother Lydia said, "Listen, my girl, sometimes we must seek out the best in people. It is like receiving a gift wrapped in coarse goat hair. When you open it up a fine jewel may be revealed. That is how I see Judah bar Cleodan."

Expecting Judah ever to be a precious gemstone was less than a mirage to me. I kept quiet, but wanted to lash out with the truth of what they had done. Nobody wanted one such as me, perhaps a gypsy spawn born to a wanton woman, and adopted out of kindness. Unattractive, weak, and dull, no one wanted Judah either, and they chose to put two misfits together. I nodded, and wondered how this could have happened to me. I wanted to be a healer. I wanted to see Mary again and be with her if she ever had a baby. Alas, I had no say in the matter. Frustration and anger dulled my senses and I became disinterested in going back to my weaving.

The tribe of Dan soon moved on to other pastures in the land of Judea. In those days I whiled away my time shuttle poised in my hand, thinking about the past and worrying about my future marriage.

Judah had been a sickly child. Grown up now, his appearance still lacked the robust look of a man. I had never in my wildest dreams imagined myself to be his wife. Our betrothal period lasted a half-year. Most betrothals were a year, but Father Moshe and Cleodan wanted to have the ceremony as soon as we settled at new grazing. I faced my wedding as a stranger to it, pretending it all happened to another person. Our wedding would surely take place despite my misgivings. While not one to ordinarily be docile, I let myself be carried along with everyone's excitement about the upcoming event.

Our marriage ceremony was to take place in the desert. I gazed with wonderment at the garments I borrowed from Serena. She brought me the most beautiful elaborate robe that had more colors than any I had ever seen. My veil of seven gauze layers completely covered my head and swept down below my waist. The creamy light embroidered linen tunic, the kind one finds among the finery of those who travel the trade routes, looked too rich for me.

"I cannot accept these beautiful garments." I looked with dismay at Serena who was enjoying dressing me for my wedding. I feared what others would think.

"I traded my healing services to a peddler who had injured his legs. He gave me this lovely colored robe. The veiling and tunic came from another, and I truly want to see you wearing them." Serena showed me how to braid my hair, and on my wedding day she fashioned it into an attractive crown.

Father Moshe accepted the gifts of two lambs and two milk goats and six flasks of olive oil from Cleodan. The guests walked in a processional line until they came to the tent. Judah's father had given him a new goatskin tent. Fresh straw mats with red and gray woven cloths to cover them were placed in the center. Young couples do not usually have their own tent. Naliah had insisted on a separate one for us, pleading they were already crowded, and she did not want to erect an addition. My future mother-in-law had never been friendly towards me, and I suspected that had influenced the decision.

As my first duty in the ritual I walked around Judah three times to ward off demons, because these evil desert spirits cannot penetrate a circle. Next, our families and friends made a great circle around us, shouting whistling to further discourage evil beings and thus protect us. A natural colored cloth canopy was set before us. A warm gentle breeze rippled its decorative streamers of white and red Egyptian cotton. With the father of Levi, our friend, presiding beneath it we made vows before Yahweh to be faithful to each other, and concluded with quaffs of wine we shared from the ceremonial cup. I went through the motions, participating as required. Judah stomped on and smashed a ceremonial wine cup. By doing so, all remaining desert devils would be scared away by the noise.

"I think Hannah is too quiet today, but maybe it means she has finally decided to settle down and become a woman."

"She will do well. Give her time," Serena said.

"She is lovely," I heard a woman say.

"Thank you." Very discomfited to be the center of attention, I hardly noticed what Judah wore or his appearance, and heard no comments about him.

"Poor Judah bar Cleodan will have his hands full with her." Ham laughed.

People talked, but I let their words disappear in the wind. Judah smiled his crooked smile when he looked at me. I bowed my head and walked among our friends and family pretending the most normal event in the world occurred. In spite of the festive atmosphere, I kept myself unyielding inside as a cold stone.

I would have much rather been racing across the sand, but I could not run anywhere. I did wish Mary would have known about our marriage and would have been among the guests.

Once inside our tent, Judah and I drank more wine and

stretched out on a soft straw mat. We peered tentatively at each other wondering how to proceed with consummating our marriage. We both were very young and inexperienced in the mating of men and women. Reclining on his back on the mat beside me, with his head resting on his hands, Judah cleared his throat, yet remained silent. He did not attempt to touch me. Amused at how big his bare feet were, I giggled.

The din of noise from our guests stifled me. People ate and drank near our tent. "I think our wedding was simply an excuse for these people to get drunk. They will be reluctant to leave the outside of this tent until they see the proof we are truly coupled."

Judah sat up, nodded, took a bone knife from his goatskin sheaf and pricked his finger with the point, and shrieked. Startled, I yelped with him when he cut himself as though I, too, were hurt, and then I giggled nervously. He squeezed blood from his finger onto the marriage cloth, an old trick I had heard about from gossiping women. Even though people were being very noisy, they heard the sounds we made. The men made rude comments, whistled, and stomped outside.

"You stained the cloth as proof of my virginity?" What he had done had surprised me, but now the tension left my shoulders.

"Um…for your father."

He waved the cloth through the tent flap, and gave it a toss. Judah blushed when men gave him advice, and made crude gestures to try to tell him what to do. They pushed on the tent walls until I feared they would come inside.

"I still am a virgin," I whispered. To thank him, I ceremoniously kissed both his cheeks. He blushed. Music began immediately and people started singing and dancing. They left us alone. We were not expected to participate until the next day. Bread, wine, dates, figs, fine herbs and goat cheese had been laid out on a cloth in the corner of our tent for us to eat. More relaxed now, I felt ravenous and picked up a handful of dates. I had no knowledge about what to expect when we were alone. Judah's first act of kindness had endeared him to me. We were in a conspiracy together. We were both hungry and ate heartily, but we had no conversation with each other. I finally said, "Judah, what do you think about this yoke they put around your neck called Hannah?"

"Um, well, good enough," he said after a long thoughtful pause.

"Would you have liked to marry a better woman? You know how I am. A short time ago I won foot races against your younger brother Benjamin."

"Um, well, Benjamin does not run very fast."

"Let us talk and learn about each other. I will go first and then you."

"Um, well, all right." He settled back.

"My thoughts often give birth to great ideas. Once I asked my mother to give me the task of dying the spun thread we used for weaving. I mixed colors in the vat, blue with yellow, and had come up with a beautiful green like the grasses in spring. Do you remember?" He nodded to me and I continued. "People ridiculed the color and said the sheep would be chewing on these garments if we wore them. I told them the sheep had never been known to chew on the hay colored robes we all wear." I had hoped to amuse him, but he had a bland expression on his face. "I have ambitions. I want to become a healer and the best weaver one can imagine. I want to be a midwife, perhaps at the birth of a king and become famous. It would be wonderful to wear fine linens instead of rough clothing." Now he stared overhead rather than look at me. I felt frustrated, and tried to make the best of our situation. "It is your turn now."

"Um, I like to herd our sheep. It is quiet in the meadow." He glanced at me with those dark brown eyes, but had nothing more to say. Silence spoke rolls of scrolls.

"Fine. It is as you wish." I turned away from him.

Judah laid back and closed his eyes. I thought I would have a long empty life ahead as I watched his silent behavior and I wondered how I would endure it. I asked myself if this was all I could expect of our marriage.

Five moons had waxed and waned from the time we were wed. Judah stayed away tending our flock much of the time. I busied myself with cooking, spinning, and weaving.

My mother-in-law, Naliah, and Mother Lydia both

kept staring at me one day while I wove a swaddling cloth. Finally Mother Lydia said, "My girl, are you with child?"

"If I am with child, you both will know even before I know it myself." I felt exasperated. "The cloth is for another."

"I did not think I saw a change in Hannah." Naliah ignored my presence when she spoke.

But things had changed. Now I must have a womanly demeanor and keep my face covering in place around men. I could no longer hoist up my tunic and run joyfully across the desert sand or play games with children. It would be scandalous to walk out to the men in the pastures and joke with them the way I had before. It was forbidden to belly dance the way I, and a few of the young girls, used to do after watching a gypsy tribe perform. Solemnness prevailed as I went through the daily routine of being a wife, caring for my husband and our tent. I often thought of the last evening I spent on the outskirts of Nazareth. It had been at least a year ago, the last night I behaved as a carefree child. I wondered if Mary had married Joseph. Had Mary's cousin Abram had his *bar mitzvah*? I remembered his fears about being grown up and having no more time to play. I could certainly understand. I would be daydreaming with my shuttle poised in the air and suddenly hear the raspy sound of my mother-in-law's voice, "Idle hands are the devil's tools." And I would resume weaving weft threads, pushing the bone shuttle in and out of the warp threads. I wanted it to be perfect.

Eventually weaving gave me hours of pleasure. I

made sitting mats from wool. The warp and the weft, the art of keeping the work neither too tight nor too loose, had finally become set in my mind and the task became easy. Mother Lydia and Serena both admired my artful shawls and gave me flaxen threads and Egyptian cotton for weaving cloth for garments.

My lessons with Serena were my balm in the whole ordeal of trying to be a good wife and daughter-in-law. At first Judah's Mother had objected, saying I would no longer have time for such idle pursuits, and besides, to her way of thought, healing arts ought to be a man's work. But one day an accident happened which changed her opinion of my usefulness.

Benjamin, the coddled younger brother of Judah had taken a walk out beyond the encampment to a dry pasture where he sought after an adventure among the rocks and caves. He came back to camp crying and bloodied with skinned knees, abrasions on his hands, and a nasty bump on his head. Naliah had taken to her bed with a headache earlier and stood back wringing her hands while I applied ointments and soothing cloths to the boy's wounds. I took over and cleaned and dressed his scratched arms and knees, saying, "You hold still now."

"Stop! That stings," he cried, but he let me take care of him. None of his scrapes became festering sores.

Afterwards, my mother-in-law decided my skills might be helpful to the family, and agreed to let me continue my studies. Serena welcomed my assistance and my ability to understand her healing methods. She taught me valuable skills in dressing wounds, treating coughs and runny noses, and recently, as an assistant midwife. I felt proud, and held my head a bit higher. I loved the challenge of bringing relief or healing to those in pain, and also reveled in the appreciation, respect, and popularity I gained with the people in camp. Besides, I had more freedom being an assistant healer than most women in camp would ever have in a role of simply wife, daughter, and mother.

Even though I was needed and satisfied learning to be a healer, I had a restless urge to become truly important. Perhaps I had been like a "nobody" because I did not know who had birthed me, or from whence I had come. I had this burning in my being to be a person that people would bring to mind and speak of forever. I wanted to be with Mary at the birth of her firstborn, but I had no idea if I would ever see her again.

I sat alone combing my hair in the warm evening twilight when Ham sauntered past my tent. His eyes consumed me as though I were a honey cake he wanted to eat. Again, I felt the awful fear I had on the night he had frightened me when I had gone back to Nazareth to see Mary. I looked away, hoping he would leave. Father Moshe and Cleopas walked near, talking animatedly. I breathed a sigh of relief when Cleopas called to him, "Ham, did you find your missing lamb?"

"Yes." He turned away, joining them.

Was I foolish to fear this man?

CHAPTER FOUR

ne last bath in the nearby stream tempted me. Along with the other women, I had washed our garments before we left to go to greener pastures. The other women had already packed up dry clothing from the banks and returned home for the day. The water felt delightfully cool and I lingered, enjoying the refreshing tingle on my body. Suddenly aware of a man standing nearby, I hastily grabbed my shawl to cover up. When he chuckled nasally I realized it was Ham. His wife, ill and with a fever for several days, had grown weak. I could tell by his stance he had not come to ask me to help with his wife. Had it been a chance encounter, or had he planned to find me alone? He walked toward me and I looked around anxiously to see if anyone else stayed near. In a panic I wanted to run or scream. Instead, I stood rooted to the bank, and my legs were to me as unbending wooden sticks that would not move.

"What a surprise to find you here. It is almost dark and you should be at home minding your tent," Ham scolded.

"I must go. Please leave so I can dress." Despite my shakiness, I tried to speak firmly as I would to a wild animal threatening one of our lambs.

"How long will you avoid me? That man of yours has failed to put a child in your belly. You are as flat as a virgin." Old wine caused his breath and sweat to reek.

"My flatness is not your concern." Backing away, I pulled my shawl tighter around me and gathered up my dry clothing. I forced my shivering legs to move.

"I could give you a child. It would be our secret." He stepped forward.

"No, if anyone saw us I would surely be stoned." I continued to back away. Fear threatened to paralyze me when he kept coming toward me. "Think about Anna, your wife."

"I have no wife," Ham rasped. "And you have no husband. He has grown no beard, and cannot give you pleasure."

"Do not talk badly about my husband." His words stung in my ears. Embarrassed by my barrenness, I thought we were young and could wait. It would be burdensome to have a baby nursing at my breast at all hours of the day and night. Why did I stupidly think about it now?

He silently continued to stare at me with heavy bloodshot eyes and sauntered forward.

"I want you to leave me." I backed away. "Everyone is moving about the camp readying for the journey. I think…" I tried to make my voice sound normal.

"You will think. Think about this!" Ham lunged and grabbed me roughly about the waist, squeezing my buttocks and lifting my body off the ground. Clothing scattered. He bent over me, pressing me against him, and planted his lips firmly on mine, forcing his tongue into my mouth. His long rough beard scratched my face.

I almost vomited from the stench of him. My shawl slipped down, revealed my breasts, and caused embarrassed thrumming there. His teeth bit my tongue. I wanted to scream, but could not. If a person saw us they would think…what would they think? Would they say I was to blame? I feared what he might do, because his strength overpowered me. I bit his lip with all my might and lifted my knee sharply between his legs. He cursed, dropping his hold on me to clutch his privates, and landed on his knees. Using all the strength I could, I got out from under him. I quickly picked up my clothing, stumbled, put on my tunic, and then retrieved my dry washed clothes. I left him doubled over in pain on the mossy bank and hurried back to camp without looking back. I bade my legs to run fast until well away from him, and then I walked fast.

Weak and trembling, I felt safer as I dropped the dry clothing on the rug on the floor of our own tent. I sank down and sobbed. Feeling terribly confused, my body burned inside and out. What happened to me? A wild thumping threatened to beat outside of my chest. What demon had caused this flaming reaction to the abhorrent advances of a rough man? While I wanted the comfort of Judah's protection, I felt thankful he had gone ahead with the flocks. From now on I vowed to be very careful to stay close to others when we went out to wash clothes.

As I lay down on my mat for the night, I heard Serena call outside my tent, "Hannah, come, I need your help."

I put on my clothing and shawl and came out into the cool, clear air.

"It is Anna. We must keep sponging her to keep down the fever. I have grown extremely tired. You will help?"

"Yes." I hesitated. "Is Ham with her?" Flaming pepper rose in my throat, and my palms were clammy.

"I am sorry if I startled you. No, Ham left in haste to join his sons and the other men with the flocks. I think he cannot bear to see her suffer so. I will be back before dawn, but until then I must have rest."

"Of course, I will help." I had a pretty good idea why Ham had left quickly. I felt fearful when I entered the tent of Ham and Anna and began my vigil. Anna lay on her bed of straw, soaked in her own perspiration. She appeared as a tiny figure, lost beneath rough woolen coverings. Her black hair matted about her face, and her eyes were closed and swollen. Recently she had given birth to a daughter who never took a breath, and had been wrinkled and ashen when she came from the womb. They had buried the tiny baby and afterbirth in the desert. Anna had become weakened even before childbirth.

"There, there, Anna." I soothed her brow with the cool

water from the jug next to her, and my heart went out to her. She opened her mouth to speak, but no words came out, and her breath stank like sour milk. A quiet woman, Anna kept to her tent and seldom participated in social gatherings. Other women placed spinners and looms near one another and visited as they worked. The younger women took turns minding each other's children, which allowed time for them to accomplish other tasks. It all worked out very well. But Anna hardly spoke to other women. People remarked about how opposite she was from rude and outspoken Ham. It must be a thorn in the side to live with such a lusty man. I had seen him ogling young girls, and wondered if he had tried to attack them the way he had me.

Through the night, I kept up the ritual of bathing her feverish forehead with rosemary tea the way Serena had taught me. Anna remained in a fitful sleep. Much time passed while I kept watch. The heat emanated from the woman's forehead as it did when I had come into the tent. My arms ached, but I pressed on with the task of bathing. Remembering how I had felt when I bathed in the cool stream earlier, I decided to remove some of her covering and cool more of her body with the water. I began with her arms, lifting one out of a wrap, bathing it, and then covering it again. My ministering continued, bathing limbs and body thus. When I went back to placing cool cloths on Anna's brow, her dark swollen eyes finally opened wide.

"Anna, are you thirsty?" I put a cool drink of white

willow tea to her lips, but she did not drink any. I put drops of wine and olive oil on a cloth and blotted Anna's parched lips. When I touched her pallid forehead with my fingertips, I realized her fever had broken. I relaxed my hands for a few moments and shrugged my shoulders several times to ease my muscle aches. I smiled through my tiredness, because the work of my hands had helped her. She appeared to be sleeping more peacefully.

The sun already peered over the horizon when Serena came to the tent. Pleased with what she saw, she said, "You have done very well with this one. I meant to come sooner, but I have been with her day and night and succumbed to my tiredness. I slept longer than I intended."

"It was no trouble. I am glad the fever has gone down."

Serena examined the patient. "See her yellow skin. She needs fresh air and sunshine, nourishing broth, tea, and water. Then we will add solid food."

"She awakened briefly and consumed nothing. I blotted her lips with the oil and wine cloth."

"You are a gifted woman." Serena placed an arm around my waist in a brief hug. "Now you must take a rest, but I fear you cannot if you want to catch up with everyone. I believe Naliah has already left, so do whatever you must. Anna is unable to travel, therefore I will stay with her until she is stronger."

"Shall we both tend her? What if her fever returns?"

"I cannot expect you to remain here. It is my duty to stay," Serena insisted. "You must go with the others. There is one, Anat, who is about to have a baby. She traveled with her husband Philip, and their children. Could you be her midwife?"

"Alone?" While I had helped Serena a few times, I had never been the sole midwife present at a birth.

"Oh, now, it is not her firstborn. The mother does most of the work, if you recall." Serena patted my arm. "You will do well."

Even though I felt extremely tired I packed, ready to go in a short while. Later I came upon Anat. Indeed, she cried out in a makeshift tent. Philip paced the earth a respectable distance from her and waved to me. I hurried to Anat and stood by while she bore a daughter. Without the ready availability of water, we got through the birth process cleansing using a salt solution I had prepared and brought in a vessel I had strapped on the back of a donkey. Flasks of oils and wine tied to my waist were put to use.

I helped Anat ceremoniously bury the blood, the cloth, and afterbirth as was customary. We were camped on a plain between our former grazing lands and greener pastures by the Jordan. The men and flocks were nearby.

Attending Anat, I gained confidence in my ability to be a midwife. In the early evening when the stars were beginning to wink above and I could finally rest outside my tent, my thoughts turned to my friend Mary. Had she married Joseph, and was she expecting a child, or barren? I tried to imagine her life now. I beheld the night sky with its endless stars and remembered the night I had been with her and Abram.

My thoughts were interrupted when Judah called,

"Hannah." I smiled as I saw him walking toward me in the twilight. Gladdened to see him after an absence, I rose to greet him, but he turned away. Of course, his mother waited in front of her tent, and embraced him, clucking like a hen. He was pulled inside his family's tent without coming to invite me. Surely he supped bread and wine with his mother. Even though I seethed with jealousy, I could not fault him for respecting her. A few other neighbors had come away from the flocks and were going home. And then I saw Ham, alone. He walked casually, strolling, but my mind shrank in fear as the moon cast a shadow that moved ominously toward me step by step.

CHAPTER FIVE

I became even more fearful of Ham after he attacked, and almost did the unthinkable to me. I dared not go outside my tent after sunset, but that night I thought Judah would emerge from his family tent soon. I hoped he would save me. Ham kept coming toward me. I quickly grabbed my mat and a sack, and began walking rapidly toward the Women's Tent where we went when we were unclean from monthly flow or childbirth. I had no urgent requirement to be in the tent, but I felt sure Ham would be loathe to follow me.

Young, unmarried Meda quietly sat inside the tent on a soft mat. She nodded and smiled when I came in. Her mother Sara, a widow, lived in a tent next to Mother Lydia. While we talked the evening away, Meda and I did not mention both of us had visited the tent two weeks before. I wondered why she sat yet again, but we did not speak about such things. Judah never asked where I had gone that evening. Maybe he heard where I went.

Untold days passed for me and we moved the encampment to new grazing. While I sat weaving, Serena returned to us. After greeting me, she said, "At the last Anna became dreadfully weak, and consumed neither food nor drink, and she died."

"A sadness for the boys who are left without a mother, but I am relieved you are here with us." I grieved for Anna.

"Have our people been well?" Serena fingered the cloth on my loom.

"Yes, I have been able to do everything requested of me, but I have missed having you near to give me advice concerning which herbs to use."

"The men say we are ready to move the flocks again." Serena shrugged her shoulders. "I will not have to set my things out here and I can use the time to help you make ready to move."

I sighed and stood up. "Once again." Serena and I kissed cheeks. We packed the contents of the healing tent.

Obediently I traveled with my mother-in-law. Judah went with the flocks. We were on our way toward the Bethlehem hills, and as I walked beside a donkey laden with Naliah's household goods I saw several people traveled on the road. "It is time to be counted and pay Caesar," I heard a man say.

A man walking up ahead of us led a donkey burdened with rolled rugs and a woman. I saw her round middle, and thought she possibly expected a child. My eyes widened in pleasant surprise. As I came nearer I recognized Mary from those times when I had camped near Nazareth in Galilee, and my heart beat as happily as a drum.

"Mary." I ran toward her. "Is it truly you?" I stopped to dislodge an annoying pebble from my sandal.

"Can it be Hannah?" Mary's face lit up with surprise, and her husband halted the donkey. "Joseph, this is the friend I told you about."

He nodded. Mary dismounted heavily with her husband's helping hand. I went to her to kiss each cheek then embrace her. Warm sand drifted lightly around us.

"How soon will your child be born?" By Mary's size I determined the birth would take place soon.

"I am sure it will be in a few days," Mary and Joseph answered together, which brought a smile to Mary's face. I felt a twinge of envy at their closeness.

"As decreed by Caesar Augustus, we must go to Bethlehem, the place of my birth, to be counted and pay our taxes." Joseph shook his head. "Mary insisted on going."

"I have heard it is very crowded now with everyone registering. Surely you know a family who will give you a room?"

"We do hope so. Relatives we seldom see live there." Mary wrinkled her forehead and gazed at stoic Joseph. Grayish clouds punctuated the deep blue horizon, and the air held a fresh earthy aroma.

We continued on and walked very slowly together. "Oh, I have gotten married. He is a shepherd, Judah." I counted the moons in my head, thinking Mary must have gotten married soon after I had left the Nazareth area. It had been about two years.

"I have wonderful news to tell you, Hannah. I hope you will believe what I have to say," Mary said. Joseph walked on a ways down the trail, stopped and tightened straps that held items on the donkey.

"I am listening. Please tell me all your news."

Mary began an account of the most incredible thing I could imagine.

"For a long time, I, as well as you and everyone else, have been awaiting the Messiah. About eight moons ago, I was in the place of prayer in the corner of our roof, and had been meditating and trying to remember prophesies Abram had recited for me. On the lovely evening, stars greeted the night sky with twinkling lights. I suppose I fell asleep. I awakened out of a deep sleep, and anxiousness fluttered inside my breast. Someone stood near. I worried that Abram had sneaked up. Had a robber come to steal and to attack me? I had heard of thefts happening, but seldom in Nazareth. And then a Voice spoke from the shadows, 'Greetings, favored one! The Lord is with you.' It could have been one of the stars from heaven had suddenly appeared on our roof, as my eyes could not gaze upon the brightness. I bowed down and covered my face with my hands."

"Oh, it must have been awfully frightful."

"Shaken and perplexed by the greeting, and afraid to say or do anything, I wondered what it meant. I asked what he wanted."

"He might have been a thief."

"If he had come to steal from me, I had no jewels or money." Mary paused, breathed deeply a couple of times.

"Are you well?"

"Yes, thank you. The being, standing tall as the ceiling, approached me even closer and shone with a light which emanated from within itself. I remember very well the astonishing words. 'Do not be afraid, Mary, for you have found favor with God. You will conceive and bear a son, and you will name him Jesus. He will be great, the Son of the Most High, and the Lord God will give to Him the throne of His ancestor David. He will reign over the house of Jacob forever and His kingdom will never end.'

"Oh, Mary." She had told me a very strange thing, and I wondered how it would end.

"I asked, 'How is this possible when I am a virgin?' Joseph and I were betrothed but unmarried. I wondered what he would think. I trembled with such fear as I have never experienced."

"I have the hair on my arm standing at what you told me."

"Then he said he was God's messenger, Gabriel. He said the Holy Spirit would come upon me, and the power of the Most High would overshadow me."

"Oh, Mary, I cannot even imagine what you must have thought and felt."

"He told me I am to bear a Holy Child. He will be the Son of God. I was dumbfounded at this revelation, but a calmness permeated my being. Perhaps the amazing event would take place the same night. Every young woman I knew wondered if she would be the one chosen to bear God's Son. It would be such an honor. Such unbelievable news made me wonder if I dreamed it. I had never known a man, and yet would bear a child."

I reached out and touched her hand. The sun on my back enveloped me in a blanket of warmth.

"I have always felt special. I almost died as a tiny baby when I turned blue and had no breath. My mother told me she used her own breath and breathed it into my mouth repeatedly. Finally I coughed. My parents gave a turtledove in sacrificial thankfulness for my life. Father told me I might do great things for my life had been spared. Dead, yet I lived. All of this went through my mind the night Gabriel came." Mary dabbed at tears on her cheeks.

I listened, but my mind failed to take in her whole experience.

She continued. "I marveled at this news quietly, overcome with emotion. Finally I said to him, 'Here I am, the servant of the Lord, let it be with me according to Your word.' Hannah, I immediately felt a warmth, lightness and ecstasy in my being as never before. I felt peaceful and excited at the same time."

When Mary finished telling me her news, my lips could not speak. She smiled, and patted my arm. She waited in silence for me to absorb what she had revealed. Reverently, bowing her head, she said, "So, here I am. I am going to have God's Son."

Awestricken, I drew back my hand. I knew the Messiah had been foretold, but that I could be in the presence of a sacred one astounded me. Mary glowed the way young expectant mothers do, but otherwise appeared completely ordinary. She waited quietly. Practical things entered my head. "Let us sit for awhile. You must not stand long." I got the mat and we settled on a patch of dry grass. Dark clouds readied themselves on the horizon. Fluffy clouds wafted over us, shading, and then lifting up to allow the sun to glow in full force.

"I wish to be with you when it happens, if you want to have me." I believed Mary told me the truth, yet it was almost too much to understand.

"I suppose so, but what would you do?" Mary reached for my hand.

"I have learned to be a midwife. If you have the child while you are in a strange place without your mother what will you do?" I wanted very much to assist with the birth of her child. Midwives were usually quiet heroines, but this one would be different. I could become highly respected and widely known. I would surely rise from my current status of being a barren wife, a former wild child, and a "nobody."

"I have been assured all will go well with me." Mary looked up at the sky when she spoke. The air stilled its blowing, the sun had disappeared, and rain clouds hovered.

"Then I suppose you will give birth without me or anyone helping." I had heard Mary's story about the virgin birth, about the fact she carried God's Son, but I still disbelieved Mary would need no assistance with a firstborn. Disappointment filled my mind, because she did not want me to be there at the birth.

"No, you misunderstand my meaning. You are a good friend, and I shall always want you to be my friend."

"I could help. Friends help each other." The sudden wind pelted us with bits of dry grass, as a storm threatened overhead.

"If your family can spare you, I would be delighted to have you with me."

"Hannah!" My mother-in-law called, "Come help me. I have to repack this lopsided load or it will all fall to the ground. Come, hurry!" The clouds ripped apart spilling rain on us.

I stood, reached down and gave Mary a hand. "Mary, I will find you again along the trail." She smiled. Joseph, now at her side, helped her settle on the donkey. We waved to each other.

"Who were those people?" Naliah asked, frowning, "There are thieves and bad people on the trail. You must stay with me. Now everything is getting wet. Hurry up and wrap the meal in a second layer of goatskin." I did not answer her or say I had been speaking with a good friend who would bear God's Son, because she would never believe such a thing. Chafing inwardly, I repacked the load and covered it all with a goat hair hide by myself, while my mother-in-law gave instructions. I completed my task at last, but when I viewed the trail I saw few people on it for a long wet way. Even if I ran with the donkey I would never catch up. I wanted to be close to Mary, but she was swallowed from my sight by the storm.

All seemed to be well while we walked. Only the old dung gatherers were behind Naliah and me. Sacks were laden with the dried stuff to make fires. When we arrived at camp the men had settled in the Bethlehem hills grazing flocks. Tents were arranged in a protective circle to form a sheepfold. The hills were especially lush with grasses and other plants the sheep and goats liked to eat. They would grow fat and healthy here. Men were singing, going off to their flocks, and smiled more at wives and children. I sensed that they were settled and happy to be in this place for several moons where the grass grew plentifully, and could be harvested for future use.

One day I received coins for one of my woven cloths Father Moshe had taken to trade in one of the towns. I tried to share in the general contentment, and in truth was too busy to think about the humdrum married life I had resigned myself to living.

I attended the birth of two children in one night. People sought me for my knowledge and comfort when they became ill. In a few short months I had become a respected healer they could count on. When Serena rejoined the group after Anna died, I thought my popularity might wane, and I would be everyone's second choice.

Then one day Meda's mother, Sara, came to me. "My daughter wants you to come see her. She has an issue of blood which will not stop."

"Serena is busy with another?" I picked up my kit of herbs and cloths to get ready to help her. I had worried Meda might be suffering from an ailment when she was in the Women's Tent too soon again the night I had dashed in there early myself to get away from Ham. Meda was a smart young woman, and I hoped I could be a friend and help her.

"Meda requested to see you, Hannah." Sara grasped my hand.

I felt needed and proud. With such an affirmation I realized I had become a healer in my own right.

CHAPTER SIX

ne night I rested outside my tent, basking in the wonder of the night sounds. The evening became very still at first and the stars shone with an unbelievable brilliance. I thought I could reach out and touch them. A wind blew. Wispy clouds descended to the earth out in the fields. I imagined it to be celestial beings. Awestricken, I thought I heard a Voice, or was the wind making a sound? It was a strange happening.

"Go seek Mary. She has need of you," the Voice, perhaps in the wind, but also deep inside of my being, urged me and caused my life pulse to beat faster. Too perplexed about what to do next, I simply went to check on Meda again.

Sara, lying next to her daughter, said, "Thank you so much, Hannah. The bleeding has stopped completely."

"Keep taking these herbs for two more days, but visit

Serena if the bleeding resumes without stopping again."
The treatment worked, and the girl would be healed soon.

"Did I hear my name?" Serena appeared outside the
tent. When I saw her, I knew my next steps. After we
had discussed Meda's condition, I walked arm in arm with
Serena.

"I am to assist with a birth in Bethlehem."

"Your fame has traveled." Serena smiled. "I wish you
Yahweh's blessing."

"Judah is with the flocks, but please let Mother Lydia
know. I must go now, and she will still be slumbering."

"I will tell her in the morning. I can tell Judah when
the men return." Serena and I embraced.

Unwilling to delay until morning, I put bread, a few
other necessities and choice herbs into my skin bag and
slung it over my shoulder. I quickly sewed a pocket of
coins inside the bodice of my tunic. I hurriedly packed a
swaddling cloth I had woven, filled a flask with wine, and
walked out of my tent into the night. Quiet buzzing and
whirring sounds of insects and night birds echoed around.
At first the sounds taunted me and I strained to hear if
any footsteps were nigh. Perhaps wild dogs or robbers
were near. It was dangerous to walk alone in the darkness,
but I did not feel afraid.

A Voice murmured from an unseen spirit, "Go seek
Mary."

Had an angel spoken to me? Did an angel guide
me to my destination, or simply my own desire? Doubts
assailed me. Perhaps it was simply a breeze. I wondered

how I would know where to begin to seek and find Mary. I walked rapidly for what could have been two hours and finally saw the vague dimly lit outline of a town ahead. My life pulse thumped in my throat from excitement. God's Son would be born to Mary. It would be an honor to assist with the birth of one greater than any king. I wondered if they were staying in the house of a relative, or in an inn. I would ask people I met in town.

My ears perked up as I heard moaning a short distance from the trail. I thought about the encounters I had with Ham and grew frightened. Even though each time I had gotten away from him, I feared I could be in grave danger. Men could be horribly evil. With Ham's wife dead, I had avoided all contact with him. Now my throat constricted. I approached the sound carefully, and in the moonlight saw someone lying down by the trail. I knew I ought to ignore the person, because it could be a way to ensnare me. Thieves might be in the bushes waiting to rob me of my meager herbs, spices and coins. Compassion bade me to take a chance. I stooped to see who lay in the moonlight. A man moaned, and I imagined his face contorted in pain. "What happened to you?" I asked.

"Terrible men came and beat me and took my donkey and all my possessions. Go away, girl, for they might be near."

"If they are near, it is better to have two of us." I kneeled beside him, and felt calm and unafraid, because a protective Spirit lingered near. With my fingers, I inspected the bloody wound on his head where a lump the size of a thumb had formed.

"May I look at your wounds? I am a healer. I will press firmly on your head injury with a cloth dipped into wine." He winced a little. Next, I made a poultice of a honey herbal mixture and applied it to the wound. "Is it only your head?"

"No, my legs hurt. I cannot walk," he said almost in a whisper.

"May I tend to them?"

"Yes, daughter, but I do not know if it will help," the man said. He pointed to his legs that were exposed where his robe had been torn.

I knelt down by him respectfully and set to work as if he were my own father. On his left foot, ankle, and leg, I found raised bruises. When I examined his right ankle I worried because it was very swollen. I removed a cloth from my pack, crushed comfrey leaves, and put them in olive oil. First I smoothed the skin with oil, and then I wrapped the ankle firmly with the herbal cloth and tied the ends.

"Can you sit up?" When he nodded, I helped him up, pulled out my flask of wine and offered him a drink.

"You have been very kind. How can I repay you? I have nothing left since the thieves have taken it all."

"Payment is unnecessary. Would you please try to stand? I will help."

"Thank you, thank you." The thin man rose unsteadily until I helped with a supporting arm. "Surely you are an angel sent from God."

"No angel. My name is Hannah, come from the shepherd tribe of Dan."

"You are from the Danites? A story I heard around a campfire long ago told all were lost at sea." The man's voice had gained strength.

"Yes, they tell such a tale." I repacked herbs and reached for his hand. "Stronger now?"

"Thank you, yes." He raised his arm and lowered it again. "What do you know of your family?"

"My Father Moshe recounted a history about our ancestors' capture of Laish which they claimed as their own land and renamed Dan." I feared too much talk would delay my journey. "Can you walk then?"

He stood up, but teetered. "No walking for me. I will lie back down," he sighed. "Go on your way, but be careful, daughter. It is dangerous for you to be alone."

"Then come with me. You must walk a ways at least. Everything will become stiff if you remain lying down for long." I draped his arm across my shoulder to help him walk. We walked thus, very slowly making our way closer to the few dim lights of Bethlehem.

Neither of us spoke. I felt disheartened by the hindrance in my quest to find Mary, but I had no thought to abandon the poor old man. In the half-light we came upon a man who had two donkeys. Seeing a young woman helping an older man, he apparently assumed I was his daughter. "I see your father could use help, eh?"

"He was attacked by thieves down the road back there, and his leg is hurt badly. Would you kindly give him a ride on your donkey?"

"Now, why would I believe your story? Perhaps you

two want to steal my donkeys, eh? How do I know, eh?" The fat, middle-aged man wore a turban on his head and he stuck a finger under the edge of it to scratch his scalp. He wore the fine, colorful garments of one who buys and sells. One donkey carried rolls of rugs, while the other one held travel packs on his rear and side bags.

"You do not know. I have these two *mites*." I thrust them out in front of me, offering to pay him. I had a few more coins, but I was fearful to let him know.

"Keep those to buy something for yourself. I am hoping to sell one of these donkeys in the town." He pulled one pack off the smaller donkey. "Get up here then, old man. I don't have all night, eh? Here, let me help you lift that game leg up onto my trusty steed," he laughed. "Maybe you want to buy him. We'll work it out. Give you a good price." He helped the man onto the donkey, first lifting him to the blanket, and then putting his leg across to straddle it. We continued our journey on the trail to Bethlehem.

I walked quietly beside them. My legs were weary, but I pressed on. My thoughts went back to Mary, and I wondered how she was doing.

"What brings you to Bethlehem? Taxes, eh?" The merchant had a flask at his side. He tipped it to his mouth and then offered it to the man.

"Taxes," rasped the injured man.

Let the merchant think whatever he wanted. He seemed friendly. But my silence simply made him more talkative. His accent amused me, because I had never heard one speak in such a way before.

"Caesar. What a terrible one, he is, eh? Poor countrymen like us have to pay in and pay in, and what does he do, eh? He lives in splendor. He lacks for nothing, the scoundrel! That's sumpin', eh? But we can't escape it, eh? Herod, now he is one who has his hands in our money sacks," he muttered. Suddenly he changed the subject. "You bandaged him all by yourself?"

"I did. I know about caring for those who are hurt or sick or having babies." I wondered if I had said too much, and warily eyed the merchant.

"Well, well, a midwife. You could set yourself up to be a healer, eh? You read fortunes, too? I know people of worth. Yes, you could do very well in the city, eh? I am called Zeke the Rug Man, by the way."

"Pleased to meet you. My name is Hannah. I am foreign to the city, and come from a nomadic tribe who follow the grass for grazing flocks."

"Good people, shepherds, but some are thieves." He mumbled to himself and then grew silent. The air smelled as fresh as a mown field, and the steady clopping of donkey hooves could have lulled me to sleep if I had been riding.

"I am actually looking for some friends when we arrive in Bethlehem. I promised to come help them." I decided to be truthful as we were getting closer to town and I was anxious to be on my way. Perhaps Zeke would take care of the old man. "The man on your donkey is not my father. I found him injured on the trail and I helped him. When you thought him to be my father, I let you believe it and

I am sorry. I must be on my way and I beg of you to take care of this man."

"Eh?" Zeke rubbed his beard thoughtfully.

"Please," the old man on the donkey said. "Please find me a straw mat where I can lay my head. When I am back on my feet I will repay you."

I inspected the bandaged ankle. "You must stay off this for a few days, but try to use it. Moving your feet now and then will help you to heal more quickly."

"Listen to the young woman, eh? She knows what she is talking about." Zeke wagged his finger.

Zeke had not answered me, but he also had not refused to help. When we came into the gates of the town, many people were wandering the streets. A few carried oil lamps and others depended on the early light of approaching dawn. Merchants were busy selling oil, wine, and food. "Sweet dates, figs, and honey cakes for sale. Come and buy." Voices droned on.

I heard the village sounds. Makeshift tents lined the main road. Farther down, the outline of buildings created a silhouette painted in my mind forever. "Hannah, tend kindly to yourself, eh? I will see to the old one. I have friends. If you ever want to set up a healing business let me know. Eh?" Zeke walked away down a side street with the donkeys. One still carried the man I had helped.

An overwhelming feeling of being alone struck me when Zeke left, and I was tempted to follow them. Where would I find Mary in Bethlehem among this throng of people? I stared at the street. Beads of sweat formed on my brow, yet I shivered in the cold air. I breathed deeply to still my rising anxiety. It was a strange place and I did not know anyone who lived in Bethlehem. The Voice had directed me to come here. I had to have faith that I would find Mary before she had her baby.

CHAPTER SEVEN

I came to an inn, and when I went inside the courtyard several people were lined up to speak with the proprietor. He waved his arms and shouted above the noise, "My rooms are all taken!" I slipped through the departing throng, felt an elbow now and then, and wondered at all these people who were still awake at this time. While the crowd of people had the appearance of a festival celebration, many were subdued and had pinched faces.

"Are you deaf?" A swarthy young man bumped into me, and raised his eyebrows. "He said he had no rooms."

"I am not in want of a room," I said. Wine servers poured drinks in an open court to my right. A nice respectable woman never went to such a place alone. Did he think I planned to enter it? What he or others thought of me was unimportant.

When I finally made my way to the host he had already turned away. "Wait, please," I said. A faint aroma of spices wafted out when he pushed through the swinging wood door.

"No room." He shouted over his shoulder as the door swung shut behind him. "Day waiting below the earth yet, and people have been up all night, crazy," a man muttered. Hospitality was usually given to travelers, but this enrollment had tried the patience of those who were normally friendly. There were simply too many guests.

As I pushed my way to follow him, I almost ran into a boy child who sat to one side building a pretend hut from small pieces of wood and sticks. The child's nose dripped and he held onto one of his ears. "Oh, little one." I knelt beside to him. "My name is Hannah."

The sick child looked curiously at me for a moment, and then shook his head, snuffled a drip, and wiped his nose on his tunic. My heart went out to him.

"Please leave, young woman." The man paused. He wore a food-spattered tan garment that showed he had been at work in the kitchen. "You must lie down on your soft blanket and go to sleep," he said to the boy, and pointed to the tan square in the corner of the room.

"Please, sir, I am seeking a young couple. The woman was, well, is, almost is, soon to give life to a child. Have you seen them?" I thought how I might be taken for one who had lost her mind the way I babbled. I stood up.

"Do you know how many people have been here today? I don't remember seeing them." He turned to leave.

I stopped momentarily and crouched next to the boy. "What a fine house you are building."

"I cannot breathe." The boy, about four years old, rubbed his dripping nose.

I pulled aromatic herbs from my pack, tied them in a small sack, and fastened it with a thin leather thong looped around his neck to dangle. "It is a gift for you. Wear this and it may help." I showed him a clean cloth that had been softened with oils. "Apply this to your sore nose. It may save your clothing from being soiled and make your nose feel better." I gave the cloth to him and he clutched it in one hand and fingered the sack of herbs. "What is your name?"

"I am Simon." He gave me a lopsided grin and continued to tug at his ear.

"Simon, let me have a peek at the ear you have been holding onto. Do you fear it will fall off if you let go?" He smiled. When he moved his hand, I looked into his red ear and dropped garlic oil into it.

"It tickles and stinks." He shook his head and made a face. "Yuk."

"Well, well, a healer." The man startled me, because I thought he had left. "Thank you."

"Yes, I am a healer. Would you like for me to put him to bed?"

"You may. Simon is my nephew, and my namesake. My brother, Peter is a fisherman and often away. His wife has her hands full with the rest of her brood of twelve children, and relatives staying for several days, so I said he could stay here. I have neglected him with my inn being filled to the brim these days."

"Simon!" The man reacted to the urgent call, shrugged his shoulders, and left me with his nephew. I took Simon's hand and led him to the blanket in the far corner of the room. I sat down and cradled his feverish brow in my lap and hummed a quiet tune, adding a word or two, "Come, my Simon, sleep my little lamb, sleep soundly." Wistfully, I thought how it might be to have a son such as this one. When he drifted off, I laid him down and tucked his soft beige shawl around him. I slipped away leaving him asleep, and walked down the street to another place.

The house was shuttered and dark, but people still milled about. I went boldly to the door and rapped. No one answered. When I kept on knocking, the people around me laughed and sneered. "Save your knuckles. They refuse to answer." A burly man waved his flask.

A woman peered out of a window. "We have no rooms. Go somewhere else."

"Please, I seek a couple." I pushed up closer to privately tell her more. "The woman is having a child soon and I am to be her midwife."

"Hah, if you are her midwife, then I suppose you would be the one to know where she abides." The shutter slammed shut. Although discouraged, I was determined to find Mary.

I asked people around me, "Have you seen a round little woman and her husband?" A very gnarled old man who stood with the help of a staff motioned for me to come near him. I approached him cautiously.

"I saw a pair such as you tell of yesterday," he whispered hoarsely. "These people turned them away, and they went on down the street." He coughed loudly then, wheezing. I feared he would take his last breath.

"Sit down, maybe I can help you," I sighed. Here was another person I could not pass by without tending. I reached into my bag until I found the right herbs. I put them in a square of white cloth the size of my hand, and tied it with a thin leather thong, sprinkled wine on the cloth to release the aroma, and then fastened it around his neck. I offered him my flask of wine and he drank several sips.

"Thank you," he whispered. His rattling chest quieted to a bubbling rasp. "I am an old man and will soon die. You have been very kind."

"I am glad I could ease your breathing." I hurried off in the direction he had indicated across the court from Simon's inn. People were still standing around, talking. Others had put sleeping mats out on the ground beside the road where they were lying down, wrapped in animal skins. A murmuring echoed in the chilly air as conversations waned. In an exhausted daze, unaware of exactly where I wandered, I trudged on. Then I heard the cry of a woman in pain off to my left.

I followed the direction of the sounds. Excitement and dread both whirled in my head at the same time. The travail of a woman panting and crying out became clearer when I neared a family tent hastily fashioned from goat hair blankets.

"Who comes here?" a man's voice said.

"Hannah. Are you Joseph?" I picked up my garment hem, and ran among the shadows to go to the tent.

"Nah, it is Iscariot and my wife is Mara." His voice was thick and slurred. "Come in."

"I am a midwife. I have come to Bethlehem to be of help to another woman who is, or will soon be having a child. I can help if your wife wants my services." Mind and spirit sank. My medical supplies dwindled as I had already reached into my pack three times to help people, all in one night. I shook my head and thought why tonight of all nights I must tend many people.

I set to work immediately, kneeling beside the woman who again cried out. The small woman's dark skin and clothing were soaked with perspiration. A closed-bowl oil lamp provided the scant light that shone and revealed two stones set nearby to be her birthing stool. An empty water jug lay on its side by a pile of bedding. Sacks of meal and other food were on the other side. Another rug for sleeping was next to the sacks.

"I can do nothing. Mostly, I can do nothing right," he slurred, shook his head, and fumbled with a depleted goatskin bag at his waist. The woman grimaced, panted rapidly and shook her fist in his direction.

Usually the husband stayed well out of the way during childbirth and afterwards he must stay away from his wife for seven days. Her husband must sleep outside, because she was deemed to be unclean. I wondered for a moment how to admonish him to leave. "Could you go find more water? I will need it."

"Where will I find a well in the dark?" Iscariot growled, and groped his way around inside the tent. He grabbed a skin bag, the empty jug, and stumbled away, mumbling to himself.

I put my hand on her abdomen, counting the times her belly hardened and released. "How long have you been going on thus?"

"A time, at daylight yesterday the waters came." Her head was clammy to the touch.

"Soon it will be daylight again." I patted her hand reassuringly. I moistened a cloth with olive oil and applied it to her parched lips. It would be a dry birth and painful. Her abdomen appeared to be hard in the wrong place. I tried to remember what Serena had said about turning a baby before it emerged. At times it would come out feet first, but be stuck in the woman, and we would have to help the birth. Much tearing of flesh could take place. I worked with her breathing, concentrating on calming her. I helped her to sit on the round stones. I wondered how she had managed to have these stones inside her tent after traveling. Perhaps she had gotten them after arriving. She continued her labor for a time.

Finally, the woman pushed mightily, but the baby stayed put. Unwanted tears came to my eyes from fatigue. Then I shook myself, squared my shoulders, took a deep breath and did what I hoped was the right thing. I reached inside the woman and attempted to move the tiny foot that had emerged. "Come on," I whispered, "Turn about for Hannah. Come into this world the right way." When nothing I tried to do helped, I withdrew, because I feared I might hurt her or the child. The woman moaned, and let her body make the hard movements. I sat back to stretch my shoulders and rest a moment.

Her eyes opened wide, and with a loud cry she pushed very hard. The baby slipped out, miraculously, its downy head first into my hands. The afterbirth remained stuck inside of her and I prayed for help. The woman could die from so much bleeding. I could hardly see in the dimly lighted tent, but knew the baby was a boy. I tied off and then cut the cord. I held the baby upside down and thumped him gently on the back to dislodge the mucus plug to help him take his first breath. A strong, lusty cry announced his entry into the world.

"You have a son." A deep satisfaction came from seeing a new life safely born into this world. The mother breathed normally and stretched comfortably on her mat. I wondered where her husband had gone for water. The healthy baby I placed in the folds of my own tunic in my lap. I could take care of him later.

As I massaged her abdomen, two women appeared in the doorway. One took the baby from me and wiped him with salted water they had brought with them. She wrapped the child with a clean swaddling cloth.

"Thank you. My name is Hannah, and I am a midwife. I happened by and offered to help when I heard her cry out in pain." I felt relieved to see these women who I thought were relatives come to help.

"We two are sisters, Martha and Sarah. We could not sleep, but prayed the night while you cared for Mara. When we heard it was over, we came to give you rest." Sarah finished binding the child, and only its pink face peeped out. Martha brought a vessel of water, a jar of oil, vinegar, and cloths, and began to clean up.

"I am most grateful. Her husband went out to draw water a while ago. I suppose you know these people?" The afterbirth tissue came out and I breathed more easily. The air smelled pungent with the aroma of salty blood and new life.

"Yes, we are cousins to Iscariot."

Why had they delayed in coming to help this woman, especially being her relatives? Perhaps strife in the family had rent them asunder.

"Out! All of you, I warned you earlier." Iscariot reeked of strong wine, reeled and teetered. He set the water jug down with a resounding thud.

"Please, Mara needs us now. We will leave when she is stronger," Martha said sternly, her dark eyes flashing. After all, childbirth was a woman's business, where the matriarch should be fully in charge.

"Mara needs us now," Iscariot mimicked. He lunged toward Martha, but she stepped aside. He fell to the ground, overturning the water he had placed there. His bread loaf sized hands covered his face and he gave in to a drunken sob.

"We are sorry to have you in the middle of this family dispute," Martha said. "I suppose you are wondering how cousins could hate each other so much. Our great grandfather Iscariot divided land unequally, favoring the younger son over the eldest. The younger son was deemed to be fairer and more responsible than the elder son. We are descended from the youngest Iscariot and Jude Iscariot from the eldest. Our house has been divided ever since."

"You have a son." Sarah quietly held the tiny bundle next to Iscariot. He uncovered his head tentatively, and stilled his sobbing, then reached out to gently touch his son. The baby made a bleating cry like a lamb. Sarah then placed him on Mara's breast, where she cuddled him in her arms. Awake now, the new mother fared well despite her tiredness. Iscariot sat quietly out of the way, with his bloodshot eyes focused affectionately on his wife and child. For these few moments the family Iscariot had become united once more through the birth of a son.

"His name will be Judas bar Iscariot," Mara announced quietly. Her husband opened his mouth to speak, then thought better of it and merely nodded. Amused at his silence, I thought the man knew when he was outnumbered. I wondered when he would leave his tent as custom demanded.

As I gathered my things and left, dawn's fading stars in the sky reminded me of the night Mary, Abram and I had gazed in wonder. I had delivered Mara's baby, but she certainly was not at all like my friend Mary.

Goosebumps prickled my skin and a chill at the base of my neck ran down my spine. Although exhausted, I moved on. Almost no people were on the road in the earliest morning, except those lying asleep on mats beside it. I sank down on a dry grassy patch beside the road to rest.

I fell into a dreamy sleep sitting with my head resting on my knees. Two baby boys toddled in my dream. One ran around a carpenter's shop among the wood shavings and the other chased him. The one being chased had a pleasant round face, but a strong chin. He laughed, and tossed his long brown hair. The heavier boy who chased the other had darker hair, an olive complexion, and resembled the man, Iscariot. He laughed also, but not with the laugh of a happy child. It sounded evil. He then picked up a stick threatening, and kept demanding, "Play with me." The pleasant boy laughed playfully and shook his head.

I awakened still sitting up the same way as when I went to sleep. At first I did not know where I sat. Then I did. Sleepy Bethlehem was alive with activity.

"Clear the path. Make way. You, old man, hurry off or we will throw you off." Helmeted soldiers wearing heavy packs and curved shields of wood and leather marched past and yelled, "Make way." When people moved too slowly to suit them, they were shoved aside. Loud tramping and more shouts and screams from men and women echoed in the streets. People, carts and donkeys scattered as a flock of sheep being chased.

I quickly stood up, gathered my meager belongings and hurried to a nearby doorstep until they passed. The sun made its first radiant appearance on the horizon.

Although the rest had refreshed me, I was chilled and helpless. Dried brown blood spots and mucus stains from the birth of Judas were spattered on my tunic. Mary's baby might already be born. Had I missed the birth I wanted so much to attend when I had taken pity on Mara in the midst of childbirth?

I smoothed my stained tunic with my hands and started walking again. A gnawing hunger pang wrenched my stomach, and I reached for my last piece of bread. I nibbled absently at the tough dry morsel. I lifted my wine flask and realized it was nearly empty. Had a multitude sipped from it last night? I could not remember. Saddened, I thought the whole world had fallen ill when I passed by.

"Where will I find Mary?" I asked the twittering birds in the olive trees.

CHAPTER EIGHT

awn had broken, painting the sky with a glorious gold, pink, and lavender glow. People talking, birds twittering, and the thrum of the soldiers filled the air. A spacious front entryway propped with sturdy wood posts came into my view a short way off the main road past Simon's place. Perhaps this was where Mary and Joseph had spent the night. When I approached, a donkey brayed. The familiar earthy aroma confirmed nearness of livestock stables. No doubt, the place had a big kitchen. Indeed, the faint aroma of spicy foods mingled with bread baking kindled my appetite before I got there. I had a coin to spend, and fresh bread would satisfy my hunger.

As I tentatively stepped inside, I saw family-sized rectangular tables covered with white cloths. Each one had a round clay oil lamp. Hewn wooden benches were next to the tables and all around against the walls of the room.

Aromatic herb stems hung in bunches on the scrubbed walls. A hum of conversation came from nearby.

"Ahem," I said, as I came to the curtained doorway entering what my nose told me was the kitchen. A man swished open the curtain and we both blinked in a cloud of steam for a moment. Olive skinned, he appeared to be Egyptian, at least a head taller than me, perhaps eighteen or twenty-years old, with a short black beard, and trimmed dark, slick hair. He wore a red tunic with a broad leather girdle around his middle, and leather sandals tied high on his muscular legs.

"Where have you been dawdling serving maid? My father has been expecting you to come and wait tables. Soon hordes will be in here for breakfast. Come." Astounded, I knew not what he meant. He grabbed my wrist, and pulled me into the kitchen. All the while my lips failed to form words.

"I am not your servant!" I finally sputtered, and I shook my arm to try to free it from his grip. "I am not anyone's hireling. I came looking for my friends who might be staying here."

"Ah." He let go of me, rubbed his chin and glanced down at my soiled garments. "Who might they be?" He spoke the local dialect with an accent.

"Mary and Joseph of Nazareth." I tried to avoid the man's questioning eyes. "She...she's great with..." I flushed, embarrassed to be speaking with this handsome man about private matters. When he continued to stare at me, I realized it would be best to explain my soiled clothing.

"I helped another woman give birth last evening. I am a midwife come to assist Mary, my friend."

"Oh, I am sorry." He wrinkled his forehead. "Well, come along out back. My father had no more rooms last night, but he took pity on a couple who might be your friends and let them stay in the stable with the donkey." He must have seen my shock for he added, "he only charged lodging for the ass." He turned away, moving through the kitchen while I trailed behind him. The servants eyed us curiously, but kept on chopping and stirring. We continued through a side door and went out toward the sound of the donkey. "Noisy bugger, is he not? The well is over there." He indicated a grassy area to one side of the stable.

"Thank you, yes, I must clean up," I murmured, when my face became hot. Knowing I had possibly found Mary, I was so overcome with fatigue and joy I could barely speak.

The innkeeper's son and I entered the rather spacious stable behind the inn next to a hillside. Clean hay had been strewn about, making the stable smell nicer than one would expect. A grey donkey stood braying at us and a few wooly lambs were bedded down on one side of the pen. In a far corner beyond the animals stood a wood trough filled with hay, big enough to hold a human. Joseph stood beside it. Mary slept on a blanket in the trough. I broke into a run, went to her, and saw she still awaited the birth of her child.

Joseph looked up, raised one hand, and put a finger

to his lips. He motioned to us to come with him, and we stepped outside together. "She had a bad night," he almost whispered. "She is asleep and she slumbers while the donkey brays, but I fear our voices would awaken her."

"I am Ramen, the son of the Hawara the innkeeper," he said to Joseph. "Let me know if you have want of a drink or some other item I can supply. I have to go back to manage the servants in the kitchen."

"I am Joseph. I met your father when we arrived here. Thank you, I appreciate your hospitality." Joseph sounded patient, despite being forced to stay in a stable.

Although very weary, I felt ecstatic to find Mary at last. I would be with her at the birth of her baby. Joseph stood awkwardly for a moment. "Come in if you wish."

"Thank you, but I am in want of a good wash. I will return shortly."

I went to the well and drew up water, then dashed the refreshing coolness onto my face and washed my hands seven times. These were cleansing rituals I should have done after I helped with the Iscariot birth. I loosened the thongs of my sandals and washed my aching feet. I put my stained outer tunic in the bucket to soak. I rubbed the stains with a coarse stone until all of the spots were gone. I dipped more water to rinse my tunic, and then laid it on the grass to dry. I retrieved a comb from my bag and pulled it through my tangled hair, but failed to put my scarf back over my head. The warm sun comforted me as I sat on my cloak to air my face and arms, still fully clothed in layers of garments. I took honeyed olive oil from my bag and rubbed it into my sore hands and feet. Lulled by the quiet hum of the cattle and gentle breeze, I closed my eyes for what I intended to be a brief moment. The sun went behind the fluffy clouds.

Suddenly, I was rudely and violently pulled to my feet. Brutal hands held my arms, and when I screamed, one massive hand quickly clamped my mouth. Another arm pinned both of mine. I could not see him because he was at my back, but I beheld a large man by his strength. He stank worse than animal dung. His rough clothing scratched my skin. A panic seized me and I thought I was as good as dead. No matter how much I kicked and struggled, the man lifted me up and lurched away carrying me over his shoulder like a lamb.

"Halt!" a man shouted. I could not see Ramen.

"She is my wife's handmaiden. She ran off again." An unfamiliar voice growled in my ear. He lowered me and swung me from side to side the way one would a sack.

"Ah, well, it is hard to keep good help these days," Ramen said. He wore a white turban tied with a red band, and he appeared to be taller and more imposing. "I am in want of a serving maid and would pay you for her."

"No, she serves me," roared my captor.

"I have silver coins." Ramen dug into his leather pouch and extracted a handful, which he offered to the man. When the brute shook his head, Ramen drew out more coins. They bartered for me until at last the evil man let go of me and flung me away from him. I landed on all my limbs. Caution held me back from completely trusting the man who now took my hand and helped me up. He threw another sack of coins at the rude man for good measure.

"Thank you for saving my life. The man lied to you as to his ownership of me." I viewed my savior with mixed emotions. "He grabbed me from beside the well where I rested." My whole body shook from the ordeal, and my knees were so wobbly I thought they could fold up like cloth.

"I was fairly sure you did not belong to him, but..." He eyed me thoughtfully, still holding my hand. "The maid we hired never came."

I shook my hand free and walked to the well to gather up my things. "You do not own me. But for your trouble were you to wish for me to wait tables in the inn, I might do that." My knees shook. "No dancing though." I wanted him to know I would refuse to perform the way some maidservants who tended eating tables did. While I realized this man had saved my life, I had no desire to become his slave.

"I would appreciate it, but ..." His dark eyes locked on mine momentarily. Then he shrugged.

"Since you were kind enough to protect me, I will wait tables to help you for now, but I want to be available for Mary when she gives birth. I want to be free to go when she needs me." I was vulnerable, aching inside. What had happened to the Voice beckoning me to come to Bethlehem? Had it been a dream, or an imagined echo in the wind?

"Rest assured, you can do your midwife duties when

the time comes. Now come, we have fresh garments for you to wear. My father insists on cleanliness." Ramen walked quickly, ready to see a job done. "We are near to the well, and we use much water here. My father dug the well himself, but of course everyone uses it."

"Ramen!" An older and shorter version of the innkeeper's son stood tapping the hard-packed earth floor with his boot. His white tunic stretched across his slightly thicker middle, and he had a red turban wrapped around his head.

"Yes, Father, I have a new serving maid who can begin to work immediately after she changes her clothes. Aren't you pleased?"

His father examined me with the shrewd eyes of a man who is accustomed to evaluating and hiring servants. "She will do." He nodded and winked at Ramen. "Where you found her is hidden from my knowing, but I trust she can do the required work. We will have people waiting. Come and show her what is to be done."

"Her name is…"

"Hannah," I interrupted.

"This is my father, Hawara."

Hawara turned away to answer a question from someone, and Ramen pulled me to the kitchen storage to tell me what my duties would be and get my apron. I took a deep breath.

Enrobed in a white tunic made to fit one twice my size, I waited on tables in the busy eating place until my feet tired from walking on the hard floor. People were mostly in a bad mood because of the enrollment and taxation. Men leered and made rude comments, but none of them touched me. "More wine here," three men tapped cups on the table. "Render unto Caesar…" Men grumbled into their wine goblets, raising empties and demanding service. After they had a few drinks, conversations grew more pleasant, mirthful, and they burst into song together. A traveling band came in playing flutes and sitars. I endured the long evening, but grew more anxious all the while, and I hoped Joseph would soon send word from the stable boy for me to come.

After hours of answering calls for more date cakes, goat cheese, bread or wine, the crowd thinned. Ramen came to me with a goblet of wine and a date cake. "Come, sit." He bade me follow him. "You have done well."

"Thank you, I have never served people at tables before." I tugged at the white garment as I walked into the room in back of the kitchen area where extra benches lined a wall. Stone jars filled with staples lined the shelves and floor. "I must go see how my friends are doing."

"I sent a slave from the kitchen to check. Nothing is happening yet." He smiled engagingly. "Since I paid for you, I thought I might be able to sit with you a moment." His eyes shone, and he motioned for me to sit on a bench. I sat down, grateful to give my feet a rest. A pleasant musty aroma from the wine casks wafted in the air.

"Thank you again, but I agreed to wait tables, nothing more." I bit into the date cake, thinking about my situation. An employer rarely, or never visited with his servant, especially a woman. Perhaps social rules were different in Bethlehem. Or perhaps this attractive man, who was obviously of foreign origin, was not accustomed to our way of doing things.

"I hope your taste is pleased with the cake." With one hand he held a wine goblet and his other hand dangled loosely at his side. Finally he sat on a bench opposite me. "Delicious," I said. Hungry and thirsty, I thought nothing had ever tasted so good. My whole body ached. He handed me the goblet of sweet dark purple wine that I gratefully sipped.

"You are very beautiful." Ramen looked directly at me. Startled at his brashness, I blushed behind my scarf. I knew of his fond interest by the way he lifted his eyes upon me. Did he now want to own my body? After all he had paid for me. But when I peered up at him, his manner was neither lecherous nor threatening.

"I am married." I smiled at his compliment, yet I felt uncomfortable sitting alone with him.

While his countenance revealed surprise, his voice recovered rapidly. "Oh, very well. Your husband did not travel with you?"

"No." I wanted details of my life to remain hidden from him, so Ramen talked, while I listened.

"With this place being overcrowded, I worry our food supply will run short. We will have plenty of bread because we bake daily in our community oven, but the meat and vegetables may want replenishment soon. Of course, cheese, dried dates and figs are always ready. Wine, we may have to start watering down." He paused, sipping his wine. "What troubles me more...those brutal soldiers who march our streets in a show of Roman power. They often kick and shove people who are in the way." Then he chuckled. "I think men sometimes come in here to be gone from the trouble in the streets. I suppose I ought to be grateful for the business."

As Ramen's voice droned on, I thought about our social rules concerning how and when a woman could be in the company of a man. Most men were grown up boys, like Abram or little Simon. The sweet wine eased the ache in my arms and legs and the cake alleviated my hunger pains. We sat in the warm room and my eyelids drooped, but I refused to give in to my tiredness.

I rose from the bench decisively. "I will go see my friends now."

"But I told you they were all right," Ramen protested. "You are very tired and ought to rest. I have a spare bed cloth I can put down in this room. I am sorry I have no private room left for you."

"It is tempting, but I will take the blanket and lie in the stable near my friends." My eyes flashed defiantly as I turned to leave.

"I am truly sorry." Ramen sounded contrite, but in my urgency to see how Mary was doing I gave no thought to it. As I hurried out the door, I glanced back and saw he watched me leave.

When I came to the stable, a camel had been bedded down in the straw next to it. A short, dark boy in white garments sat next to the camel. When I entered the stable, I saw Mary sitting on a low stool beside her bed, albeit a feeding trough. Her light brown robe enfolded her.

"Hannah. Joseph told me you were here." When Mary saw me she rose heavily and walked stiffly with one hand massaging the small of her back. I could see by her sallow face restful sleep had eluded her. We hugged and kissed each other's cheeks as we both wept for joy.

"Does your belly grow hard and then ease? Are these coming evenly spaced?"

"Yes, I am having pains, but they come and go." Mary smiled. "So glad you are here to help."

"If you will lie down, I will have a look at your huge lump, soon to be a child." We giggled together at the thought.

"The child cannot come soon enough," Mary said.

"I will go tend the donkey." Joseph hurried away. He had been sitting quietly on the hay pile in the corner. He wore a brown woven robe over a wheat colored tunic, had a light brown covering on his head, and wore dark brown leather sandals on his feet.

The hay smelled fresh as the stable boy had recently cleaned the animal dung from the area to make it a tolerable place for people. When Mary settled on the blanket, I put my hand on her belly. I could tell she experienced an abdominal tightening, but truly hard labor was still to come. "Are you ready for this?" My spoken words remained in the air, despite my thought to recover the poor question.

"I am ready. Oh, I humbly desire to hold my precious baby in my arms. Any pain I must bear will recede in the wake of my joy." Mary spoke breathlessly. "My aunt lives in town, but Joseph told me the house is already full of other traveling families."

"The town overflows with travelers," I murmured. I had a flask of rosemary steeped in olive oil. I blended the oil with more herbs and splashes of wine in a bowl. I gently massaged her abdomen with the herbal oils. "Is the pain too great for you to stand?" I helped her up, taking time until she was finally stable.

"It is not so bad." Mary cupped her hands across her middle to caress the baby cradled inside.

"It will be awhile, and it would be good for you to walk around if you can." I put my arm around Mary's back and we strolled outside the stable.

"Tell me about your husband. Will he miss you terribly?"

"Judah bar Cleodan is busy with the flocks. Unless they have returned, he does not know I have left my tent."

"And if he has returned?"

"He will miss me, but he will understand my place is here helping with a birth." I lied. I knew not what he thought about my being a midwife, because we had never discussed it. I assumed he accepted my being a healer, but he would hate that I had traveled to Bethlehem alone.

"Then I shall not feel badly about keeping you away from Judah. How is it with you and your husband? I suppose you are happy." Mary breathed deeply and sighed.

The clean golden hay crunched beneath our sandals while we paced, going into and out of the stable.

"Yes, I am happy. His demands are few, and he is frequently away with the flocks." I tried to answer honestly. "He is a quiet man. My mother-in-law is a different story. She constantly stares at my middle to see if I am with child. She thinks I am shunning my wifely duties and is forever asking me to do chores. 'Pack these rugs. Wash these cloths. Give me a hand with this pot of stew.' I can never please her."

"Poor Hannah." Mary giggled, presumably at the way I had changed my voice to mimic Naliah's rasp. "We all have to please our mother-in-laws." She bent her knees suddenly in a bearing down pain.

I caught Mary and put an arm around her back to help her stand. "Let us go back inside, but try to keep walking even while these pangs start." The sunset lit the partly cloudy sky and painted pale pink and gold wisps of color on the horizon. It was a beautiful, cold night. I praised God for the wonderful friend he had given me in Mary. I gently guided her back into the stable, lit the oil lamp, and placed it on a low wood stool. The simple round pot lamp with a cloth wick flickered a flame and attracted a moth that danced playfully in front of the light.

"Lie down for a while, now. Let me see how things are progressing." I felt her belly, grown hard again, but knew it might be hours before the baby would appear.

"What shall I do?" She gazed up at me with trusting eyes.

"You may do whatever you wish. If it pleases you to lie down, then it would be well to do so. If it feels better to walk a short way, it may hurry the baby. You are doing nicely, but this is your first child and it will take its time to come into the world."

"Son," Mary affirmed. "It will be a boy." Her face was cherubic in the lamplight. We both turned then as we heard footsteps crunching the hay-strewn dirt floor.

"Hannah." Benjamin called from the stable entry. "You are a hard one to find. You must come home now. Mother's got a fever." His voice took on a bold authority, but cracked before he finished talking. "You...you must come."

"I cannot. Mary is in the midst of childbirth and her baby is coming. Has Serena been summoned?"

He paused in the gateway to the stable enclosure. Because a woman was in labor he halted, but he insisted, "Serena is there, but it is your job to take care of Mother." He stood wide legged and firm, stretching his full height, a hand taller than me. At twelve years, the spoiled youngest son puffed with self-importance.

"No." Though troubled, I disbelieved his urgency for me to return. "I am needed more here."

"So, our mother can die while you take care of strangers."

"Ben..." I wanted to lash out at him, but feared it would be upsetting to Mary. I composed myself. "Go sup, have a bite to eat, and I will speak with you in awhile." I felt exasperated. He hesitated and I asked, "Do you want coins?"

"I have enough money." Benjamin reddened, turned quickly and left.

You may go take care of his mother." Mary smiled up at me. "The birth will happen the way it has been foretold."

"Yes, I know, Mary." I became torn because of the request from Benjamin, but I determined I should stay with her.

CHAPTER NINE

While I was busy with Mary, I hoped Benjamin went into the inn for refreshment. When her pangs eased for a time and she rested, I went to find him. Ramen waved to me to come toward the kitchen where he stirred something in a steaming vessel. Benjamin was off in a corner talking with two men I recognized from home.

"So have you met Benjamin, my brother-in-law?" I gestured to where he sat.

"The boy in the corner?"

I nodded.

"I wondered at him coming in here alone. The appearance of his cloak and the way he smelled put no doubt in my mind he was a shepherd. When I asked what I could do for him, he scowled and demanded service, saying he wanted figs, dates, bread, and stew, but then he reached in a pouch dangling from his belt and turned away. It amused me when he mumbled he wanted only wine. Thinking back to my young self, I brought him watered wine. I gave him a bowl of pottage with a round of bread and told him it cost no money today."

"He does have an appetite. Can he see me when I stand behind this post?"

"No." I smiled gratefully when Ramen placed a cup of wine in my hands.

"Thank you. He is not alone, but traveled in the company of others. The man is Cleopas, the father of Laban, the boy who is sitting next to Benjamin. They probably came here to trade wool for fresh supplies they needed."

"When I asked Benjamin if his family traveled here to pay taxes, he told me no, but he came to bring his sister home to take care of his ill mother. He wolfed down his food while he talked, and told me his sister did not want to come home because she attended a poor woman having a baby in a stable." Ramen had a half smile on his face.

Still hidden from Benjamin's view, I turned to leave, but Ramen firmly laid his hand on my arm, flashed his dark eyes at me, and continued to talk. Even though I wanted to go back to the stable, I sipped more wine and listened.

"The boy told me how you used to play and run races with him, but now you were too grown up and were married to his brother. His eyes grew wide with surprise when I asked if he had traveled all this way to bring

Hannah home. He told me his mother had commanded him to fetch you, because she has a fever. Apparently another healer tried to coax her to drink a soothing tea, but she refused it. I think he is afraid."

I broke in on Ramen's account. "She is my mother-in law and, of course, Benjamin is fearful. Although he is usually lazy and takes no more steps than asked, his fears sent him running off with the family donkey to Bethlehem to find me." I took the last sip of purple wine and left Ramen managing his servants in the foggy kitchen.

The cool night sky studded with glittering expectant stars. I watched as Mary continued to labor. Unlike other women I had seen, Mary never complained or cried out. Her waters had issued while she had squatted on the makeshift birthing stool. Everything seemed to be normal. Joseph continued to stay away, but I knew if Mary called to him he was close enough to hear. The bleating of a lamb prompted, "Baa," from its mother. The atmosphere felt still, almost breathless. I believed the very air awaited this blessed event.

Suddenly Mary gave a hard push, cried out, and the Baby emerged. First babies were usually more difficult than this. The Boy had a crown of dark fuzz on His head, and He was plump, slippery and warm. He shone royally, a tiny beam from a bright heavenly star. I tied off, and then quickly cut His cord with a sharp bone knife. I turned the Baby upside down to spit out any mucus in His throat. I would have smacked Him smartly to cause Him to take in air, but He already breathed and made suckling noises.

The Blessed Child cried out in a resounding newborn wail and I placed Him on Mary's breast.

I cleaned everything with the water from the ewers the stable boy provided. I rubbed the baby's pink skin with salted water to clean off the blood and fluids and helped Mary clean herself as well. I reached into my sack of supplies and drew out a white cloth I had woven. With it, I swaddled the newborn. When we finished bundling Him, His sweet shining face peered from the folds of cloth. "Thank you for his wrapper. Who made it?"

"I did."

"It is fine linen cloth. I had a swaddling cloth in my sack, but I am happy we used what you have given us." Mary enjoyed a few silent moments with the Child. A heavenly light emanated from His face. His dark eyes expressed an indescribable ageless wisdom. There lay an ancient intelligence and truly the Son of God.

Joseph, who had been a few feet outside the stable, came inside and knelt next to his wife and son. He touched them each tenderly with his capable brown hands, and his face beamed with wonder. Her head covering had been cast aside. He brushed both her cheeks with his lips. Proud, vigilant and protective, he stayed beside them all night.

Suddenly, the sky which had been still was alive with what I thought at first to be a windstorm. Chaff blew around. Skins that hung over the railings moved with the breeze. And everywhere a whooshing noise along with humming and singing voices permeated the air. At first,

I thought the beautiful sounds of choral voices came from the inn where guests sometimes gathered to sing. But then I became aware of what appeared to be people entering the stable. They were not humans; they were airy silvery cloud-like beings, and they moved about on gossamer wings. Two at a time, the heavenly visitors came in and hovered in adoration over the manger where the radiant Infant and Mary were bedded down in the hay. Mary lay entranced. I blinked when the trail of angels flew in and then soared away to form an assembly over the stable at Hawara Inn.

Never had I gazed upon such splendor. I was overly tired, and thought perhaps I dreamed. I became overwhelmed and speech left my tongue. Joseph stood next to Mary. She smiled benignantly and peacefully. Mary may have expected the company. Truly, she had given birth to the Messiah.

My heart sang and my joy filled my entire being. Awestricken by it all, I wondered how a poor girl such as I had been given the blessing to be the first human to touch the Messiah. It had been a calling, a desire to help my friend Mary, to be in on the excitement, to be important, but now I sank to my knees in the scratchy hay, praising God with these heavenly beings. In adoration, I bowed before the Baby I had helped into the world, and had bundled with a cloth woven with my hands. If it was all a dream, I did not want to wake up.

Those watchful sentinels hovered above the stable. All quieted by the time I curled up in the hay on the floor near the manger bed. Peaceful and secure, I fell into an exhausted sleep.

Dawn came. The sun had slowly begun to cast its golden rays on the horizon when I awoke with a start. Now more visitors arrived, but these I recognized. Father Moshe, who walked with the aid of his staff, Noa, Cleopas, Jonah, and other shepherds stood at a respectful distance from the stable. Upon waking out of a heavy sleep, I thought they were coming to capture me and force me to go home. How had they known to come? The men bowed courteously and shyly near the entrance, remaining outside the stable. I stood up and went to Father Moshe, and greeted him with a kiss. "Do you know who is in the manger?"

"Yes," said Father Moshe. He pointed to the heavens. "The wind spoke to us. Praise to the King, hosanna, praise Him! The Messiah has come. We left our flocks asleep and followed the angels' singing voices. I want to see Him." It was difficult for him to walk, but Moshe, with my help made his way to the manger where the Baby lay. He groaned as his old his knees creaked when he kneeled in the hay. He had tears in his eyes. "The Promised One has come."

Benjamin and Ramen were standing nearby. They had come to find out what the excitement was all about. "So, the baby is finally here. Now I have more men to help me bring you home. If the worst has happened to mother, you are to blame." Benjamin faced me, wagging his finger toward my face as a menacing threat.

Nothing could cause me to worry now. I had accomplished my mission. What had occurred revealed to me so much more than I had ever dreamed when I first had the mysterious call to come and be with Mary.

"I caught Him when He came into the world," I murmured to Father Moshe as I helped him stand.

"Daughter, thank you." He patted my arm, let go of me, and straightened his body.

More visitors rushed into the stable, stirring up the scent of hay in the air.

"Mary, I did not know you already had the child." A round-faced woman in a blue tunic rushed into the stable, brushing past everyone, waving her arms with flapping sleeves to shoo the men away. "I am sorely vexed at not having been with you." She ran to embrace Mary. "My guests left, and now I have room for you." She lifted the Baby and cuddled Him.

"Thank you. Hannah, this is my aunt Mary. She and Uncle Eleazer will care for us. You go home with your people. I will be fine now."

"Mary." I embraced my friend, kissing her wet cheeks and mingling our tears. My life had been changed forever.

"I will go back with you, Father Moshe."

"I hope you get back to our mother in time." Benjamin squinted meanly at me when he spoke.

CHAPTER TEN

By the time we reached camp the golden sun dazzled the horizon. A bright star lingered near the rim of the earth and soon faded. "It is another sign," Father Moshe said.

Creamy white blankets for extra shade were tied around the tent of Naliah and Cleodan, giving the appearance of a celebration instead of a person near death. I found her lying on her bed. "I will never be well again," she sighed.

I knelt and touched her cool forehead. "Truly, how are you?" When she failed to answer, I said, "You are well then?"

"No help from you." Her eyes flashed angrily. "When will you learn where your place is? Do you know it at all? I should never have allowed Judah to become your husband. You went away without his permission." She waved her hand at me, the way she would if she were swatting a flying bug. "Go! I do not want to see you again."

"But, I was..." It was no use trying to explain. I regretted I had not stayed with Mary for more days instead of coming here at my mother-in-law's bidding. "Rest well." Normally I would have wanted to argue with her, but I felt tired and still had such a sense of peace I could say no more. I gratefully returned to my tent.

My husband sat in front of the open flap of our tent, gazing off into the distance. While the air felt comfortable, the intense anger on his face chilled me. His dark eyes focused on me and tried to bore into my soul. I said nothing to him, but stood quietly waiting for him to speak. Finally he said, "I never speak ill to you, Hannah, about your work as a midwife or healer, but this time you went too far. I was embarrassed when you had to be summoned home to care for Mother. And you traveled alone. I became even more humiliated when I saw you come back to camp accompanied by the sorriest of the lot of shepherds. They were in charge of the sheep on the east hill. They simply left them because they said they heard angels in the wind." His voice held an uncharacteristic sneer. Unlike his normal silent demeanor, Judah continued to talk. "They told a wild story about the Messiah, born in a stable in Bethlehem. The Messiah was born in a stable? I doubt it. They all left me behind on the other side of the rise and I gathered their flocks with my own to keep for the night."

"I was with them, because I assisted at the birth of

the Messiah. I wish you had been there too. It is all too amazing for me to tell of it."

"Oh, truly? I suppose you saw a bunch of angels. People are whispering about you running off alone." The hard tone in his voice sounded much like his mother's. "Benjamin says the son of an innkeeper appeared to be fond of you." He shook his finger at me.

"No, he is not." Heat began creeping up my neck. "What has happened to you? I did speak with the man, but only for business. I waited tables in the inn to repay him for…" I stopped. How would all of this sound to a jealous and angry husband? How could I explain what had happened? I had taken Judah for granted, because he had always been meek and agreeable. I wondered if the painful, hardened lump behind his ear had gone away. I had rubbed herbal ointment onto it two days before I left. He was not usually one to speak out the way he did now. Something was terribly wrong.

"I have much to tell you. Come inside where we may talk." My whole being sagged with weariness, yet I knew we had to talk this thing out.

"You worked like a common servant at the inn?" His red face contorted with anger. He stood suddenly, raised his hand as if he wanted to strike me, lowered it, shook his head, and stomped off toward his mother's tent.

"No, not what you think, Judah." He did not turn around as I spoke, but I decided it would gain nothing for me to call him back. He had never been this angry with me. I sank to the ground and dissolved into wrenching tears. Perhaps he was very tired like I was, since he had the responsibility of several flocks last night. Bone weary, I thought I could fall asleep right here on the ground in front of my tent. I managed to crawl inside and fall on my sleeping mat. When I tried to think about my options, all I visualized was a darling Baby with the light emanating from His very being. I slept alone, unknowing whether Judah had returned to his flocks or stayed in his mother's tent. Most young couples lived in an extra wing of the family tent. Now I was grateful his mother had refused to have us live with them when we married.

The next day Judah left. "Good morning," I said to the wives of Cleopas and Noa. They did not look at me and kept shaking rugs. People were polite, but they avoided talking with me. Maybe I imagined all of the insults. I knew I had done nothing wrong.

Mother Lydia sat in the sunlight spinning cream-colored wool into yarn. I wanted to talk with her and hear her motherly voice. Seeing her by her tent, I brought my lap loom and sat next to her for several minutes before she set her work aside. "So, Hannah, my girl, what have you to say for yourself?"

"I was midwife to Mary of Nazareth who bore the Messiah in Bethlehem. He is absolutely beautiful. I am sure of the truth of it." Seeing the uncertain expression on Mother Lydia's face, I said, "I suppose you disbelieve what I say. But I wish you could have been there. Father Moshe knew."

"He is crazy like the rest of them." She refrained from

casting her eyes on me. "How could he have left our flocks unattended? They claim angels told them to go see the Blessed Baby. Whoever heard of such a thing?"

"I believe there were angels. They were white and pure and one could almost see through them, they were so…" I struggled for descriptive words. I raised my shuttle, yet I plied no weave.

"Well, my girl, you had better ask the angels to tell you about your marriage. People are talking. You ran off to Bethlehem alone, Naliah ill. Because you are not yet with child after all this time, Judah bar Cleodan can leave you and take a new wife."

My peacefulness shattered. I never expected Mother Lydia to sorely lecture me. "Would he do that? It has been about a year, but is not my fault a baby refuses to grow in my womb. Judah is seldom at home. I am not the one who stays away tending the sheep every chance I get." I was close to tears, and when I saw the shocked expression on her countenance I went to her. I would have buried my face on her shoulder and asked for forgiveness for my outburst, but she put up a hand to stop me. I bowed my head before her. "I am sorry, Mother. I am very upset by all of this. I would never intend to cause anyone so much trouble, especially you. Please forgive me."

Mother Lydia smiled sadly then, and tears trickled down her face. "Oh, my girl, the same words I often heard when you were a child and I scolded you." She reached her arms up to embrace me. I thought wistfully how my life had been uncomplicated when I had been younger.

"I was barren and Moshe did not put me away. We took a foundling to rear as our own child. That was you, my girl." She quieted for a time. "What will you do?" Her sad eyes pleaded with me.

I gave her another hug. "I must speak with Judah, but I believe he is out grazing sheep." I wondered if I would ever be able to convince my husband to stay with me. "And I shall try to talk with Naliah." My heart and mind rebelled, but I wanted to give Mother Lydia hope. More than anything else, I wanted to be with Mary and her Child. What had happened to the peace encircling me in the stable?

"Go with God, then, my girl." She patted my arm. "Moshe and you are all the family I have."

I rolled my eyes up toward the heavens when I left Mother Lydia's tent, hoping for a sign. The clear blue sky had a haze near the horizon where the dust from a herd of sheep lingered in the still air. I walked back toward my tent and the dust clung to my sandals. Even though it was improper for me to go to the fields alone, I wanted to find Judah and confront him. I would make him listen to me. I would ask him what he thought about our childless marriage. I packed a waist bag of herbs, a skin with watered wine, and picked up a staff from beside my tent.

I strolled casually past the women and children keeping my eyes downcast, and avoided conversation. I felt the icy stares. What gossip had started? I walked past the tent of Naliah, giving it a wide berth. I wanted to avoid speaking with either her or Benjamin. I held my head up high and walked toward the grazing pasture. I hesitated, worrying about what would happen, but I did not return to the encampment. I kept going. Deep inside, I knew I had done nothing wrong, but could see how people could misunderstand my going to Bethlehem secretively and alone. Judah would have to understand, because I wanted to help Mary in these first critical days after the delivery of the Child. I wanted to go back to Bethlehem.

When I saw Judah in the distance, he looked like a young boy leaning on his staff and singing to his sheep. I felt both pity and love at the sight of him. How hurt he must have been when the whole encampment scorned me. I stopped and took a deep breath of the cool morning air. I walked faster. He held a new lamb in the folds of his cloak. I was more than a stone's throw away from him, and he looked up at me. When I came nearer, a thrumming in my chest threatened to undo my resolve. Sunshine dazzled my eyes as the breeze lifted my head covering. "Judah." I hesitated to say anything else.

He turned away from me. "Why have you come? You will frighten the sheep."

"The sheep are showing not as much as a grain of fear." Indeed, the flock still bedded down, and only the lead ram, Caesar, stood. "Perhaps you are the frightened one?"

"No." He cast his eyes toward the earth to avoid me.

"I will tell you what happened. I went to Bethlehem to be with Mary when she bore the Baby. I knew it would come soon." I avoided telling him about the angel voice in the wind, because of the attitude he had about the herders who had left their flocks at the angel's bidding. "On the way I found a man who had been beset by thieves and I bound his wounds and…"

"Thieves?" He turned to face me and his eyes were ringed with dark circles and puffed from crying or lack of sleep. "That is the reason you must not ever journey alone. Hannah, it is unsafe for you to be by yourself in the desert. How could you have done such a thing? You dreadfully worried me."

"A Voice called and bade me to go there."

"Why did you have to be there? What about me? Do you forget you are married to me? Why go alone?"

"Would you have come with me?"

"No, I have to work, but Benjamin could have gone." His voice spewed in a defensive whine.

"Benjamin? He is too lazy to accompany me." I took another step forward.

"You were disobedient to me and our fathers. You told no one you were going. "

"I told Serena." A sudden gust of wind blew my head covering off, and I stood before him with my long dark unbraided hair tangling in the breeze. His dark eyes widened with an expression of wonder and anger at the same time.

"Why tell her, and not tell the family? When Mother became ill everyone searched for you until Serena told them where you had gone."

"I am sorry I caused you worry and trouble. What

do you want me to do?" My eyes failed to make contact with his.

He became silent and turned his face toward the flocks. The lamb in his cloak kicked and bleated so he set it down. It hobbled away unsteadily for a few steps, then broke into an amusing sideways caper toward its mother. The ram stood up, and the rest of the flock gradually rose from the brown stubble. The odor of sheep dung and wool filled the dusty air around us.

The antics of the lamb caused me to smile, and I watched Judah also enjoying its capering. Our thoughts came together and we grasped arms in a formal embrace, kissing each other's cheeks. "What shall I do?"

He shook his head, threw up his hands and frowned. "I do not know. Mother is very angry with you and she wants me to give you a divorcement."

"Why?" I knew his mother's reasons, but wondered if they were his as well.

"Hannah, we have not, I mean, you have not yet…" At a loss for words, he blushed.

"You mean she wants to see a grandchild. The fault is all mine?" I was angry, frightened. Did my husband truly intend to put me away?

"You must go back. Did you tell your mother where you were going?"

"We are not through talking." Out here with the sheep, and no one to hear us, I knew I had to share my inmost thoughts. "In time, I do want to have our children. After the first time when you failed to do what a husband should do with me, you... You know what must be done."

"I know I cannot do..." A croaking catch in his voice halted his words. "What shall I do? I wonder if I will always be the same way." He rubbed his almost beardless chin thoughtfully. "Maybe it will be better if I put you aside."

"No." I was stunned. I had thought in time the boy I had married would become a man and we would have children. We needed more time. The lump behind his ear caused me to worry. I wanted to ask if I could have a look at it, but decided to wait until we were through discussing our problems. Tears trickled down my cheeks and I wiped my face with my coarse sleeve.

"Hannah, Hannah, I care for you very much. I wish we two could go away and be far from our families, simply you and me and our sheep. Then in time I believe I could be a better husband to you." It sounded to me like he had second thoughts.

"Judah, you are such a dreamer. I care for you, too." I reached for him and hugged him tightly. "If you want to go away we can, but it will be impossible without the protection of the others."

He did not resist my hug, but did not hug me back. He stared off into the distance. "There are greener fields over those hills, and I want to take our flocks there."

"You have your father's sheep as well as those of Father Moshe. Would you take them all with you?"

"There is naught I could do to separate them." His words came out flat. He raised his hands as if defeated.

"No. Please listen to me. You know we cannot live without the protection of our families." Neither of us spoke. We watched as the sheep lazily nibbled at the sparse grass stubble.

"Judah, I want to go back to Bethlehem." I decided to distract him from his foolish idea.

"To be with that woman and her baby?" He scowled and doubled a fist at his side.

"Yes, the Baby is the Messiah. I know it. I heard it. I feel it inside my soul. I truly want to be with them again." My inner peace and joy remained.

"Hannah, you are deluded. You must come with me." He grasped my hand.

"Why? Why must I go with you? Why do you wish to go now? The flocks have enough to eat right over there." A patch of greener grass grew in a low place beyond the chewed dry remnant at our feet. I pointed with one hand and he let go the other.

"The grazing pasture is more abundant where I am going. I can no longer stay with the others and be humiliated. They say you are a wild woman, and men say I am not a man." His head was downcast, his arms dangled at his sides, and he cast his eyes away from me. "You would be unprotected to face it alone. Therefore you must come with me."

"Will we tell them we are leaving?"

"No." He looked straight at me, and his voice echoed in my ears.

"Judah, we cannot think of such a thing. Your mother

and Mother Lydia will be beside themselves with grief and even anger. At least let me go back and pack a few provisions and bid our mothers farewell." I thought to pacify him until I could talk him out of this unwise move.

"They will stop us." He avoided my eyes.

We were so intent on our problems that the man who approached gave us no notice until we saw his shadow near. He shouted, "Greetings, you two." He walked, lazily swinging his staff.

Judah sighed and clenched his fists as we watched Ham walk toward us. I replaced my head covering that had blown aside earlier.

"Well, did I interrupt you two?" Ham sneered. "Your mother wants you and is searching for you, Hannah."

"Mother Lydia or Naliah?"

"Naliah."

"Is she then ill once more?"

"Not ill, but ill tempered." He chuckled at his own joke.

"I am glad you came. Judah and I are going to move our flocks off beyond those hills. When you go back to camp you can tell them where we have gone to ease the burden of worry."

"Why would a man ask his woman to come grazing with him?"

"I suppose you think I should be back at camp tending to my spinning and weaving." I jutted out my chin.

"You have quite a woman there." Ham wagged his finger at Judah. "Hannah and I had a good time together out by the river bank one time. She almost let me know her."

Judah stared at me with dark eyes. I shook my head. "No!"

"You are telling me a lie, Ham. What do you want from us?" Judah's fists clenched.

"I want your woman. When you put her away, which is what your mother wants, I will take her," Ham leered. "She can give me strong sons."

Judah raised his staff and swung it mightily at Ham. Ham ducked and lunged at him. The staff was flung aside. I screamed. The two of them wrestled in the sand briefly, but heavy Ham, twice as strong, had easily thrown my husband to the earth. He held him face down in the dry stubble and sand for several moments. Blood flowed from Judah's nose when he lifted his face from the ground. I yelled, "Stop, stop," but it landed on deaf ears.

I picked up Judah's staff and hit Ham over the head with it from behind. Ham swore, "Ooh, camel dung!" He sprang to his feet. "Ah, you wish to wrestle with me. Ha! I could have a good time with both of you." He reached for me, but I sidestepped him quickly. I gathered up the hem of my robe and sped across the sand. I ran with all my power. I did not look back, but heard Ham laughing. "Run, girl. Soon you will be all mine."

I ran faster. I had no knowledge of where I rushed blindly to escape from harm. I gazed back to see if Ham followed, and he did not, but I feared to return to where I had left them. I slowed down to a walk, thinking I might go back to Judah in awhile. As I walked the sun grew higher and I saw no shelter. I also had no water because I had dropped my flask of watered wine when I fled. My mouth felt parched. I cast my eyes ahead where thankfully, a stream of water shone. I ran toward it, but it eluded me, and I never got closer to it. I was fearful and frustrated and I dropped to the sand and caught my breath. I remembered a bag of mint leaves at my waist. One bit of leaf on my tongue tasted fresh and moist.

Judah could follow because I went in the general direction he told me he wanted us to move. If he were to catch up, I had to stop. With my outer cloak I made a tent over my whole body. And thus I sat for a long while, thinking, but not coming up with a workable plan. In the heat my mind wandered in delirium. I dreamed of an angel coming to rescue me. At times my thoughts went back to Bethlehem and Mary. I tried to imagine how they were getting along. Truly her Baby was the Messiah, so what could happen? They would both be well, and I could stop worrying. Mary's life would be full now.

"My life is empty," I said aloud. In reality, no angel came to rescue me. I was afraid and entirely alone. My body wracked with sobs, but I had no more tears. "Oh, Messiah, I want to see you. I must know that you both are well. Please keep Mary safe. Rescue me from harm, and help me sort out my life." I prayed to Him and drifted off to sleep.

In my dream I stood on a high mountain where dark green shrubs grew in dense thickets. Thunder and lightning flashed from the dark clouds overhead. The clouds floated close enough to envelop me. I felt excited, unafraid. An invisible spirit lingered near, very kind and loving, that I could depend upon and speak with. Perhaps it could be the kind spirit of Mary. I had been at peace with her, but the gentle Voice I heard in the wind had the deep tone of a man. "My child, you are never alone. I am always with you." A protective arm enfolded my shoulders the way Father Moshe would hold me safely when I had been a child.

When I awakened I still had the blissful feeling of having been visited by the kindest, most caring soul I had ever met. And the words abided in my mind and soul. "I am always with you." When I threw back the cloak the sun created long shadows from small rocks and desert plants. When I looked toward the mountains, I saw clouds forming. A shiver went through me. Had I been up there in my dream? In the distance where I had run from earlier in the day, dust billowed, hopefully being kicked up by a flock of sheep or goats. Judah? I thirsted, but could not make myself move from where I sat. My legs were like old rolled-up rugs that refused to stand at first, and crumpled when upright. I stood and waved my cloak, hoping to attract his attention.

As the flock came nearer, I felt afraid and let down. No one led them. I recognized our lead ram, about a half a head taller than the rest of the sheep, holding his head up majestically. His horns curled forward in twin arcs and he had a black crescent on his nose. "Caesar," I called to him. It was, of course, an irreverent act to name a ram thus, but no authorities would hear us in the desert. Caesar came to me and stopped. When he did, the whole flock shuffled to a stop. "Where have you left my husband?" It was unusual for the sheep to go away without their shepherd, unless they were frightened.

All around the gently rolling hills I saw nothing save scrub brush and stones. I wondered why Judah would have wanted to come to this place, as grazing appeared to be sparse. Perhaps farther on, closer to the mountains, we would find water and greener grass. I wanted to follow the sheep tracks back from where they had come to find Judah. I worried about his injuries, knowing Ham had attacked him. I had few herbs with me. "Rest a moment all of you." I rubbed my head, which throbbed fiercely. When I put my arms about the wooly neck of our ram, I saw a flask hanging there. I thanked him profusely and unknotted the tie that secured it. I took a big gulp of the water and wine mixture, and then closed the flask. "Caesar, let us go find your master before darkness descends and we cannot see your trail."

I walked back the way I had come, following the sheep tracks, and the flock obediently followed me. Our pace slowed, because my legs were very tired. I kept my eyes on the trail for signs of a person, or of a struggle. A wind blew. "You are a blessing," I told the wind. "You are cooling things off, but if you become too strong, you will take away the sheep trail." My life pulse quickened, but I did not panic. While I saw no person, I sensed a benevolent Being was nearby. The sky became darker and

Caesar and other sheep let out a plaintive, "Baa-baa." He stopped and peered at me with his bland dark eyes. I kept walking, trying to ignore his pleas to stop.

"Come." I tugged at his wooly neck. Caesar nodded his head and started to walk again. Several of the flock started a fretful bleating, and ewes stopped to nurse the lambs. "Oh, all right, sorry." I threw up my hands. "You may all rest for awhile." On a different day, I could have been coming home at this time with a jug of water on my shoulders. Judah would have been bedding the sheep down in the pastures or a sheepfold for the evening. I thought over the last few days and felt saddened by the turn of events. I wept quietly, wondered if he felt dire pain, or did he lie dead among stones? He was too dedicated to his flock to let his sheep wander off without him. The worry gave me a hollow ache. Caesar knelt down to rest next to me. I sat down, and curled up with my arm thrown across his comforting wooly neck that smelled of his special oil and salt. I noted his coat had grown quickly after the last shearing. I closed my eyes for a moment to rest them.

When I awakened, the stars were shining brightly overhead on a night filled with occasional bug whirs and rasps. I hoped no lions, wolves, or wild dogs roamed in the area. My whole being became alert to the assorted noises of the desert, the snuffling of sleeping sheep, and a different strange sound. I listened again, straining my ears. Echoes carried far in the desert, because nothing stood in the way to absorb them. It could almost be human, a faint moaning wafting over the sands. The hair on my arms prickled. I listened and wondered if it was Judah. Could he be near enough for me to reach him? The dimly lighted moon hung overhead like less than half a melon, yet I decided to walk toward the sound. I removed the flask from Caesar's neck, patted him firmly and said, "Stay here." He lifted his head when I stood, but remained in his reclined sleepy position.

Visions of being lost in the desert came to me as I rushed toward the moaning sound. I tripped over gray rocks and tufts of grass and came to a stony rise. The noise grew louder. A shadowy outcropping loomed ahead. When I drew near, I saw an opening. It was a cave in whose mouth the wind sang a mournful tune. I stopped at the shadowy hole. "Judah! Judah bar Cleodan, are you in there?"

The moan lured me to come closer. I had heard of caves such as this one. People said spirits lived there. Father Moshe once told me he thought the sound came from the wind humming as it worked its way through a cavern. Frightened, I could not decide if I would stay and look further or return to the flock. I saw the faint outline of our sheep in the valley below. I kneeled on the ground, bent and buried my face in the folds of my robe and I gave in to great racking sobs. After a time, I shrugged myself up and stood, clearing my thoughts. I berated myself for being a crybaby. The night air was cool. Thoughts of Mary and the Messiah came wafting back into my mind, and a calm came over me once more. I tried to reason what to do next. I must find Judah. Responsible for our flock, I did not know whether to search more now or go back.

At the cave entrance, I thought I heard labored breathing. I hoped it was Judah, but it could also be a desert wanderer or animal. I stepped cautiously inside the mouth of the cave and tried to gain night vision. In the darkness, I inched forward feeling the rough walls. The rocky ceiling scraped at my head making it necessary for me to stoop. I stopped, life pulse pounding. How far should I go? Nearby I heard labored breathing. Sweat beaded my forehead. My foot bumped against what I thought to be an animal or body. I heard short wheezy breaths.

"Judah," I whispered, and hoped for an answer. I kneeled down and groped in the dark, and my hands touched his rough robe. He made no reply, and my hand worked its way to his head. He lay face down, and I explored his matted uncovered hair. "Judah, Judah." I wondered if I could pull him out of the cave to see in the moonlight if this actually was my husband. I put both my hands on his shoulders and shook them, trying to rouse him. My hand explored his face and went directly behind his left ear. I touched upon the lump and wetness I thought to be blood. "What happened to you? Did Ham abuse you?"

A plaintive moan came from his lips. I cradled his head in my lap and sat stroking his sweaty, bloody hair. I reached for the flask at his waist, untied it, and dripped water onto my fingertips, then applied the moisture to his lips. I was fearful for his life. My mind traveled back to our earlier quarrel when he had threatened a divorcement. If we left the others and went off on a nomadic life by ourselves, could we survive? The desert held bushels of unpredictable events. Weather changed abruptly provoking strong winds and flash floods to destroy our tents. Marauding tribes or bandits might overpower us and take our flock and goods. Wild animals killed lambs. If he wanted me to go with him, I should, and I did not want to return home without him. While I cradled his head, his breath weakened and came in short gasps. How much blood had he lost? I felt his skull and I found oozing blood. He had a gaping, squishy wound. Had he taken a hard fall on the rocks? Or had Ham applied a rock to his skull? I wished I had a lamp.

From deeper inside the cave I now heard another sound, the scratching noise of what I imagined could be wild dogs or a lion. Fear clutched at my insides. The hair at the back of my neck tingled, but I could not give in to terror. I tugged at Judah's body. Again and again I pulled and prodded. It was useless. I envisioned wild animals attacking, tearing at flesh. "Oh, Yahweh, oh, Messiah, please give me strength." I laid my body across the limp one of my husband to protect him. The noise subsided. Hours passed. While his life pulse faded, his breath became shallow. Everything grew quiet.

CHAPTER ELEVEN

Judah had died. Eyes almost blinded with tears, I slipped from the cave carrying his flask and staff. A pang struck my inward being at leaving him, but I did not know what else to do. Then I raced away and breathed a sigh of relief as I saw our flock in the valley. The ram stood. When I reached him, I kneeled by him and buried my wet face in his fluffy coat of wool. I babbled, "Our master is gone. What shall I do?" I came to my senses as the sun lightened the horizon.

"Come, Caesar." We led the flock toward camp. I saw two men in the distance. One was Father Moshe, walking with the aid of a staff. I knew he anxiously sought me, but feared the sheep would scatter if I ran to him. Cleopas came with him.

"Oh, Father Moshe," I briefly collapsed against his frail body. "Judah is dead. Men must now be burdened to bring him from the cave a half day journey away."

"Dead? Are you sure?" He stroked my head. "Daughter, I am sorry. Did a lion or wild dog take his life from him?"

"There were sounds in the cave, perhaps dogs, maybe a lion. It was dark when I found him badly injured, still breathing, but his tongue gave me no words. He died in my arms."

"You are brave, my daughter. I will ask someone strong to help, perhaps Ham."

"No," I blurted. Had Ham caused Judah's death? "I mean, yes, thank you, I need help with the sheep and we must take care of his body." Why had the flock of sheep been protected from the beasts?

"The men will have a ways to travel from camp." Father Moshe cleared his throat.

"I will go back to Judah and be the *shomeret*, because his body must not be left alone." I had been reluctant to leave him, because our practice required someone to stay out of respect for the deceased.

"I will go and stay with Judah's body," Cleopas said. "He was a friend, a fine shepherd and I will miss him."

Nothing seemed real to me afterward. Numbness prevailed. Benjamin came to herd and tend our flocks. Ham and two other men went to take care of Judah's body. When they returned, they said his torn flesh, with bite marks, proved a wild animal killed him. After pouring water on the floor of the cave, they wrapped and buried him inside a cavern near where he had died. The women wailed loudly as was the custom. All who had touched his dead body were ceremonially unclean.

Since I had been with Judah, our laws deemed me to be unclean. In the dry area where we were, no nearby *mikva* existed in which to immerse myself, so the women took a jug of water and poured it over me three times for my ritual cleansing.

Serena walked me to my tent. Mother Lydia dressed me in black haircloth for mourning. Concerned only about me, she wiped my brow with cool water and made me sip wine. She offered me barley cakes and broth, but I had no appetite. Days passed and I continued to stay in my tent. For seven days people came to quietly express sympathy. I nodded, saying little. Even though I had initially objected to my marriage, I had grown to love Judah. As a married woman I had status. I had belonged to him. Now it was as though I too had died. For days I went about my life half aware of those near me. "My girl, you must have a bowl of this stew I made especially for you," Mother Lydia coaxed.

"Thank you." Nothing smelled or tasted savory to me. How long ago had Judah died? While my strength slowly returned, my faith felt as dry as the desert sand. Yahweh had failed to answer my prayers to protect my husband.

Father Moshe and Mother Lydia came to my tent together. "How are you two this fine day?" I asked. "Please sit in the shade and I will bring wine."

"We are well, thank you." Mother Lydia settled on the mat next to Father Moshe.

The two of them together seldom talked with me. I knew something troubled them. "What important news do you have?" I handed a goblet of wine to Father Moshe.

Father Moshe took it, cleared his throat and began, "Six moons have risen and waned after the death of Judah. The time of mourning has passed, and you must have a husband."

"No. Must I?" I became suddenly on guard.

"Ah, my girl, but if you have no husband, what will you do?"

"I shall be a good healer. People will be kind." I gave Mother Lydia a cup of wine.

"You have a flock to tend, and you cannot do it alone." Father Moshe set the cup down and directed his eyes toward me.

"Who has been tending them?" I had neglected our flocks and felt ashamed. Layers of mist were lifted from my mind. I saw more clearly for the first time in a while. The day was crisp and bright. Skies were a deep blue with a few wispy strands of cloud. I thought of Mary and the Messiah, and I longed to see them. I forced myself to listen to Father Moshe.

"At first Benjamin and I tended the flock. Ham has been caring for them along with his own," Father Moshe said. "Ham…" A long silence prevailed as the single name hung in the air. He took a swallow of wine. "Ham wants to take you as a wife."

"No!" I seethed, outraged. Ham had not made an idle threat in the desert. "No."

"He is strong and can provide well for you, my girl."

"I think he murdered Judah. I cannot go to the tent of

such a man." My face flushed with anger. My fists doubled. Father Moshe watched in shocked, pained silence for minutes, scratching his beard thoughtfully before he spoke. "That is a strong accusation. Judah took a nasty fall on rocks and then a wild animal finished the job. His broken skull and torn face tell what happened. It is a wonder no wild animal attacked you. The cave where you found him is some distance from the grazing area."

"I know very well where the cave is. I will tell you what happened." My chin jutted out. "Judah and I were talking about going away on our own, moving our flocks. Ham came to tell us Naliah sought me, and the men argued and fought. When I tried to stop them, Ham threatened me. I made a bad choice when I ran away, even for a short distance. The flock was without a shepherd when they came to me. After sunset I heard a moaning sound and followed it. Inside the resounding cave, I found Judah injured and dying. Perhaps a wild animal did cause his death, but Ham attacked and fought with him, and I believe, caused him to die."

Father Moshe and Mother Lydia listened with rapt attention. A language of unspoken understanding passed between them. The air became still in the breezeway. My brow trickled drops of sweat. The sallow face of Father Moshe was still as a statue.

"I hear your words, yet I know we cannot prove what you say. Ham will deny it." He looked toward the horizon. "What then will you do?"

"I must go to Bethlehem to be with Mary and the baby

Messiah." I cast my eyes to Father Moshe alone, because the disappointed countenance of Mother Lydia sorely tried me.

"I forbid it." He raised his voice. "It is unsafe to go alone."

Her breath came out in a snort, and my mother shook her head. "My girl, it is nonsense. You will waste your life."

"I cannot stay here." I searched for understanding in her eyes. "I may lose my life, but I believe I must try to find my purpose in it."

"You are very stubborn, my girl." Mother Lydia smoothed her head covering and rose to leave. Father Moshe sat silently watching.

"Moshe. She will not listen to reason," Mother Lydia appealed to him as she turned away.

"And what about Benjamin?" He placed his open palms on his knees.

"Benjamin bar Cleodan?" First shock, and then disbelief hit my mind. But I knew it was true. The younger brother of Judah could take me to be his wife in two years when he grew old enough. It would be a simple transaction.

"Think about it." Father Moshe now rose to leave, and left me sitting with our empty clay goblets. It would have been respectful for me to stand when they did, but the moment passed.

I had hardly gathered my wits when Judah's mother rushed toward me. I rose politely and kissed her cheeks, and motioned for her to sit on the woven reed pallet, bracing myself for what she might ask. "Mother Naliah, how are you?" I poured from a goatskin flask a portion of red wine for her.

"You know why I have come." She refused the clay goblet with a hand wave.

"We are both sad women. You have lost a son, and I a husband." I gestured a hand toward the mat. "Please sit."

She wiped a tear from her bony cheek, and then squatted like a locust ready to spring up. "You have lost a husband, but you shall have another. Benjamin is young. Long ago we made an agreement for the daughter of Cleopas for him. You may be a second wife when the time arrives for him to marry."

"Mother, I appreciate your offer, but…"

"I did not have to come to you," Naliah interrupted. "We could go directly to your father to arrange everything."

"I thank you. It is such a courtesy. Yet, because I am barren I shall relieve Benjamin of his obligation to me."

"Humph, well, what will you do?" Her arched eyebrows formed the appearance of blackbird wings.

"Like Serena, I can heal people."

"Serena is the only healer we need."

"I am sorry, I must think. You have been most kind to make the offer." I bowed my head and folded my hands calmly.

"I came to you because Ham has expressed a desire to have you as his wife. He spoke first with us and then with Moshe. You must have impressed the man as he has made a generous offer." Her dark eyes stared at me trying to penetrate the stony expression on my countenance. She rose, wrapping her cloak around herself in a sweeping gesture. "You are fortunate to have a choice. We will talk again."

"I thank you." I watched her bustle away, with her brown cloak flapping noisily about her legs. Her untouched cup of wine stood before me as an insult.

My mind cleared after the period of mourning the way the sky becomes blue again after a storm has passed. Neighbors had generously given me time to let me to grieve. Now, after almost six moons, they thought I must be done with it and go on with my life. Time could be bought if I favored my rightful marriage to Benjamin. It was not what I desired, and I made plans to leave.

I gazed at the clear blue heavens. "Messiah, You are a baby, but God's son. Please hear my prayer. Help me know what to do." I sat for a while, watching the heavens. Perhaps a Voice would answer me, or call me to action the way it did before the Messiah came. But all I heard was the distant bleating of sheep, the children in the camp calling to each other, a baby crying, and the murmur of women going about chores.

I sat down with a bit of wool in a basket and twirled the gray and white fibers into yarn, but I had no patience for it. The black haircloth cloak felt too warm, so I went into my tent and took it off. Among my neatly folded garments, I found the colorful green cloak I had woven and dyed long ago. A giggle puckered my lips as I remembered the impudent girl I had been. I joyfully pulled the cloak on and found it light and cool, the best choice for me. I moved to the shade behind my tent, and I went back to my spinning with a renewed vigor. By sunset I stopped, as the next day would be Sabbath. My supply of bread was enough for me to eat the next day.

Everyone gathered in camp. The men met for evening prayer. Women were in their tents putting children to bed. Flocks were in the fold created by our circle of tents. A quiet murmur of voices filled the clear starry night with neighborly comfort. Sabbath meals had been prepared for the next day. Goat milk, wine, savory soup, pottage, bread, honey, cheese, figs and dates were ready. No work would be necessary on the day of rest.

That night my eyes became misty when the sun was setting, and I saw the last flock being brought in. A short while ago, Judah and our sheep would have been home. We would sit outside the back of our tent together, often saying nothing at all, enjoying quiet companionship. I missed our time together. As I stayed behind my tent in the starlit night, and sat thinking, Benjamin came quietly and squatted facing me. He had come from prayers and his simple fringed *talit* draped loosely about his round shoulders.

"Stay away from me," I murmured. "Your mother will…"

"Hush." He pressed a finger to his lips. "Back here no one can see us.

I want to know what truly happened to my brother."

"What have you heard?"

"Those who prepared him for burial are whispering maybe it was not a wild animal killed him. A lump on his skull appeared to be the result of being hit with a stone."

"I believe it is true." I gave Benjamin the same account I had given Father Moshe and Mother Lydia.

"Why on earth would Ham fight Judah? I am going to kill him," Benjamin whispered hoarsely. Realization dawned slowly across his face. "Ah, Ham wants you."

"Yes, but threatening or killing Ham could cast you into a trough of trouble, or even death." I reached across and ruffled my young brother-in-law's brown curls that poked out beneath his cap.

"I care for you as a sister, not the same as Judah did. Will you go to Ham then, even if he killed Judah?"

"No," I hissed. "I loathe such a cruel man. I could never be his wife."

"Then my wife?" he squeaked.

CHAPTER TWELVE

My faith in all I had been taught to believe faded in the darkness as I gazed at the heavens. Where had Yahweh gone? Had I been dreaming deeply enough I had imagined everything? I wanted to start a new life in a different place. Next time the camp broke to move, I decided to leave. I would begin by going back to Bethlehem, even though I was sure that by now Mary would have gone to Nazareth.

After a night of fitful sleep, I was awakened as men called to each other in the still morning air. Bursting into the quietness, I heard barking and frantic shouting. Wild dogs were attacking our flocks. People ran toward them, carrying sticks. Our sheep and goats might be torn, killed, scattered and lost. I threw on my head covering and cloak, grabbed Judah's staff, and ran toward the dust and noise. Mother Lydia lingered in front of her tent wringing her hands. Naliah paced. Young women ran with me. It would take all our hands to control the flocks, even if the dogs were beaten off by the time we arrived at the furor.

When I got close, the dogs were gone. Seven lambs had been killed. Others maimed. The men moved with hurried steps and carried rods and staffs. In all directions, they went in search of flocks. I knelt by an injured lamb whose leg was badly torn and bleeding. I picked him up and cuddled him in my arms, and pressed his wound to stop the bleeding. He smelled fresh and salty like a woolen cloth hung out in the sun to dry. He bleated and struggled mightily to escape, but I held him until he calmed down. His dark winsome eyes closed in slumber. "You will be fine, little Caesar." He had the distinctive black crescent on his nose. I thought it was odd Judah had named a ram Caesar, the opposite of a bloodthirsty, cruel leader.

"He is one of ours, I think." Benjamin said, walking toward me. "Our flocks are safe behind the thicket, while others have run to the four winds. Caesar is an incredible ram. I cannot believe how he bleated and skillfully circled them to safety when the wild dogs attacked."

"Thank you." I listened to the implication when he had referred to the sheep as "our flocks." Did he think he had taken control?

"Let us talk about things." His eyes were still bright with the excitement and terror he experienced. "When I saw you with the lamb, well, I, um…felt differently about you."

"What do you mean?" He reminded me of his brother when a serious expression knit his brow.

"I said I had only brotherly affections for you. That was not honest."

"Oh, it is because of the ordeal with the dogs. Your blood is racing and you have impulses you know not what to do with yet."

"Hannah, see my beard. I am becoming a man."

I smiled, thinking about the spoiled, petulant one who now tried very hard to be grown up. In fact, he did have short facial hair, proof of his budding maleness.

"I see your beard, but that alone does not make you a man." With my full head cover in place against the wind and sand, my eyes alone peered out. Hopefully they kept secret the mirth I covered up. His betrothal to Esther, the daughter of Cleopas had been arranged since right after she was born. Now I had become his responsibility whenever he became of age to marry.

Esther was ten, therefore Benjamin would wait two, or even four, years to marry her. With Benjamin two years younger than me, as a second wife, I would still be like a sister. I pictured myself as an obnoxious old woman admonishing the young couple to be careful, telling Esther how to cook or weave, doctoring their wounds, imparting wisdom, and generally being a "thorn in the flesh."

Father Moshe hobbled toward us. "Halloo," he called, waving his staff in the air. "Hannah, please stay with my flock over there. Benjamin and I have to help the others." The flock lay quietly while the sun coursed onto midday.

Clouds drifted, forming shapes of fluffy sheep in the blue sky. Idle, I had mixed feelings, wanting to stay with the people I knew well, yet wanting to leave everything behind.

How much could I carry on my person? I would wear extra garments. I wished I could have a donkey. I could carry my tent, all of my herbs, flasks of wine and water, money, a blanket, meal, yarn, dried fruits, and a rug. That would do.

Benjamin did not return with Father Moshe after the sheep and goats had been gathered. A young ewe was still missing and he had taken off into the brush to find her. I thought about him going after one sheep. He seemed changed from the mischievous younger brother. But he could be thinking of seeking a sheep in the wilderness as an adventure, giving no thought to where he was going. I hoped he would not get lost.

"Will you tend the flock now? I will seek to find where Benjamin went," I said. Father Moshe held up well in spite of all the activity.

"Be careful." He nodded and patted my shoulder.

I grabbed my cloak and staff and walked purposefully east from where Father Moshe had come. It no longer mattered to me what people thought. Even though Benjamin had always been such a brat, I loved him like a brother and feared a terrible outcome for him. The vicious dog attack had left no clear footsteps to follow. Sand and dry grass were torn and tossed as wind stirred them with unseen hands.

I gazed toward the rim of the earth where the sun had risen and thought I saw a tiny dot moving east. As I headed toward it for hours, the wind gusts flung bits of dry grass that stung my hands. Directly overhead white clouds drifted, but on the horizon darker gray ones threatened. The oncoming storm spurred me to walk faster toward the spot I hoped was Benjamin. I folded up the hem of my cloak and tunic in my hand and ran. My breathing calmed and I felt exhilarated to be racing away across the sands.

So intent was I on the dot in the distance, I tripped on a rock and landed with a thud face down in the sand. Grit clung to my lips and nostrils. At first nothing hurt except my pride. Then a stinging ache began where the brush had abraded my right hand and both elbows. I lay for a moment embarrassed, and wondered if I had been seen. I dusted off and stood to survey the terrain ahead. The spot had disappeared. How could he have vanished? Perhaps it had not been Benjamin after all. The wind whipped my cloak and stung my uncovered face with bits of sand. Behind me I could no longer see our distant tents. My knee burned. I lifted my tunic and saw my skin scraped raw and bleeding lightly. I tore strips from my under tunic to bind my wounds and stanch the bleeding.

Blowing sand now covered everything. I wondered if I could continue walking into the wind where grit stung my eyes, or should I wisely sit and wait. Fear crept into the corners of my mind. Were Benjamin and I both lost? There was nothing to do but throw my ample haircloth cloak over my face and body and huddle under it for protection. I sat for ages as wind slapped my back. Fine pebbles and sand relentlessly pelted my cloak, and I wondered if this could be how it would feel to be stoned to death. I was thirsty. As I sipped at my flask, the tepid liquid served as a balm to my parched tongue and lips. I remembered the birth of the Messiah. A warm feeling washed over me like morning sunshine. I smiled in spite of the raging wind. Will I see them again? My chilly faithlessness in ever making our reunion possible sent the thought flying with the wind.

Something nudged my cloak and alerted all my senses. I sat perfectly still, but it bumped me again. I smelled wool. Could it be the missing ewe? No matter, the sheep likely belonged to someone I knew. I reached a tentative hand out and grabbed a wooly leg. "Maa," it bleated and jerked to try to free itself. I threw back my cloak to enfold the young ewe. She struggled again when I covered us up. Almost as suddenly as it had begun, the gale died down, leaving the grains of sand to drift carelessly wherever they willed. I heard granules pelting idly on my cloak tent. I peered out finally and tried to determine my location by the position of the sun. I thought I had walked on an eastward course. If I wanted to go back to camp I must go the opposite way. The ewe did not run away as I continued on, but stayed beside me. My legs grew weary and my skinned knee and elbows burned. I trekked on and on, but our camp was lost to my sight.

Perhaps our tents had blown away in the storm.

No familiar landmarks came into view. Now I feared I might have traveled in the wrong direction. Had my eyes deceived me? Soon the sun would disappear, and I had no means of protection except my cloak and the young ewe to keep me warm.

I wondered about Benjamin. Had he also lost his way? Was he the dot I had run toward, or had it been a mirage? Should I have continued to try to find him? Could he be hurt and unable to stand up? I had grabbed my emergency pouch of herbs and tied the bag around my waist before I left in case he needed care. Many questions plagued my muddled mind. I walked blindly onward, unsure of direction. My stomach growled. The ewe stopped to chew on tufts of grass. I tipped my flask to drink and found one swallow remained. It refreshed me. The ewe settled down and I sat next to her resting my arm across her.

The next morning I awoke with a start. I had dreamed of angels hovering and a baby crying. I dusted off and moved swiftly. An unseen Spirit guided me. I recognized landmarks near the trail to Bethlehem, the one I had taken before. My strides became purposeful, lighthearted. The little ewe kept pace. Father Moshe and Mother Lydia would be worried, and Naliah would be angry when I did not return home. But the regretful thought was a mere bump in my determination to continue on. What was ahead for me? I had to know.

In Bethlehem I soon recognized the neatly swept covered porch of Hawara Inn, and I saw Ramen out front wiping his hands on his apron. His face glowed in the sunlight. I paused, realized I blushed, and made sure my head covering was mostly in place before I walked up to him. "Blessed morning to you."

"Well, it is still morning." Smiling, his dark eyes twinkling with surprise. "It is Hannah, isn't it? What brings you and your ewe to Bethlehem?"

"Are Mary and Joseph still here?"

"No, I'm afraid not." He shook his head. "They left, oh, when did they go? Several, uh, two or more moons, ago. Shortly after the baby was born they lived with relatives here, and then threats and trouble filled the town with dismay. Joseph feared for the life of the young Prince."

"Prince? Oh, yes, of course. Did she, I mean, did they name him at the *brit*? I left too soon to know."

"Jesus, I think. The locals are whispering He will overthrow Herod when He grows up. It caused such a problem." He put his hand to his head. "Hannah, you must be tired. Come inside."

"What about her?" I suddenly remembered the ewe.

"Come, I am sure you remember the way." Ramen and I walked the sheep quietly to the stable and poured fresh water from the well. The ewe eyed the clay trough briefly and began lapping.

When I went inside, the inn was deserted. The tables gleamed from being scrubbed, and the plain benches were tucked close to them.

"How is business?" I asked, already knowing his answer.

"Hah! Slow, it's very slow."

"But, why? What has happened?"

Ramen studied me before he spoke. Finally, he sat down heavily on a bench and gestured for me to sit across from him. "After the enrollment, of course, travelers went back home. But then I have another bit to tell. It had to do with the birth of the Child you delivered." He looked away from me.

"Tell me. What is it? Are they dead?" Not knowing what had taken place, I was fearful.

"Dead? I don't know about Him, or them, but I hate to tell you many others were slain. Young boy babies, all the soldiers could find, they were all killed." The silence in the inn echoed his words.

Tears trickled down my cheeks and words escaped my bidding. Finally I found my voice. "Since I am a woman, I am unknowing of the words of the old prophets, yet I believe this may have been foretold."

"I do not know your ancient stories either. All I know is what happened here. Three men, who were riding on camels, following a bright star, came to search for the Child, because they thought He was to become the next King. They arrived at the stable too late. Nonetheless, these three men found the relative's house where Jesus and His parents were staying. I heard these were Magi, men who read signs in the heavens. They brought costly gifts. People said Herod's decree to kill baby boys was the fault of these three men, because they had spoken with Herod about the quest to find the newborn King. The birth of this King had been foretold from ancient times. Of course, Herod forbade such a Child would grow up and take his place. He did not know where the Baby Boy lived in Bethlehem, therefore he ordered all boys under the age of two to be slain. By ordering them all to be eliminated, he probably thought he could be sure he killed the right One."

"Ramen." His father's raspy voice startled me. "Do we have a guest?" I saw Hawara who stood with a hand on the doorframe, hunched over with an air of defeat.

"Yes, indeed." Ramen stood up and went toward his father. He took his arm and led him to the table. "It is Hannah, our serving maid. Do you remember that she worked during the busy census when we had the couple in the stable?"

"Yes, but she has come to the wrong place at the wrong time. We have no work for her now." The old man stood next to the table and braced himself with one hand.

"Forgive me, sir, I did not come to work. I came to ask about Mary and Joseph, the people who had the Baby in your stable." I bowed my head.

"Ah," said the old man as he rubbed his chin thoughtfully, and spoke in a disgusted whisper. "The soldiers came and tore this place apart. They threatened to beat me. They beat Ramen. We have been questioned again and again about them. I pretended I thought nothing of the couple and Child, and had settled them in the stable as being no better than animals. I know where they may have gone, but you must swear to tell no one.

Unless robbers assailed them, they have traveled to a safe place far away."

"But where?"

"I cannot tell you." The old man wheezed. Ramen shook his head when my eyes questioned him. He stood and walked off to the kitchen. When he came back, he carried an earthen pitcher from which he poured three cups of wine. He sat down and gave Hawara the first cup, and then handed me one before he lifted a cup to his lips.

"Thank you." I gratefully accepted the wine. My mind whirled about. Shall I continue to search for them, or simply believe they were all right and go back to my tent at home? "If you tell me where they have gone, are you afraid the authorities will follow me and harm them?"

"Or do you harm." Ramen's eyes sought mine again, and his quiet voice was as a caress for me.

His father began a coughing fit. Ramen took his father's arm and led him from the room.

"He has not been well." When Ramen came back, he touched his wine cup, but remained standing.

"May I help your father?" I dug into my bag, trying to find the right herbs. "I have a remedy which may loosen the phlegm. Do you have any honey? I can boil water and make a healing tea for him." I got up and walked toward the kitchen area. Ramen followed me.

"What are you brewing?" He seemed almost amused.

"A balm for his cough," I said.

Soon the steamy air smelled of lemon balm and honey.

I added a bit of strong wine and gave the cup to Ramen to take to his father.

"I might even drink this myself," he said as he left the room.

I browsed the rooms. Webs laced the wall sconces, telling a tale of neglect the clean tables had not betrayed. The place where we sat to take a rest when I worked as his serving maid was the same as then. My mind traveled back to the angel visitors that kept watch over the stable the night He was born. It was difficult to believe the Child was in danger. With the dire news of the threat to the Messiah I feared for Mary's life too. Was He truly the promised One? How could it be? I wondered if Benjamin had arrived safely back at camp, and I became conflicted for stopping my search for him. Were people worried about me and would they seek after me? I was returning to the serving area when Ramen came back.

"Did it help?"

"Yes, when I could finally convince him to take a swallow." Ramen chuckled.

"Does he not trust me?" I brushed my beige head covering to one side, and thus exposed all my face.

"I trust you." Ramen came nearer to me, and gazed at me with a question in his eyes. "You are thinner and have older eyes than before. What has happened during the time you were away?"

"My husband died." My voice broke in spite of my resolve. "He was killed by a wild animal they said, but I believe his fight with a bullish man caused his death."

Unsure of myself, I wondered why I revealed all this to Ramen. My breath caught. "I...well, my time of mourning is over."

"I am sorry for you. And I suppose his young brother will take you as his wife when he is old enough." Ramen's brow creased.

"Yes." I simply could not tell him about Ham. A dreadful thought came into my mind as I wished Ham were dead, but I tried to remove my murderous thoughts.

"Will you go back to your father now?"

"No, at least not yet." Where had Mary and the Baby gone? I wanted to take care of the young Jesus. I was lost in thought for a moment, but when I heard Ramen's father coughing a deep phlegmy cough, I was ready to do whatever I could to help ease his misery.

"Shall I prepare a room for you?" Ramen tapped the table with his hand and directed his eyes anxiously in the direction of his father's coughing.

"Thank you. I could help with your father." I produced a tied bag of pungent smelling herbs. "Here, keep this near him. When he gets up he can tie it around his neck. It will help him breathe easier. Here is willow bark for more tea if he becomes fevered." Normal activity of healing someone calmed me. It was good to be busy.

That night as I lay on my mat trying to sleep in the dank stillness of a windowless inner room, I thought about the fact these innkeepers were originally from Egypt. Could Mary and Joseph have escaped to a secure place in Egypt? My life pulse raced with the idea. But where in

Egypt had they fled? I had heard of Alexandria, but I did not know where the borders were or anything. Of course, Ramen would have knowledge of it. I closed my eyes, but hardly slept. My thoughts wove between hateful ones for Ham, and hopeful feelings about seeking Mary and her Son.

The utter quietness of the inn again struck me the next morning when I awakened. I went out to the well to do my morning wash, and stopped by the stable to check on the ewe. When I had left the ewe, it had been alone with a donkey and a couple of goats. A flock of a few sheep were now bedded down in the stable. A shepherd had stopped for the night. This time I was very cautious as I slipped off my outer garment to wash at the well. I exposed one arm at a time and replaced the folds. I kept my eyes on the trail to the well. I would not be taken off guard this time.

When I came back into the inn, Ramen had brewed a pot of sweet smelling tea and put thick cakes of bread, cheese and figs on the table. "My father slept well, and he is grateful."

"I am glad he is well. I will be on my way today."

"Must you go? Please sit and eat with me. We have fresh fish."

"Where is Egypt?" I ignored his invitation.

"Several days journey," Ramen said, raising an eyebrow. "You suppose they are there?"

"Your father helped them."

"No, my father does not know anything about it."

"Do you? Did you advise them?"

Ramen came close and spoke in a whisper. "We told them of our relatives who live across the border."

"I must go to them. Tell me the way to journey there."

"No, it is too dangerous for you to go alone." His voice rose.

"I have traveled alone more than once. What about you? You were born in another place, I think."

"It seems as though I have always lived here. My family came from Egypt when I was young. Of course, my father and I do not have the same appearance as the other townspeople. He decided to wear a turban so he would appear to be as one who came from the East." Ramen chuckled. "Our hair is more straight and black, and our noses are triangular."

Hawara slowly entered the room. His face was ashen, yet more rested. Ramen went to him. "Have a cup of tea, Father. You can help me with family history. Hannah wants to know more about where we came from."

Hawara sat heavily and lifted the cup of warm tea to his mouth. He sighed, "Yes, I came from Egypt when I was young. My father owned land, servants, and a spacious home, but political unrest had made life in my country difficult. After many years of Greek rule in which my father was a royal scribe, our part of the country had come under Roman rule. However, one would not be counted as having Roman citizenship without serving in the military. Egypt proved to be a difficult place for me as a young man after my father went to Rome and never returned. In order to provide for my mother and sister, I became a bread baker. I baked and sold flat bread in a street market."

"Your bread is delicious."

"Thank you." Hawara coughed, tilted his head back and gazed at the ceiling before he continued. "Bread baking suited me well, but when Roman tax collectors regularly came by my booth and took coins from my successful business, I decided I must turn to another trade or leave the country entirely. When my beautiful young wife died during the birth of our first child, Ramen, I was grief stricken. My sister, Medina, and brother-in-law took care of my mother and baby son. When my mother died, I packed up Ramen and our few belongings, bid my sister and her husband farewell, and set off for the Judean hills. But these are the ramblings of an old man." He was overcome by a coughing spasm that reddened his face.

"Please go on when you can. Tell me about how you and Ramen came to be in Bethlehem."

"I am fluent in many languages as my father had been an educated man and taught me well. I became the proprietor of this inn, and I was able to speak with any number of strangers who darkened my door. As an innkeeper I make a fair living here, and as long as I observe local customs nobody bothers us. I still pay taxes, but I think it is more logical, based on earnings, rather than whatever the tax collector takes. Lately the situation has changed for the worse." He wheezed.

"Up until now," Ramen said. "I'm sure even though we

are making no money, they will still collect tax."

Hawara cast his eyes on me, sizing me up the way he did on the night he thought I was the servant they hired. "Are you married?"

"No, I am widowed." Startled by his bold question, my face grew hot, and I wondered why he asked.

"Father, you must be tired." Ramen sounded embarrassed. "Let me help you to your bed."

"Ramen, I am not finished." Hawara coughed, curled his gnarled hands around his wine cup and continued. "Business people are too busy for such things as betrothal and marriage. Ramen is twenty-five. They have different customs here, and I have always thought Ramen had to establish himself as an innkeeper before he should take a wife."

Now I understood why Ramen's father had asked.

Ramen grabbed a towel and wiped tables. "Father, could you ..."

"All right, I will go." Hawara shook his head and sighed. "I cannot do anything for you if you do not want my help."

I watched the two of them leave the room and smiled. Hawara was a straight talking old man and had caused his son discomfort.

The man came quietly enough that I did not hear him, but saw his shadow. How long he stood in the doorway, or how much he heard, was unknown to me. He cleared his throat.

"Benjamin," I breathed, glad to see him alive. How had he gotten here?

"Greetings, both of you," said Benjamin, as Ramen came back into the room. Benjamin wiped his moist face with his sleeve. He grasped my shoulders, kissing both of my cheeks. "Is our ewe in the stable?"

I nodded, too surprised to say anything.

"You must be hungry." Ramen pointed toward the table.

"Only a drink." Benjamin tossed his head of long hair and squared his shoulders.

Ramen chuckled to himself, brought more bread, figs, and a cup of wine. "Is your mother ill again?"

"No. I came seeking Hannah, my wife."

"Wife?" Ramen appeared to be as disappointed as I felt.

CHAPTER THIRTEEN

My thoughts whirled like a sudden dust devil in the desert. I was uncertain about my future. "Is this your trick to make me return home?" I narrowed my eyes at Benjamin.

"It is no trick. I speak the truth." Benjamin folded his arms across his chest, stone-faced.

"Tell them you could not find me."

"You are asking me to lie." He unfolded his arms, made fists with his hands, and hit the table once.

"I cannot believe this. You are my young brother-in-law. I could never think of you as a husband."

Benjamin glared, refolded his arms and pursed his lips. Ramen, embarrassed to be in the midst of a family situation, nodded his head and left the room. I paced, trying to sort things out. The flap of my sandals echoed on the hard earthen floor. Neither of us spoke for a while.

Then Benjamin broke the awkward silence.

"You must help me bring the sheep back. No one at camp knows I came here. I am grazing a herd as far as anyone knows." He made a scraping noise with the toe of his sandal.

"Not anyone? Who helped you bring the sheep here?"

"You did. When I came back to camp after being lost, my mother, delighted and grateful I was alive, told me she would give me anything I wanted. I held counsel with my father. I told him plainly I wanted to revoke my original betrothal to Esther, the daughter of Cleopas, and take you as my first wife. Later, when she became old enough to marry, I would take Esther as a second wife. Mother was in such a fit of anger she would not speak to me at first, and Father pointed out you had disappeared in a sand storm."

"It is as I would expect." I frowned.

"After she calmed, they talked. Breaking the betrothal to Esther was not easy. At first, her father would not hear of it. When two ewes with lamb went into the bargain along with two large woven rugs, they were satisfied."

"Costly. Words seal themselves inside my lips at such a fine gift, and nobody even knew if I still lived." I did know why, of course, with Benjamin now their only son.

"I was almost sure I would find you here in Bethlehem."

"You were?" My face probably shone with my amazement.

"Yes, you told me how much you wanted to see Mary." He faced me, standing tall. "Now, come back with me."

His plea sounded like an order.

"No. How could you have done such a thing?" I was on a mission to find Mary and be sure she and her Baby were all right, but now Benjamin tried to stop me.

"I thought it would be a favor for you. Ham would have taken you if I had not struck this bargain with Esther's father and mine." His chin jutted forward and he curled his lip.

"Ham would never have me as his. I would die first."

"I wanted to spare you." His voice had the old childish whine. "Hannah, I was thinking of you."

"I can take care of myself." Inside, I wondered if it would be best to go home to straighten things out. "If I come with you, will you please set me aside for being barren?"

"I might think about it." A smile creased his face. "Remember the night I came to you secretly behind your tent after my prayer time, and I told you I had a plan?"

"Was this it?" I cuffed him on the arm. "Why you, you are teasing me. I ought to give you a good thrashing." I lunged at him to tackle him, but he stepped aside. I fell forward. Both of us were laughing as he caught me to keep me from hitting the floor.

"I will tell my father and your father I have thought better of it and since you are barren, I will put you away quietly. I do not want anyone except the immediate family to know of it. I will pretend to be too embarrassed. Do you approve of my idea?" He stretched himself up to his full height, and I realized he had grown taller than me.

"Why are you doing this?"

"For my brother, I suppose." He dangled his arms.

I turned away from him with many thoughts going around in my head. Already free to travel wherever I wished, why did I consider going back? With tradition being such an enmeshed part of our lives, it was nearly impossible to do anything else. I walked outside to the courtyard and the stable trying to recapture the wonder of the night of the Messiah's birth. The decision to temporarily abandon my trek to seek Mary was a difficult one to make. No Voice in the wind and no inner thoughts gave me wise counsel about what to do. I went to the well, drew cool water and splashed it on my face. I thought about Father Moshe and Mother Lydia who would be worried about me.

As I struggled with my thoughts and feelings for hours, both Benjamin and Ramen avoided me. Defeated by my indecision, I came back into the inn. Almost as a sudden storm, the words came out of my mouth, "Benjamin, let us go herd the sheep to the grazing." We left and waved to Ramen. He looked dismayed, and slowly raised one hand.

Father Moshe and Mother Lydia saw us coming on the trail. Happy tears fogged their eyes and both of them hugged me warmly. "You are alive, my girl." Mother Lydia kept patting my arm and hugging me. It felt good.

Friends who were weaving called, "Welcome home, Hannah."

Serena stood in the doorway of her tent and said, "Hannah, well and good to see you."

Once back, I went directly to my tent and put on my black haircloth garment. Having followed me, Mother Lydia said, "My girl, Naliah and I have been talking about your wedding, but why are you once again wearing your mourning clothing?"

"My sadness drove me to do it. There will be no marriage. Benjamin has plenty of time, and he could have a more suitable wife in Esther than in me."

"Hannah, my girl, why are you always so difficult? And what shall we tell Naliah?" She wrung her hands. "Everything has been settled."

"How will you live?" Father Moshe demanded. Until now he had patiently waited for Mother Lydia to have her say. "We did not take you in as a baby to have you waste your life due to your own foolishness."

"I can take care of flocks as well as any man, if you will allow it." When they both sat staring at the floor mat, I added, "And I can continue my work as a healer. I am barren. Truly no man would want me."

"You cannot care for the sheep and goats alone," he said, rubbing his forehead.

"Tell me why." I looked directly at him.

"You are a woman. It is true a few women attend the flocks with men, but you will not accept any husband. I do love you Hannah, but what do you expect me to do?" Father Moshe threw up his hands. "Shall I defy tradition?"

"My girl, do you ask us to face the scorn of our neighbors?" Mother Lydia wrung her hands. "Naliah…"

"Oh, I would not want to stain your good reputation."

The words escaped before I thought how disrespectful they were. I quavered with anger. "It would have been best for me to have stayed in Bethlehem." When I saw pain etch their faces, I said, "I am sorry." It was no use trying to convince them Benjamin was unacceptable. The whole idea of a marriage, even with a quick divorcement, did not set well at all with me.

I spent a few weeks resting and dealing with everyone's plans for my life. While I had been undecided in Bethlehem, I knew now I must leave. My life would be miserable trying to satisfy Naliah's or anyone else's demands. I should never have come back with Benjamin. I came to my parents and spoke to them plainly.

"Thank you for what you have done for me. I must go now and live my life. I want to find my friend Mary and her Child." I hugged and kissed Father Moshe and Mother Lydia warmly as I told them. Father Moshe rubbed his forehead, and Mother Lydia shook her head and folded her arms, but they knew they could not stand in my way once my mind was set on a plan.

"Please be careful, my girl," Mother Lydia said as she watched me pack. I wore my clothing in layers and carried herbs and other necessities in a bag tied around my waist. Water and wine flasks dangled from my shoulders.

"You may never be welcomed back among our people," Father Moshe warned, and looked up at me with sad eyes, and then away. "Sometimes there is no Voice in the wind, but your mind and spirit will direct what your next steps must be." He faced me with teary eyes, touched his hand to his chest, hugged me to him quickly, and turned away. I was determined to go. Both the thrill of freedom and the sadness of parting filled my being as I began to walk away from the life I knew.

As I kept going, Benjamin fell in step with me. He was quiet for a while and then he said, "I understand."

"How could you, a mere boy, ever know my feelings?" I spat out the words, flooding tears. I felt bad about my reaction to him, but I wanted to be alone with my thoughts. I wanted no reason to turn back.

"I saw him gaze at you with fondness."

"Who did?"

"Ramen, the innkeeper's son, has an eye for you."

"No, and even if he does, it can never come to anything." My life pulse quickened and my face flushed. "I would have a difficult life there. It is not like being in this simple place."

"Then where are you going all alone? Tradition says you are my wife unless I divorce you."

"I belong to no person but myself, and I am never truly alone. I have a Spirit with me all the time." I expressed a faith I now questioned, but continued on. "I want to find Mary and her Baby, to help her take care of Him."

"Hannah." Benjamin paused, and touched my spirit with his glistening brown eyes. "I hope you know what you are doing. I will miss you, especially when I fall and scrape my knees." He pulled my head covering aside and kissed me goodbye quickly on each cheek, turned to hide his wet eyes, and walked away.

Tears stung my eyes. I cried a lot lately. While I had been reluctant to come here, I did not want to leave this way. Now I was unsure where my feet were taking me. I walked in a daze much the same as the last time I went to Bethlehem after being lost in the sandstorm. I prayed for protection. The presence, the angel, or spirit all eluded me as I traveled.

On the trail ahead, I noticed a caravan of richly dressed people. They went slowly, and I knew at the pace I walked, I would soon be up with them. While my curiosity heightened, I knew anyone dressed in fine dyed robes, wearing rich cloth and jewels, and riding on a camel would not even acknowledge a shepherd girl. I cast my eyes downward as I walked, thinking I could steal a glance at the people as I passed. One man who walked beside a donkey appeared to have the trappings of a rabbi, perhaps a student. Now I wondered if they all traveled together or had happened to meet on the trail.

"Good blessings this day," the young man said. He sounded congenial, friendly as fellow travelers often are. I skirted around him on the trail. "Are you from the people who are of the tribe of Dan?" My outer travel cloak had the distinct striped markings of my fellows.

"Why, yes," I said, being polite. I ensured my face was covered with the plain beige cloth.

"Your people often graze in the pastures outside of Nazareth."

I was not sure whether to answer or not, but I slowed my pace. "They do, in green seasons, yes." We walked side by side, yet a ways apart, and I thought he would say no more.

"I once met a girl from your tribe," he said, keeping up with me even though I tried to walk away from him.

I slowed, as I thought I recognized his face. Could this be Mary's cousin? "Would your name be Abram?"

"The same," he said. "And would you know anyone named Hannah?" I heard the smile in his voice.

"I cannot believe this," I said. "I am Hannah, and I am searching for your cousin Mary and her Baby."

"Well, what fate brings us to see each other again?" Abram paused. "Mary, poor Mary, I do not know how to tell you about her."

"Oh, please, do you have any news of her? Please tell me she is alive. Do you know where she has gone?"

"I am sure we are forbidden to speak together." He cast his eyes on one of the older men, and started a faster pace.

I hurried after him. "I fear I am troubling you, but I know Mary and Joseph and the baby had to flee from Bethlehem because of a murderous decree from that madman Herod to kill all boy babies."

"Yes." The grown up Abram, with a bearded, pleasant face, turned toward me and led his donkey off the trail a ways, waving the others on. We stopped. "I remember the night under the stars with you and Mary. It was the last time I was able to play with my cousin, or to do anything young boys do. My studies consumed me then, and still do. For Mary's sake, I will talk with you, and explain it to my father later."

"Thank you," I said, and offered him my flask of wine. He smiled a crooked smile and took a sip. I caught his quick wink.

"Here it is. Mary rather disgraced the family as she was betrothed, but unwed, and became with child. Joseph took her as his wife anyway, as he is a good man."

"I attended as midwife at the birth of her Boy Child. It was a special night, one I shall never forget, and I am compelled to see them again. Do you know where they have gone? If you tell me, I will stop bothering you." I looked at him earnestly, and hoped for more news.

"They fled to Egypt. An innkeeper, who put them up first in the stable at Hawara Inn, has relatives who live in Egypt. His name is Hawara. He told them he would be happy to guide them, but they decided to flee by night. I learned of the trip to Egypt through relatives in Bethlehem. Whether they made it there without dire consequence, no one knows."

"I know Hawara and his son Ramen, because Mary had her baby in a stable by their inn." I stood open-mouthed at the revelation. "I pray they made it safely to Hawara's relatives in Egypt."

"You travel alone. Are you married, Hannah?"

"I am widowed." I knew it was improper for me to be talking to a man, but I pressed on. "I trust Mary and the Baby are all right."

"I, too, hope they are safe. And for your protection, walk with us." His dark hair fell as a long silky mane cascading across the broad shoulders of his rich brown cloak. A boyish twinkle lit up his smiling eyes.

"Your father would not approve of my traveling beside you. I will go." I turned away from him.

"Abram." A man, wearing purple, I presumed to be his teacher or his father, called to him.

Abram made the sign of a traditional blessing as we parted. "The Lord bless you and keep you. May the Lord make His face to shine upon you and be gracious unto you, and may He turn his face toward you and give you peace."

I followed a short distance behind them until we reached Bethlehem. Abram turned and waved. "*Shalom.*"

When I got back to Hawara Inn, the entrance porch stood cluttered with sand and leaves, doors were closed, and the inn appeared to be deserted. I called, and when nobody answered, I went around back to the stable. A gray donkey munched on hay, two milk goats stood in silence, but no other sign of life stirred. I went to the well to wash and wondered where I would go and what I would do. My dread and despair almost consumed me. Bewildered the inn had been abandoned in such a short while, I wondered if Ramen and his father had gone to Egypt. Had my coming here been a mistake? I sat on the ground next to the well to let my arms dry in the sun. The air was very warm and still, with few insects buzzing. A fearful element saturated the quietness of the air. I rose, resettled my garments, and adjusted my head covering. As I gradually calmed, I decided to go down the road to the other inns and question them. Surely the neighbors would know what had happened.

On impulse, I knocked on the door to Hawara Inn. I thought I heard someone inside, and waited. Finally the door opened a crack. A stale musty coolness wafted out. The dark eyes of a boy around ten years old peered from around the corner. "Where are the innkeeper and his son?" I asked.

The boy kept staring at me with luminous eyes, and shook his head. He was as olive skinned as Ramen, but not likely his son. He might be a new stable boy, or a house servant.

"Is Ramen anywhere about? I am a friend. Peaceful." I tried again to communicate, using a different dialect. Perhaps he was deaf and mute, or spoke a foreign tongue.

"Not here. Ramen is sad, because his father is gone." He did not move or open the door further.

"Oh, did his father die? I am sorry." My thoughts went back to my last visit. "Where is Ramen?" I demanded, quietly, stepping closer to the doorway. I held out a mite.

"I am to tell no one," the boy answered in a whisper. He squinted his eyes in the light as he opened the door and reached for the coin, but then jerked his hand back.

"But, why are your lips sealed against speaking of it? What is this all about? Is he in trouble?" I still held the mite. "May I come in?"

The boy peered around warily, opened the door a bit wider, turned, and left it ajar as he scurried back into the room.

"Where are you going now?" I asked, sniffing the stale air. "I want to speak with Ramen." I felt exasperated, but did not want to barge in. I peered inside the open door and felt a hollow in the pit of my stomach at seeing the dark emptiness of the room, which had once been alive with people. No aromas wafted from the silent kitchen. All the benches and bare wooden tables were shoved up against a far wall as was done when a thorough sweeping was under way.

The shadowy ghost of Ramen's voice confronted the boy. "Did I hear you speaking with a visitor?"

The boy quavered, "Yes, master, a woman. She says she is a friend."

Ramen shuffled toward the door. When he appeared in the daylight of the open doorway, blinking, I could see his eyes were puffed with grief. His shoulders drooped, and he wore no turban or decoration save for a black armband on his loose gray robe. My whole being gave sympathy to his despair.

"Ramen, I am sorry. I am saddened to hear of your father passing on." I spoke calmly and wanted to touch him and take his sadness away.

"Come, come in," he said, gesturing.

"When did it happen?"

"Not long after you left. He had taken a turn for the worse and talked deliriously. I had run out of the tea you made for his fever."

"Are you in trouble?" I reached out and impulsively grasped Ramen's left forearm.

"No, but if I carry out the murderous thoughts I have had, I will be." He covered my hand with his right hand, and we stood quietly for a time. Ramen finally straightened his posture, snapped his fingers and pointed at the benches. The young boy pulled out a bench for us, bowed slightly, and then politely left the room.

"Tell me more." I sat on the bench.

"Business had picked up a little. We had a couple of guests and a kitchen crew the day the officers came. I tried to keep things together while these men were questioning my father." Ramen pulled out a table and sat on the bench beside me. "Naturally, people were watching and listening from the kitchen and doorways, which compounded the embarrassment for us. Officials questioned him again about the disappearance of the family who had been in our stable. Father became very angry and his face reddened as he spoke. Then his breaths came out in gasps and he fell to the earth, clutched his chest, showed his startled face, and died. Hannah, I am beyond angry. How could they have done this to a sick old man?"

I saw how devastated Ramen was and did not know what to do for him, so I simply rested my hand in his.

He patted my hand absently. I now had more questions troubling my mind and few answers I could come up with as to what to do now. Shall I return to Father Moshe and beg forgiveness? Shall I go to Egypt? How could I help Ramen? Why did I want to help him? Was the boy his servant or related to him?

"Who is the boy?" I asked.

CHAPTER FOURTEEN

Ramen said, "The boy's name is Pel. He was a slave to one of the Roman officers who came here. I became outraged and murderous with them when my father died, and they had to restrain me. That officer gave the boy to me for the rest of the day to help around here. I don't know why. Maybe he wasn't such a bad sort, simply following orders. I sent a note offering a fair slave price for Pel. I did not receive a word back."

"It is good you have help." I felt relieved to find out who Pel was. "Have you given your father a traditional burial?"

"Yes, he is in a cave outside the city. He was anointed with sweet oils, wrapped in a grave cloth, and sprinkled with herbs and spices from our kitchen. I put his knife beside him for protection. His favorite bowl and wine cup were filled and buried with him. I wanted to put one of the milk goats with him, but when it came time to slaughter her, I could not do it. Humph, sometimes I do not know what I believe." He gazed toward the ceiling, "My mother, who died in Egypt, was wrapped in fine linens, and buried along with fruits and meats, a cloak for travel, and her favorite white, longhaired dog." Ramen stood and paced as he continued.

"Religion has been of no concern to me for a long time. The cult of the godess Isis once intrigued me. My relatives held on to older beliefs in the *Ptolemies*. My father was not particularly religious. After he came to Bethlehem, for the sake of business, he bowed to the local authorities. If anyone was in our establishment who believed in Yahweh, father respected them as well. In fact, he believed a nameless God existed in the heavens who controlled all of life on earth and all gods."

"Interesting. Except for the neighboring desert gods of harvest, rain, and seasons, I am solely acquainted with Yahweh, Whose name we are not supposed to say."

"Father used to bow to the rising sun as well as the setting sun for a short time. He was very tolerant, and didn't ask me to join him in this practice. Father told me his father's father had simply worshipped the sun. For the sake of business and safety, they paid homage to the official god, or gods of the time."

"Have you a belief?" I asked.

"I suppose it is similar to my father's thinking. He told me I would find my life one day. All of life depends on the sun. It is simply there. Perhaps even death depends on it. Life goes on as people are buried. I no longer bow to any God because it makes no difference to God or to me. Even the Baby born in our stable everyone made such a fuss about has God in Him. God is God."

His words made sense and I wondered at his eloquence and his openness to talk with me. "Are you grieving deeply?" I asked. I had watched his brow creased in thought above his triangular nose as he paced.

"I suppose." His eyes glistened. "I do miss him. I simply do not know where to begin or what to do next."

"Will you keep the inn open?" I asked.

"I can't decide." Ramen's smooth hands opened and closed. "All our hirelings have been relieved of duty due to lack of customers. All I have is the boy slave."

Ramen and I sat quietly for a time with an unseen emotion coursing between us. I could hear his heart beating, or was it my own? Finally I said, "I have left the encampment for good. I am not marrying Benjamin. And I must search for Mary and Jesus to help them in any way I can." My words rushed out until they were all spoken.

Ramen cast earnest eyes on me. "Will you marry again?"

His question surprised me. Flustered, I blushed beneath my veil. "I think not." My life pulse hammered under layers of clothing. I bit my lip and shut my eyes trying to think clearly.

"Never?" He seemed unaware of my embarrassment.

While I admit he was a rather handsome man, I did not know why his nearness affected my whole being. I prayed inwardly for guidance in what to say next. "I still want to find Mary and the Baby." I raised my voice without meaning to. "Do you know where they are?"

"Is this an official questioning?" He stood, turned away from me and began pacing rapidly. He came back angry, yet controlled. "I do know where they went, but not where they are now. Does that help you?"

"Ramen, I am sorry. I suppose you cannot understand my desire to be with them." I stood and went to him, facing him, but his eyes avoided mine.

"There is much I wish I could tell you. But I think you would not understand my needs." His voice came out low and husky.

"Perhaps you underestimate me." I impulsively pulled back the flaxen scarf I wore around my head. It drifted to the floor.

Ramen became rigid and stepped backward, possibly taking this as a brazen invitation. "Hannah, I would like..." His voice was a low sensual whisper, with each syllable enunciated clearly. His countenance expressed pleasure and his dark eyes shone.

"Whatever it is you would like, I would probably fear it." I remembered Ham. I had simply meant for Ramen to tell me where Mary had gone. But now I felt drawn to him, and did not understand my desires. My resolve to remain free crumbled in the face of Ramen's open arms. I drew back and hesitated, unsure of myself.

"Help! My Lord. Help! I don't want to go with him." Pel's voice echoed from somewhere in the courtyard.

Ramen ran out. I retrieved my scarf and covered my hair.

It sounded like Pel's original master had come for him. I heard loud voices.

"The boy was on loan to you. He is mine and I am taking him back."

"Sir, I will pay you well for him," Ramen yelled. "Here, is this enough? Please let me keep him."

"He is not your slave. I will not bargain," boomed a man's voice.

"No! No, Master!" Pel yelled. His master had come to claim him. I heard horses, whips cracking, and carriage wheels on packed earth. Presumably Ramen ran after them. The sounds grew farther away. I walked to the front doorway of the inn and waited. Ramen returned, downcast.

"The officer wouldn't even listen to my offer. I fear he mistreats the boy, but perhaps not. Pel liked it here because the work wasn't hard and he had plenty to eat. I will miss him." Ramen gestured, palms up, shrugging. We stood by the doorway for a time. "Would you care to have a bite of food and wine?" He put his hand on my shoulder as he ushered me inside.

Ramen lit a round oil lamp and placed it on a wood table. He went to the kitchen and came back with slices of cold lamb, bread, cheese, olives, dates, and figs. He filled two clay wine goblets. I sat at one of the tables and waited. My mind had been full of plans earlier in the day, but now I could think of nothing except Ramen and the young boy slave.

"Thank you." I marveled at the food and chose a date to savor its sweetness.

We were silent. The room warmed in the glow of the lamplight. Even though I had sat and visited with him before, I found it difficult to look at his face, and I was glad he kept his eyes averted. The air smelled sweet and damp like new wine.

"What will I do now?" Ramen sliced a piece of goat cheese and put it onto flat bread. "Business is poor, and you can see the place is truly empty. I have no more than an occasional traveler, with the census long past."

"Come with me to find Mary." My words escaped before I thought. I wondered if I should have proposed such a thing, but kept talking. "Close the inn and leave it to Simon to watch. I want you to show me how to find my way to Egypt where they have gone."

Ramen held his bread in midair, staring at a dark corner of the room. "I thought of going back to Egypt to visit Aunt Medina, who is the only family I have now. I hate to put extra work on Simon, but then the inn is as good as closed anyway."

"So you will come?"

"I, well…I must show you how to get there. Yes, I think it would be good to go to Egypt and for you to meet my Aunt Medina, as I do want to see her. She is a wonderful host." A smile creased his face. Ramen had forgotten his food and sipped his wine absently. "We cannot simply pack and go. I will tell Simon to take care of the inn. We must have two donkeys, water, food, clothing, bedding, and tents. It will take time to prepare."

I smiled, but stifled a giggle. I recalled how quickly I had put on all of my clothing, packed sacks of food and herbs, and tied them about my waist. I thought of how rapidly the whole encampment departed at the threat of a sandstorm. "Have you ever traveled, besides the time you were a young boy and came here?"

"Yes, we went back to Egypt twice to visit, but it has been a long time."

"Good, you have experience. Let us begin packing." I rose and cleared the table. As far as I knew, almost everything I required was already attached to, or worn on, my person.

"All right then. I shall miss Pel. He was such a good boy to have around when I wanted chores done."

We spent a great deal of time packing. Ramen was methodical and meticulous about how he rolled up the bedding and rugs. He took care to make sure the load on the donkey rested evenly across its back. In the interest of time, I had talked him out of purchasing a second donkey for the trip, so he took even more pains to choose those items he deemed essential. He placed a clay water jug on one side of the donkey and bedding and tents on the other. I put food in a packing basket and placed it on the donkey's rump. It was in front of a rug draped across his back to serve as a sitting place were either of us to be in want of a ride.

"He is burdened," I murmured, seeing the donkey shift his feet from one side to the other.

"The very reason why I wanted a second donkey. I have a few more things to do."

"Impossible." I gritted my teeth. "We have enough for a family, and I count two of us."

"Another pot for cooking." He placed a medium sized clay vessel into the basket, and rearranged the food packed inside to make everything fit. "In case the other breaks." He tied the basket closed.

I tapped my foot impatiently. He was certainly different from any man I had known who would trek into the wilderness with almost no thought of provisions. Had I erred and been too hasty asking him to make this trip with me? My spirit told me otherwise when he gazed at me with his wonderful dark eyes. I smelled his clean, manly scent and stifled my strong urge to fall into his arms.

"I think we have finished." Ramen broke the silence, smiling down at me. He was elegant in his Egyptian head covering and embroidered linen travel cloak.

"Have you spoken with Simon?" I wanted to have all arrangements in order when we left to reassure we would have no reason to turn back.

"Yes, he wishes us well. He promised to open the inn for guests while I'm away."

We walked fast, sleeping and resting as little as possible. Sixteen sunrises and sunsets passed with each day very much the same. As we approached Medina's home, I felt uneasy. I hoped Mary would be there. I wondered if his aunt would approve of my appearance. If she did not, we would have a very short visit and I would insist on leaving. "Ramen, how do I look?" I smoothed my linen tunic.

"All right." He absently plodded alongside the donkey. "Why?"

"Nothing." I kicked at the sand. "Forget I asked."

"You are worried about my aunt? Well, you are a sight better than when I first met you all covered with birthing muck." He laughed.

I scooped up a handful of sand, threw it at him and ran.

"What was that for?" He ran to catch up, and left the donkey shaking its head to get rid of the stray granules.

"Because." I ran. Now I laughed in spite of myself. Chasing felt joyful, like being young again.

Ramen smiled ruefully and rapidly overtook me. "Ha," he said as he caught me and grabbed my arm. I twisted in an attempt to free myself, and we tumbled to the sandy earth in a heap. He planted juicy kisses all over my face and licked it as a mother animal does its young.

"Ouch, stop. You will choke on the sand." I lay flat on my back, and he on all his limbs like a crawling child, held me down.

"Shush, I'm cleaning you."

"Oh, you," I began, but he put his lips to mine so my words stopped. The whole world spun, stars sparkled, and I thought his kiss was the most wonderful thing ever to happen to me. He pulled back and our eyes met and held.

"Hannah, I desire very much for us to be married. Would you be my wife?"

I was unable to talk, but my whole body wanted this man more than I had wanted anyone. Love shone from his smiling eyes. I reached up and traced the sandy outline of his face, now very dear to me. I knew not how to answer him, and I remained mute. The grittiness of my situation disappeared, as I felt safe in his arms.

"Ahem." A man nearby cleared his throat. "Who are you?" He greeted us in an Egyptian dialect.

We both hastily arose, dusting off our clothing, to see a tall, thin man leaning on a walking stick, dressed in linen garments. His stoic expression said nothing.

"I am Ramen." Ramen raised his hand in a peace greeting.

"I am Orem, the overseer of Hawara." The man also lifted his hand.

"Medina is my father's sister. It has been a long while since I came here, and even longer since I lived on this place. Now I do recognize you."

"You are the image of your father," Orem said. Nearby two white dogs barked, and lumbered up to meet us, tails wagging. "Maki, Teli, sit." When the big dogs sat, their heads were even with his waist. "Medina did not say she expected anyone."

"My betrothed and I left hastily after my father's death. I sent a message to Medina about his passing, but I did not tell her of my plans to come home." Ramen's voice became commanding. "Orem, please take my donkey and see it to water and the stable. Come, Hannah, we will refresh ourselves at the spring by those shade trees." Orem gathered the reins of the donkey, spoke to the dogs, and they all left.

"Betrothed?" I felt amused that within a short time I heard the claim applied to me with yet another man. This one had proposed to me while he had me trapped on my back in the sand. "Well, I suppose it makes a better appearance since we traveled together."

Ramen smiled and nodded.

"Orem was a trusted servant when I was here as a boy. My aunt must have raised his position to overseer."

"Oh." I wondered if his family had great wealth.

The spring was clear, and I first splashed my face with handfuls of water, and then dangled my feet in the soothing coolness to refresh them. When Ramen removed his top tunic and washed his arms, face, neck, and chest, I saw how well sculpted and muscular he was. We shook our garments, and I took a comb and plied it as best I could to my tangled hair. When I felt presentable, we walked together toward the sprawling white stone house. The dogs sat as sentinels at the front gate.

My life pulse quickened. I hoped I would see Mary at any moment. A small, dark servant girl, wearing a simple white tunic, greeted us with a bow and beckoned us with a wave of her hand. She motioned us to follow her to Medina who sat in the shade in the inner courtyard.

I had never seen such a beautiful place. Two large white statues of dogs, the image of the live ones, stood on either side of the pebbled pathway. Colorful painted images of half-animal, half-human creatures decorated the walls, and murals of battles and hunting expeditions were depicted in the art. I could not take in all the spaciousness of this abode at once. Palm and olive trees provided shade. Stone and wooden benches and a round table were placed in the shade. Large feathered fans that reminded me of small colorful trees, rested against one of the benches.

Medina rose from her woven chair and hurried to greet us. Her gauzy white garment floated around her like mist. Ramen embraced her warmly, but they did not speak at first. "Look at you." She was teary-eyed, and held him at arm's length to see his face. "In your countenance I see your father."

Ramen stood solemnly, stoically, with his jaw set firmly. "And you, my aunt, are as lovely as ever." He stepped away from her. "This is Hannah, my betrothed."

"What a surprise! Hannah, how good to meet you, my sister." Medina cast her eyes intently at me to read more than a name from the greeting.

"And it is good to meet you as well." I offered both hands and Medina took them, drew me close, and kissed both my cheeks. I kissed hers. I wondered if I should excuse myself and leave them to share their grief over the loss of Hawara. I felt anxious and fidgety, and my eyes darted beyond Medina to the doorways leading off the courtyard. It was nice to meet his aunt, but my real concern was Mary. I wondered if they would tell me where she was. The air became hotter than before and flies buzzed.

"You must be thirsty and hungry. Shanika, please

serve refreshments." Medina clapped her hands and the servant who had shown us to the courtyard ran to get our drinks.

"I want to hear everything," Medina gushed, winking at me with her kohl-darkened eyelid. "Will we have a great party to celebrate your wedding?" Her shiny dark hair was held in place by a gold and black circlet around the crown of her head. She gestured for us to sit.

"I… I…" I wanted for words and questioned Ramen with pleading eyes. We sat at the table the servant prepared. She poured sweet red wine into goblets and set out a woven basket laden with cheese and bread.

"Yes, yes, of course we will celebrate, but I thought we would keep it small. We can discuss it later." He sat and lifted his wine goblet. "Right now, let us drink to our health. And tell me, how is your health and what is new here?"

"I am sure you know I had guests," Medina said. "Mary and Joseph stayed here for several weeks because of the terrible thing your father sent word to us about, where they killed the boy babies. They are horrendous beasts to do such a thing. I was happy to keep the family here out of harm's way. At first they were reluctant to accept my hospitality, not wanting to impose. I insisted they would be safe here, and they stayed. Such a dear Baby, well behaved, He crawled around, explored, and even pulled Himself up to stand. And such lovely eyes appeared to see right through me and beyond. Oh, I do miss Him."

"How long ago did they leave?" I felt disappointed.

"Oh, around two weeks ago. One morning Joseph woke up and announced it was time they went home to Nazareth. He is a carpenter and said he had neglected his workbench too long. He avoided traveling to Bethlehem, and took a different route. I encouraged them to stay here and start a business. He could have established himself well here. See this exquisite myrtle wood table? He made it for me as a gift."

"It is lovely." I marveled at the smooth oiled finish on the table, thinking I had never seen a myrtle tree. While I was not happy missing Mary, I was glad to know she had gone home to Nazareth.

"Have you an extra room for weary travelers?" Ramen smiled at his aunt.

"Forgive me, yes, yes, of course." She rose from her chair and motioned us to follow.

"Have Orem bring our things," Ramen said. Shanika was already on her way out, but without having been asked, Orem came in toting some of our belongings.

"Come, this way." We followed Medina until she came to a room with an open curtain. We walked up two steps to a narrow corridor where another room was situated in the inner part of the house. "Orem, their things go here." She gestured, with a wave of her hand, to the floor on the right side of the doorway. He and the servant girl bowed politely and went away.

"I trust you will be comfortable here. If there is anything else, please let me know."

Our room, cool and dark, was open near the ceiling

to let in air. A curtain divided the room to make separate sleeping places for us. The simple, woven reed mats on the floor were a welcome sight. I flopped down and sat cross-legged, thinking about our situation. I supposed this meant I was to be Ramen's wife, but tradition still had me bound to my brother-in-law. I decided not to dwell on it, but enjoy my stay, and sort it out another time.

Ramen slowly paced his part of our room, examining it. He chuckled, drawing aside the curtain to let me see. Three small, carved dog figurines were on the washbasin stand in the corner. I watched curiously as he picked them up, one at a time, handling them reverently. I knew instantly we were in his childhood bedroom, or his aunt had placed his old things here. His eyes glistened with pleasure.

"My dogs. I cannot believe Aunt Medina saved them all these years. I thought they were lost. As a boy I played with my things and left them wherever I pleased. When we went away, Father allowed me to take the barest necessities. I asked for my dogs, but he said he didn't know where they were. I have been back a few times, but this is the first time I have seen them. Wonder why she decided to unearth them now?"

"Perhaps for Mary's Baby?"

"Better yet, for our son when we have one." Ramen's voice was husky.

"Not so fast. You know I have been barren."

"The right man can change that." He moved closer.

"Hmm, if you remember correctly, I have not agreed

to marry you." I wanted to change the subject, to discuss it later. "Remember I seek Mary and her child."

"Well, they've gone to Nazareth. I promised to bring you here and you are here." He sounded edgy.

I felt exhausted from travel. I had to sort things out. Perhaps it was too soon to prod Ramen further. "Not now, but soon I must go to Nazareth."

Ramen looked at me with a pained expression, but said nothing. He held me gently for a moment before he went back to Medina. I stayed in the room and arranged our beds on opposite sides of the curtain.

In the next few days Ramen spent time visiting with his aunt, getting caught up on the news. In the evening before we drew the curtain closed to sleep separately, he related a bit of family history. "Medina's husband, a military captain, died about a year ago in battle. She cared for the Hawara property by herself afterwards. Years ago she had twin boys who died at birth. She had no other children." I listened thoughtfully.

I respected their mutual grief and his desire to talk with Medina of bygone days. After meals, I excused myself from them, and I wandered about the well-kept spacious grounds. One of the servants walked within my sight at all times, and I first appreciated the attention. Then it occurred to me maybe it was not hospitality. Had they been told to watch me? Perhaps Ramen thought I would go to Nazareth without him. I wanted to leave. While my faith wavered, a mysterious Voice was ever present to beckon me.

Any time I looked over my shoulder, either Orem or

Shanika watched me. I chafed with annoyance Ramen or Medina might mistrust me until one day I was very grateful for my follower. I went to the spring to gather herbs, and became startled by a stir in the tall rushes. Chills ran through me, prickling my arms.

Was it the dogs? No. A man appeared suddenly as a specter among the parted reeds. He must have followed me to Bethlehem and then here. I was stricken with terror. I could not feel my feet, much less run. He leered at me and stepped closer. *Ham!*

CHAPTER FIFTEEN

A scream stopped in my throat. I stared in thankful disbelief when I saw Orem followed me at a distance, but quickly drew closer. What happened next blurred my sight. Orem raised his arm high and masterfully whirled a stone flinger. Ham toppled like a felled tree, landing face down with a resounding splat in the swampy mud by the spring.

Orem hurried to me. "Are you all right?"

"Yes, oh, thank you." I still trembled from fear. "Your name suits you well."

"My mother named me." He rubbed his bearded chin, shaking his head. He bent down on one knee next to Ham. I wondered if he had knocked him out, or if he had killed him with the stone, and I wanted to examine him. When I came closer he waved me away. "Go. I will take care of this." I hesitated a moment, then went to the house. Maki and Teli followed me.

The dogs sniffed me, then twirled as twins and settled in the shade of the wall at the entrance. Weak in the knees and afraid, I wanted to share with Ramen what had happened, and all that had occurred between Ham and me before now. If Ham had been slain as it appeared, justice had been done. If he lived despite the hard blow, I was sorely in need of protection. Whether Ham lived or died, I wanted to be far away from him. Tonight I would ask Ramen to come with me to Nazareth to find Mary and her Baby. After a good meal with wine I would convince him we had to leave.

When I walked through the portals to the courtyard Medina sat alone, sobbing. She wiped her nose with a soft white cloth. A tiny white dog, Popo, was on her lap. I went to her. "What is wrong?" I stooped and took her hand.

"Nothing. You are too kind."

"Why are you weeping?"

"You have so much. You and Ramen have your whole lives ahead of you, but my life is bleak and empty. Soon you will go and all I will have are my dogs and servants. Would that you could stay." Her teary eyes pleaded. With her brow furrowed with worry, she appeared older to me now. "Please make your home here. Hawara is the dearest place I have known, and Ramen is all the family I have."

I sat on the floor next to her, speechless. My mind spun. An image of Mary and her Baby, then Ham, floated before me and disappeared. I wondered how Ramen would react to his aunt's tears. Or had she already asked, and he had made up his mind? I had to think.

"This could be a thriving place again. Please influence Ramen. Tell him you want to stay." She stopped crying, dabbing at her hazel eyes. "He insists you will live in Bethlehem."

For an unknown reason the dogs in the outer courtyard barked and howled. Popo leapt from Medina's lap, and dashed about in circles, barking shrilly. I stood up. I wondered where Ramen had gone and what had started the commotion. Were Ramen and Orem taking Ham's body away for burial? I heard shouting and pounding hooves in the distance.

"Hurry!" Medina jumped to her feet and grabbed my hand, and almost dragged me across the inner court.

"What is it?" I freed my hand, but followed her to the gate. A company of soldiers approached on horses and chariots.

"Romans. We must hide." Medina was wild-eyed. "I don't know what they want, but they are not going to find us women. Come." She grabbed my hand again and pulled me toward the kitchen storage area. She directed me to a curtained cupboard where foodstuffs were kept. The rings on her hand sparkled as she pointed. "Let us go under here."

We squeezed inside and worked our way behind heavy pottery filled with grain or oil. Our hiding place was warm and stuffy and smelled of rancid oil spills and spices. Afraid to speak, I worried about the danger we faced. My life pulse echoed very loudly in my ears, and I feared it would lead the soldiers to us.

Boots tramped loudly into the inner courts. I heard the terrifying sound of crashing pottery. Popo howled pitifully in the courtyard. The relentless barking of Maki and Teli suddenly stopped. Medina sobbed plaintively. The harsh voices and sounds of crashing objects and loud footfalls went on endlessly. Where was Ramen? Where was Shanika? Orem might be dealing with Ham or his body. I did not let my mind dwell on their fate for long. Footsteps neared our hiding place. I took no breath. I pinched my nose to stifle a sneeze. Heavy breathing and a coarse foreign language unknown to me met my ears. Someone poured wine or other liquid and swallowed noisily. A man shouted, and then there were many boots tramping into the kitchen. I felt doomed.

The curtain covering our hiding place suddenly ripped open by a man's hand. Unless the men stooped to peer inside they would be unable to see us behind the bins and crocks, tall enough to hold a child of two years. Men snorted rudely, laughed, and ridiculed one of the fellows. The earthy perspiration and stink of the marauders was sickening. I got a cramp in my leg and wanted to stretch it. The soldiers drank and laughed while I perspired and grew cold. After an eternal duration, boots echoed down the hall and faded. Possibly, an officer had summoned them. When I started to move, Medina put a hand on me to warn me to remain where I was. I prayed quietly in my mind for protection and calm.

Clicking footsteps padded into the kitchen. It was Popo. He set up a cacophony of pitiful barks and howls. Popo squeezed between ewers, and wriggled in until he found Medina and excitedly licked her face. She sniffled and whispered, "Popo, shh..."

With the cupboard open, I watched the light change from day to dusk. It became eerily quiet. Where was Ramen?

"Shall we?" I touched Medina's arm.

She slowly crawled out. We had to shove aside the bin we had drawn in front of us. I worked my way around to help in the cramped quarters, but it took forever. I was unsure I could stand, as my body felt stiff and hurting. We crept in the semi-darkness warily. Popo whined. "He is probably hungry," Medina whispered as she emerged from our hiding place.

"Do you think they left?" I pulled myself out. Fear gripped me, prickled the hair on my head, and waves of nausea burned in my throat, as I straightened and finally stood up next to Medina.

"No, I think they are camped, perhaps near the spring." Medina pulled a small bowl from a shelf and put bits of cooked rice and lamb into it for Popo. "But we could not stay cramped in the cupboard forever."

"What now? Shall I go check things out?"

"No, I will. Hold Popo for me. I still hear them a short distance away."

"I want to go with you. I want to know where Ramen is." I wanted to walk as the cramp still seized my leg.

"I think he is hiding. I cannot stop you, but we must go in opposite directions in case anyone is still here. You go upstairs and I will go through the court toward the servant quarters. If at any time you hear them, go back into hiding. We will meet here."

I walked, easing the stiffness in my leg, and kept to the shadows. I should have told Medina where Orem was when I had last seen him. I held Popo and would have backtracked to give him to her, but she was gone. "You better be good." I nuzzled his pink fuzzy ear. I was at the bottom step of the stairway when I heard a rustling sound. My skin prickled. I hoped it was Ramen, but it could be one of the men who would harm us. Hide, stay put, or continue?

I crept up the stairs, thinking each footfall I made sounded loud as a thunderclap. To still my fears, I forced myself to think of the Messiah, but it did not help. Darkness fell. I came to the landing outside the bedroom area. I stood very still, listening. Slowly I pulled aside the curtain in the doorway to our room. I could see nothing and wished I had a lamp or a candle. Popo panted loudly and made snuffling noises. Anyone near would have heard us. I made my way around the room to the corner where we kept an oil lamp. I put Popo down and groped for it. With flint next to it, soon I had lamplight. To my dismay the room had been ransacked. When I shone the light toward the washstand, I saw the pitcher had been broken and the toy dogs were gone.

I went out of our room and on to the next, carrying

the lamp. I found, it too, had been torn apart. A rug was thrown into a heap in one corner. I walked toward the rug. Fearfully and hesitantly, I reached to throw it back, and stifled a scream when the rug moved. Shanika's face appeared wild-eyed as she emerged from beneath the rug.

"What happened?" I threw it aside, and saw she lay in a pool of blood. "Oh, dear girl, stay where you are lying down." I gently covered her. Popo cried, so I petted him. "Stay, Popo." He curled up next to her.

The brutality of men who did this horrible, sinful act to a young girl made my blood boil. Trembling, I went back to our room to find herbs, but of course the water pitcher had been smashed. I headed for the kitchen. I had no more thought for my safety, but took the stairs quickly carrying the lamp. Thankfully, the house was deserted. The kitchen fire still burned in the hearth and a water kettle was there. I filled one jug with warm water and another with wine and hurried upstairs. I poured a cup of water mixed with wine and an herbal sedative and lifted Shanika's head for her to drink. She did not speak, but did whatever I said. I removed the blood-soaked clothing and cleansed her frail body with a salt solution. I tore bits of cloth from my under tunic and placed them beneath the girl's bottom to soak up blood seepage, and then wrapped her in my cloak. She finally sighed and closed her eyes. I felt her wrist, a technique Serena had shown me, and smiled when I found her life pulse.

A methodical thud echoed as someone neared. I covered the lamp with a rug. The person stopped at the top of the stairs. Popo shook himself and ran barking excitedly.

"There you are," whispered Medina. She let out a sigh. I uncovered the lamp and stood. We hugged.

"Oh, no." She saw Shanika.

"Ravaged brutally." I tried to control my trembling.

"It is unsafe to stay here, because if they come back we would be trapped."

"Shanika has to refrain from walking until the bleeding stops, and I do not know how we can move her. Where do you suggest we go?"

"Let me first see if the servant quarters are clear. At least it has more than one doorway to the room. I will come back for you." Medina grabbed the lamp, turned, and left the room.

I sat for a long while, and I held Popo until he settled next to us and was asleep. Shanika slumbered fitfully. It seemed almost safe in the darkness. The high window in the room revealed the starlit night. I was worried Medina might run into the soldiers and be hurt, and I hoped Ramen was hiding somewhere unharmed. I refused to think of what might have happened. It was all too horrific to comprehend, and I sobbed, wiping tears with my sleeve. My thoughts went back to the night I had helped Mary as she gave birth, and I wondered if they were safe. In such a dangerous world, I thought about what could be happening at this moment. I calmed as I focused on the Messiah, yet slumber did not visit my eyes.

Shanika awakened and wept. I hugged her to calm

her. Popo licked her tears. I cast my eyes on them with pity, but disallowed dwelling on the horrors of the moment. I had to find out what happened to Ramen and Medina. Would I find their bodies meanly cast aside?

"What do I do now?" I sat quietly for a long time, watching Shanika, touching her brow, listening keenly to the hushed sounds of the house.

My skin prickled as I heard thrumming footsteps. I was afraid to hope it was Ramen. I froze, and then quickly drew rugs over us as though they had been carelessly tossed. The heavy footsteps paused at the landing and shuffled toward the next room. I let no breath come and hoped Popo would be quiet. Suddenly he let out a muffled growl, darted from under the rug, raced out of the room, and barked shrilly.

"Hey!" shouted a deep voice that reminded me of Ham. I heard rustling when the person bent down to pet Popo or pick him up. A man chuckled. I wondered why he had come into the house and if he would try to find us. Popo stopped barking, but I still heard him panting noisily. The sounds grew fainter as the heavy footfalls descended. Shanika and I signaled to each other with hand squeezes. I strained my ears for more sounds, hoping against hope I would hear Ramen. I worried what the soldier would do with Popo.

Could it be Ham? Why would he be with Roman soldiers? I thought he was dead.

CHAPTER SIXTEEN

It was very early in the morning as the moon began to set, and a fading purple streaked with a golden glow of promised day appeared on the horizon. Shanika stirred and blinked her eyes in the half-light. I reached out and patted her hand to let her know I was still there. "How do you feel?" The girl made a breathy sound. I offered her a sip of water. "May I check on how things are going for you?" When I placed my hand beneath her garments I found the bleeding had almost ceased. "You are going to be all right. I want you to stay here quietly while I go find Medina. I will be gone a short while."

I went down the stairs and kept to the shadows in the courtyard. Everything quieted except for birdsongs coming from the olive trees. I stopped and listened, then moved forward again. My nerves were taut, and I felt as though I were outside of my own body. I thought I heard a rustling noise coming from the kitchen. I stopped. No sound was present except my own barefooted steps. When I went toward the servant quarters where Medina had gone, I felt vulnerable, as I knew of no hiding place there. I raced across the open court and then huddled in the shadow of an overhang from the planked covering of the hut. Once I was inside the place, my foot bumped against something hairy and I squealed. I bent down and felt the stiffening body of one of the white dogs. My skin prickled as I tried to see in the dimness. A dark figure lay on the floor. I groped in the semi-darkness and found the face of a still, warm body. It brought back memories of finding Judah in the cave and I felt the sting of unshed tears. He had a long beard. The face did not feel like Ramen. I was unsure whether to be relieved or frightened. "Orem?" My hand shook as I touched him.

The man mumbled and struggled to sit, but collapsed again. If this was not Orem, I could be abetting one of the soldiers. I reached and found his weak life pulse. As a healer I wanted to help, but my greater quest was to find Medina. I rose and tried to get my bearings. The musty air in the hut stank of old hides and tallow, and curled around my nose where I smelled my own fear. My hands crept over the rough chalky walls as I discovered a square room with woven reed curtains separating the two sleeping areas. As I inched along, I heard his shallow breathing. Groping around in the dimness, I found a small oil lamp. With no flint nearby I set it aside as useless. Fear clutched me when I did not find Medina in the hut. My throat constricted as I wondered if she had ever made it there. Was she suffering in the same horrible state as Shanika? A burning fear seared my stomach and crept up my throat. Could I be next?

I forced myself to go back to the man lying on the floor. Reason returned as I touched him. The perspiration soaked garments felt coarsely woven like those Orem wore. As I felt his leathery face and assured it to be him, relief cautiously flooded my mind. A welt the size of a fig rose on his forehead. "Orem, it is Hannah. I have come to help you. Do you know where Medina is?"

Only a moan came from his lips. "Please." I shook him gently. "What happened to Ramen? Medina?"

"Maki," he sighed.

"Dead, I know. I am saddened, too." The dogs belonged to Medina, but Orem was in charge of their care and was the master. "I will go look for them." Perspiration dripped from my face.

"Gone." Orem's breath came in labored puffs. Each rail sounded as though it would be his last.

"Ramen? Medina?" I felt icy with fear. If they were all gone, what would I do?

The old man was surely dying and I had no medicine to help him. I placed my hand on his. I sat with him even though I had an urgency to find the others and get back to the servant girl. He did not try to speak again. A peace settled over Orem, and his large, rough hand relaxed. He panted, and then a, "humph," escaped from his lips. My tears flowed as I thought he had died. With shaking hands, I reached to close his eyelids and found they were already shut. I left him lying in his sweat and blood on the cool dirt floor.

Back in the house, as I slipped cautiously upstairs I heard the voices of men and the neighing of horses, which announced the company of soldiers had bedded down a short distance away. I hoped they were leaving at daylight. Thankfully, they had chosen to leave the house in favor of camping elsewhere. I wondered if Popo had escaped from the man and come back into the house, or if any soldiers had returned. I willed my bare feet to make no sound on the icy stone floor.

Shanika was lying down and awake when I returned. "I did not find them." I kneeled beside the girl to check on her. Perhaps it would be easier to tell her about Orem later.

The curtains hung limp and lifeless. Horses neighed far away. Ashen Shanika slept. While I tried to sleep, I spent my night keeping vigil, and dozed only a moment after day dawned. In the late afternoon I finally decided it was safe to go down to greet the sunlit day. I carried a staff for protection. Insects buzzed about in the courtyard. I wanted to find an implement with which to dig to bury the dog, but soon abandoned the idea. While I had seen no other people, surely Medina had neighbors. My arms felt numb and useless and my legs felt heavy as I walked about the place, looking for footprints, for signs of either Medina or Ramen. I felt a hollow cavern fill where hunger should have been. Had they been taken alive? Were they now slaves to the soldiers? Or were they dead? I felt too weak to go back to the kitchen. As I stood like a lifeless desert stone, grief streamed through my soul and mind and engulfed me in its flood.

Messiah, Mary, Yahweh, why did this horrible thing have to happen?

Finally I gathered my courage and searched cautiously, as I followed a set of ominous boot prints and smaller footprints in the sand leading to the spring. Signs of a struggle were evident in the muddy grass and torn apart low rushes where Ham had appeared earlier. Horse hooves had made imprints, indicating the soldiers had watered horses. The sight of a woman's sandal footprints in the damp dirt filled me with dread. The men were gone at last as echoing sounds had faded. I was about to go back to the house when I spotted a white form among the reeds.

Fearfully, I walked step by step. I found the body of Medina, lying on her side with her arm shielding her face. Her gauzy garment lay askew and exposed her flesh. Teli, alive but with a bleeding paw, guarded Medina. When I felt for her life pulse it was gone. With what she had endured at the hands of these rough men I felt an indescribable pain and rage. No doubt, she had fought them until she could no longer hold on. I wondered if Teli had defended her or had crept to her side after his own injury. Nagging guilt haunted me. Had I come sooner, I might have saved her, but maybe the same thing would have been done to me. I retched violently, and bile burned my throat. Teli stood and followed me for a ways, then turned back to lie next to her.

When I got to the house, Shanika sat on a floor mat in

the kitchen. She sat silently and stared straight ahead. After a while, I pointed limply at the bowl of cold boiled barley by the hearthstones. We sat in the kitchen, spooned the gruel into bowls, then dipped into it with our fingers and let the nourishment appease our hunger. I needed strength for what I had to do. When Teli limped in Shanika looked past him. Her eyes reflected her fear.

Words caught in my throat, so I said nothing at first. I examined Teli and cleaned the blood from his leg. "Teli will heal." I went to Shanika and put my arms around her. "Medina is dead. I am sorry." While we clung together for comfort, our wrenching sobs and fear shook me to the core. "At least the terrible men are gone. I must check on Orem."

I entered the servant's hut with dread, smelling the damp earth and death, wondering how I would deal with the body of Orem. My life pulse quickened as I passed Maki's lifeless form and found Orem's body had moved from where I left it. He lay on his side, not quite on a mat in the corner of the room. "Orem?"

He groaned.

"Alive!" I could have kissed him. He tried to roll onto the mat, and I helped him. He was terribly injured, which meant now I would have two people to heal.

I spoke to him in a language I hoped he would understand. "Medina is dead. Shanika is sorely injured as you are. Do you know where Ramen is?" I spoke in a rush. I wanted to ask what happened to Ham, but thought better to wait until later.

"No. Ramen is gone? It is terrible," he said barely

above a whisper. He sipped the wine I offered, taking in the gravity of our situation. His face was stoic, but tears trickled down his weathered cheeks. "Horrible."

"Gilead oil would be best to treat your injury, but the one I have here is comfrey."

Orem shook his head, saying in a stronger voice. "I am not badly hurt, little mother."

I smiled at the irony of being called little mother. At least he could understand me. I wanted to treat the old man's wounds. "I am a healer."

"Sorceress?"

"No, no, I do not use magic powers. I apply herbs and oils to do what I can to alleviate pain. You have to rest. I want to know if there are neighbors nearby who can help me bury Medina."

"Yes, Pasin and Farouk." He pointed in the opposite direction from the pond, past the Hawara home. While he was by no means healed, I thought him to be as well as he could be now. I turned to leave, but fear stopped me.

"Orem, the man you hit earlier, did he truly die? Where is his body?"

Orem nodded his head, but looked away. He cleared his throat. "I know not. I think the soldiers took him."

The question still bothered me why the soldiers would have removed a dead body. Had he been alive, and they took him to fight with them because he was a strong man? I decided I might never find out. I made myself think about what more I had to do. "Are you well enough to walk to show me where the neighbors live? We will need help."

"You must stay here. I will go." Orem stood tall and took up his staff.

I shook my head, thinking Orem must have brought himself back to life. I let him go to his neighbors for help. A neighbor, Farouk came that afternoon. After he heard the bad news, he told me the men had taken his livestock, but had done no other harm. He and Orem led me to the Hawara family tomb, a manmade cavern for burial a short distance beyond the spring. Medina's deceased husband and other relatives were laid to rest there.

We set about preparing Medina's body for the next life. Even though I would be unclean afterwards, I bathed Medina, generously applied spices and perfume, and wrapped her in her most beautiful red robe. I put a many-colored stone necklace on her and a circlet of jewels around her hair. Orem and his neighbors prepared wine and food to be buried with her. Among her provisions were figs, dates, honey, olive oil, and barley grains. Maki would be near her.

Her body was wrapped tightly with a burial cloth and placed on a cart pulled by Orem. We all went down into the tomb where she would be placed. We stopped inside at the entrance as the men respectfully took her body from the cart. The remains of her husband were nearby on a raised rectangle, and they put her body on a similar bed. I had never been inside a grave before, and I looked on with curious interest in the darkened place until the lamplight shone to reveal it more clearly. It was done.

I wailed loudly and Shanika sobbed quietly. Afterwards we went to the house where Pasin, Farouk's wife had prepared a feast of roast lamb. Farouk talked quietly with Orem. Pasin appeared to understand nothing I said. Waggling her eyes to catch his attention, she let her husband know she was ready to leave. I thanked them for all they had done. They bid us farewell and went home.

While Orem healed, he never regained his strength and walked with a more labored step than before. He took care of Teli, but could do nothing else. One day he came to me. "I am no use to you. Please relieve me of my duties. You should go back to your people, and I must go to mine." He bowed his head before me.

"Where will you go?" I felt a growing panic. How would I handle things alone if Ramen never returned? "You were Medina's servant, therefore I have neither the authority to keep you here nor to let you go."

"Medina has gone to the afterworld. My brother is in Alexandria. Farouk has promised to take me there." I did not try to stop him, and I wished him well.

Days flowed on as I nursed Shanika back to health, but her tongue was still without words. I asked where she had come from and if she wished to return to her people, but she shook her head. I pondered on whether to wait a while longer for Ramen to return. Each morning I hoped for signs of dust or a figure on the horizon, but none appeared. Were we in danger of the return of the dreadful company of soldiers? The man who had taken

Popo haunted me. What would happen to us alone?

No animals remained here except Teli, as the mules, goats, and even Ramen's donkey had been stolen or driven off into the desert. The soldiers had ransacked the kitchen, but had left us with enough food to eat. I thought that living in Bethlehem at Hawara Inn or returning to Father Moshe would be preferable to staying in Egypt. After a time, I asked Shanika if she wanted to come with me, but she shook her head sadly and turned away. The words of Father Moshe still haunted my thoughts. "You may never be welcomed back." I struggled inwardly about what to do, and I could not pray. I decided to wait awhile longer before I traveled anywhere.

During these moons of helping to heal Shanika and to recover from the damage to my spirit, I planted seeds near the spring. Orem had stored herb and grain seeds in bags in the servant hut. I used his old walking staff to make rows and coaxed watering ditches from the spring. One bright day as we were gardening there, I felt nostalgic and sang old shepherd songs. Shanika smiled. I nodded to her and sang the same song again and again.

Na-nah na-nah na-nah nah

> *My lamb is leaping*
> *My lamb is leaping*
> *My ewe is sleeping*
> *The wind is keeping*
> *My flock tonight*

To my delight, she stood and swayed to the rhythm. When I clapped my hands, she clapped hers. We both clapped and danced to my song. Soon we were laughing. I collapsed to the grassy bank, saying, "It is joyful to sing and dance again."

"Good," said Shanika, the first word she had spoken after her ordeal. Now I was speechless. I stood up and we hugged. We both had tears rolling down our cheeks. Something precious had happened. Teli wagged his tail and came up to me. I looked at his injury and found, while he still favored the leg, it had healed.

"All praise to Yahweh." The words came naturally to my lips and startled me. My spirit still existed even though my faith had fled from my thoughts.

"Thank you, Hannah." Shanika pointed to herself and then to me. "I will stay here with you and serve you. I want to learn your language." She motioned to my lips and then to hers.

"You are my friend." I hugged her.

As we sat together admiring the green sprouts of our tiny crop, we saw a puff of dust rising steadily above the horizon and coming closer. Both of us stiffened in fear. It had been around five moons after the band of rough soldiers came to wreak destruction on our lives. I hoped it was Ramen, but I rose and grabbed Shanika's hand. "Let us hide among the reeds in case it is one who would hurt us. We can watch them approach from here. When they find the house empty they may leave. We shall see what happens." My knees threatened to give way and my life pulse drummed as we ducked behind the reeds, and kneeled on the bank in the wet grass.

CHAPTER SEVENTEEN

t was a lone rider on a gray donkey, with a second donkey laden with packs. The man's form appeared not anything like that of Ramen. My whole being shook with fear. As he came nearer I could see he appeared to be short of stature and rather rotund, wore billowing colorful clothing, and had a silken purple turban on his head. He came directly toward the spring, dismounted and led the donkeys to drink, and then he bent down and splashed his face with water. He opened a pack on one of the donkeys and pulled out a piece of flat bread, tore it apart and ate it with relish, dribbling crumbs. He talked to his donkeys. "Ever see such a place, eh? Someone's growing a smart crop of sumpin', eh? Nice house over there, but we don't want to bother folks. Even so, might be the woman of the house would want a new carpet or two, eh?"

I had heard the voice before, and could hardly keep quiet. "I know him," I whispered. Zeke, the Rug Man was certainly no threat. One of the donkeys brayed and sniffed the air. The ass walked toward the place where we were partially hidden. At first, I was too surprised to stand.

Teli ran out to meet the man, barking. "Good dog," Zeke said, but when he reached down to pet him, Teli let out a low growl. The donkey kept walking.

"What you got there, eh? Like a dog, you are." Zeke followed the gray donkey. Teli barked more loudly.

I had no reason to hide from him, and decided I had best make an appearance if I did not want these oafs to walk on us. "Good day to you, Zeke, the Rug Man." I popped up out of the reeds. Shanika followed. Teli stopped barking, and came up to us with his tail wagging.

"Ahh!" Zeke stood openmouthed for a moment. He recovered, ever the merchant. "Would you ladies be wanting one of my fine wool rugs, eh?"

"Well, come in and we might talk about it."

The day was bright with sunshine as we sat at the round pedestal table in the courtyard. Shanika brought out wine and cakes.

"Very good cakes, here. A man could become used to this, eh? Thank you for your hospitality." We were eating fresh barley and honey cakes with everything calm and routine. Teli waited nearby for morsels to drop. I had invited Zeke to stay and rest a few days, as I had an idea.

My insides were churning with my plan. I wanted

to leave the Hawara estate as soon as I could. I decided to ply the man with good food and ask him directly. "Would you see the two of us to Bethlehem?"

"That would be a bit of a stretch, eh?" His eyebrows drew up in surprise. "Not going there, no, was going on to Alexandria." Zeke scratched his forehead under his turban. He reached for another cake and ate it with good appetite.

"I will stay." Shanika turned her head away.

"No," I rested my hand on hers as she set another plate of cakes on the table. "There is no question. You told me you would stay with me. If I go, you must come with me. It would be too dangerous for you to stay here alone."

"Sumpin' happened here, eh? Last I saw you were in Bethlehem. You have said nothing of a tragedy, but your face shows the strain of it. Tell old Zeke if you want, eh?"

As I told Zeke of the atrocities, the senseless death Medina had experienced, and how we were now alone on the deserted Hawara place, he listened with uncharacteristic quietness. His eyes widened and his face held a grave expression. He had the appearance of a patient old uncle as he waited.

"Since I never found Ramen's body, I do not know where he is or if he is alive or dead." My hands were clammy and my eyes stung as I recounted the awful tale.

"Eh?" Zeke shook his head. "Maybe he went with them."

"If true, I think he went unwillingly." Ramen's strong arms, his flashing eyes, and the way he talked with me filled my mind. I could almost smell his salty perspiration as he worked. I wanted to be with him. I felt joyful at the possibility of finding him.

"He was a strong young 'un, they took him to fight with them is my guess, eh?" Zeke wiped his beard of crumbs, and stood.

"I want to find him. If he escaped from the soldiers, he might have gone back to the inn in Bethlehem. I want to go see for myself."

"All right, ladies I can sell my wares in Bethlehem as well as anywhere. Pack up your things, and we leave before the next sun rises, eh? But you can't take many robes and jewels, simply what you must have with you. Bring a sack of these tasty barley and honey cakes."

"Thank you." I could have kissed the old man. Evidently I had appealed to his sense of charity and protectiveness.

Next morning, as promised, Zeke packed up the donkeys and the three of us began our trek. It was cool and still dark, with stars beginning to fade away. "Teli," I called, "Come." He walked toward us, stopped, and ran back toward the servant quarters where he used to sleep with Orem. He whined mournfully. Shanika called him, holding out her hand. The dog could not stay without anyone to care for him.

We all continued on our walk and I kept looking back, remorsefully, thinking I should have tied Teli to the donkey. The outline of the buildings grew smaller and we were past the spring. I was sad to leave our herb garden to succumb to weather on its own. It was all I could do to keep from turning back, when Teli trotted up to me and nudged my leg. "There you are." I scratched him behind the ears. He stayed by my side the remainder of the journey.

The trip was long and uneventful, with the three of us taking turns riding the donkey. But many times, I would give my turn at riding to Shanika whose weakened body needed more rest. The desert wind was kind to us. We met a few travelers along the way. One told us of a renegade band of soldiers who had been going about the countryside pillaging homes and property and conscripting men into service of the Romans. It had been moons ago. When I described Ramen and asked the man if he had seen him, he shook his head sympathetically, and told me he had not.

When we arrived in Bethlehem at the Hawara Inn, the pathway in front was dappled with leaves and sand, and webs crossed the neglected entrance. I called out, hoping for a response, but got no answer. It was deserted. I motioned to Zeke to bring the donkeys to the well, where he drew water for everyone to drink. We walked inside the courtyard gates to the inn and entered the dusty dining area where I had served tables long ago. Memories came flooding back. The faint musty scents of old wine, stale bread, and dried fruit lingered in the air.

Shanika and Zeke stood respectfully at the doorway. I suddenly realized I was regarded as the hostess, and invited them inside. We pulled up benches and sat by a table with wine stains on it. "It's a shame, what the governing men do with what good people earn. Few can eke a living these days, eh? Used to be a busy place, eh?"

"We can stay here." I ran a finger across the dusty table. "The inn is in want of a good cleaning, but we have rooms." I wandered around the place and found every room was musty and abandoned. Evidently Simon had not had extra tenants that needed to stay here. Nobody had been in the kitchen to prepare a meal for a long time. Rat tracks were visible everywhere, and mainly led to and from the stale flour bins and rancid oil jugs.

I sat heavily on the bench next to Shanika. All hopes I had that Ramen had returned were gone. The three of us sat fidgeting at the table, silent for a time.

"Hannah, they still request healers here, eh?" Zeke put his hands palms up in front of him on the table.

"But will they accept a woman?" I felt so exhausted my head was muddled and my tongue almost mute, but I thought it impolite not to respond to Zeke.

"Don't know, but if you are good and they are sick or injured, it may not matter, eh? I know people here." Zeke had removed his turban and put a simple band around the crown of his head. His dark and greying hair curled comically around his balding pate.

"Thank you. I may soon have this place cleaned up and busy again." I tried to sound enthusiastic, but my words fell flat. "The casks may still have good wine."

"No, no wine for me. Good enough. I have to go on now, eh? Carpets and fine wares to sell, you know." Zeke tipped an imaginary cup of wine, stood, bowed to us, and walked toward the door.

"Will we see you again?" I hurried after him, as I wanted to repay him, by giving him lodging. "Will you stay here tonight? I can go to the markets and buy fresh food."

"I have a friend here, eh? I will be staying with him a day, and then off on travels again. I'm heading for Jerusalem."

Zeke unloaded our things. He lifted a bundle from his donkey and handed it to me. "It has been a pleasure to travel with you. Use this fine flaxen thread to weave something special."

"Thank you. These are for you." I handed him several cakes we had left from the trip. He went off, waving congenially.

"Shanika, you can choose a room."

"You choose first." She looked dazed, dangling her sack of belongings from her arm.

I picked the closest room to the kitchen and she took the one next to it. The brushes and cloths were hanging on the wall next to the kitchen. I soon grabbed a broom and swept the floors and wiped tables. She took the broom from me and swept the front porch.

"I will go for water," Shanika said. "Can we make soup?"

"Yes, I hope so." The pots and bins in the kitchen held stale meal and rotten food. I relished finding one bit of dried meat I could boil for soup. Vermin had eaten the grain, and left behind stinking droppings and coarse hulls. We tossed the spoiled goods on a trash heap behind the stable area. I made our supper of thin soup. We still had some cakes we had brought, and a few preserved figs. I only found a cask of purple wine which had turned to vinegar, so I settled for the water from the well that tasted cool and fresh.

"What shall we do?" My head was in a fog. Shanika only shrugged. Teli came up wagging his tail, and I searched the kitchen to find more food. He would simply have to accept stale fare today. We ate in silence.

As soon as it grew dark enough for a lamp, I went to my soft pallet and tried to sleep. I could hear Shanika's even breathing on the other side of the curtain of woven cloth that divided the room. My thoughts went again to the night I helped with the birth of Jesus. Sometimes I knew the Messiah was near and I could talk with Him. Other times, doubt assailed me and it seemed as though the whole event had been an illusion. I wondered if the Messiah would know me, or if He would recognize me as the woman who caught Him at birth. He must be walking and even running around by now as He was born around two years ago. So much had happened. I had lost any sense of how many moons or seasons had passed.

While sleep eluded me, I explored my options. I could stay here and try to open Ramen's inn and do a midwifery business on the side. I could go back to Hawara's place in Egypt and grow vegetables and barley, perhaps buy milk goats or other livestock. I could try to find my shepherd family and take care of Father Moshe and Mother Lydia if they were still alive. I hoped they were. In spite of the lack of faith I often felt, I still wanted to continue on my quest to see Mary. It would take at least a three-day trip to go to Nazareth, where they had probably settled. I lay awake pondering it all, listening to the lonely call of a night bird. I smiled, remembering Mary and her cousin Abram. I pictured Abram the student with his talit and tefilin and wondered if he still resided in Nazareth.

The sun was already high in the sky when I awakened with a start the next morning. After my busy thoughts the night before, I finally had slept a sound and dreamless sleep. I smelled delicious bread baking and remembered the outdoor oven used by all the inns surrounding the courtyard. I pulled on my light flaxen robe and went outside into the warm air. Shanika sat on the ground next to the oven. How childlike she appeared; but I regretted her innocence had been robbed from her.

"Whose bread are you tending?" I smiled at Shanika.

"A nice man. He has an inn down over there." She pointed. "He said he would share bread with us if I stayed here and did not let it burn."

"Wonderful." I brightened. Simon, the proprietor of a nearby inn, came striding toward us. I had treated his nephew on the night I sought Mary before the birth of the Messiah.

"Well," he said, surprised. "I know you."

"We met briefly one evening. I took care of your nephew Simon who had a nose drip."

"Is Ramen here?" Simon looked at me earnestly.

"No."

"And you are?" Being a businessman he appeared not to have a problem speaking with women as other men might.

"I am Ramen's betrothed, Hannah, and this is Shanika." I had stretched the truth, as no formal betrothal ever happened.

"Simon, your neighbor. Thank you for taking care of my nephew. I was not able to thank you then. Some bread?" He set aside the stone to open the oven, and placed a flat shovel inside to draw out the hot loaves. Perfect toasty golden ovals came out.

"Yes, thank you, it smells delicious, and we are hungry. We arrived here yesterday." I gratefully accepted two of the loaves into the folds of my outer garment.

"If any food or other thing you find you are lacking, please let me know." Simon took his bread and left.

Over the next few weeks, Simon helped me in many practical ways. He showed me the local market where I could find the best prices on fresh produce and goods.

"This stall over here has a better price for flour, and that man will let you bargain for a lower price for his vegetables."

The street teemed with people and vendors, children playing tag, or finding stones and wood chips to play with. Mixed aromas of human perspiration, spices, sugary dates, and smoky dried meats scented the air. I lived, yet I ached inside. Deep within I felt dull, as I failed to carry out my mission to find Mary, and I still had no word from Ramen.

My motivation to work soon took precedence over my feelings. I opened the inn for business, and the eating room for meals. In the village, I let it be known I was a healer. In fact, Simon had told many people how I had treated his nephew. I felt as though I had a purpose.

When we had been at the inn for nearly a year, I was gathering herbs in the fields a short way from the inn when Shanika came to tell me a strange young man had come. He had shown up, and without saying much, grabbed a broom and swept the floors.

It was Pel. When I came back, I motioned to him with a wave of my hand.

"Sit here where we shall talk. Did you run away from your master?" I looked him in the eyes, but he did not flinch.

"Who me?" His face shone with bright expectation. "No, he set me free."

"Free?"

"He say, 'Go, go,' and I went away to see this place. They tell me it is in business again."

"And you want to work for me? What makes you think I want you to work here?" I looked at the boy, Pel, who was about the same age as Shanika.

"I like it here." Pel's shoulders drooped as he shrugged.

"What do you think?" I asked Shanika.

"I do not know." Shanika spoke in a whisper as she stood in the doorway, hiding her sweet brown face. She had begun to bud into womanhood, and lately begun to wear the head covering as the local women did.

"I will see how you do. Go on with the sweeping. When you are done, please clean up after the donkey and put fresh hay in the stable. Then come ask me what to do next." I stopped to catch my breath.

"I will." He looked down at the floor, then back up at me as if waiting for me to say more.

"Do you need lodging?" He had come with no more than the clothes he wore. Had he run away from his master? I wondered if he told me the truth.

"Yes." Pel's voice was tentative as he realized he had barged in. "My small room, is it still behind the kitchen?" It had once been a storage area.

"You may stay in your old room."

As I had feared, the next day Pel's master showed up. He sat at a table and had wine and bread, then asked Shanika if she could fetch for him the proprietress of the inn. Pel was well out of the way cleaning the stable and laying in fresh hay.

When I heard that Pel's master had come, I properly covered my head and most of my face and came to his table. If he wanted Pel, I would promptly return the boy to him. Perhaps the boy had been cuffed now and then for misbehavior as he had a couple of bruises, but he appeared to be well fed.

"Please, sit," said the soldier, who wore the vestments of an officer. I thought it rude to be asked to sit since I ran this inn.

"What can I do for you?" I remained standing, my hands on my hips. I tried to look impatient and extremely busy.

"Ah. I will get right down to it. A number of men in my company are bereft of womanly companionship here. They could use such female comfort at night while they are away from their wives and we would pay…"

"Sir, this is not that kind of establishment. I know we two women are alone here, but it is no fault of mine. My husband was taken away by a band of soldiers." Terribly shaken, I had trouble controlling the outrage in my voice. I was insulted and even ashamed anyone would think of me, or young Shanika as a prostitute.

"The men would pay well. And the work will come natural to women such as you, one Nubian, one white. The men could choose."

I pointed toward the door. "No. Please leave." My voice was ice cold, and my face was hot. It was all I could do to control my anger. It was fortunate that no other customers sat in the eating room at this time of day to overhear the embarrassing proposition. I wished now I had not banished Teli from entering the food areas.

The officer rose, walked over to me, ripped off my face covering, and chuckled. "I'll be back." He dodged the kick I meant to plant, threw the scarf on the floor, and walked out laughing. As I collapsed onto a bench I realized the man had said nothing at all about Pel.

Shanika and Pel came running in when he had left.

215

"What did he do to you?" They chorused.

"He was rude, very rude." I would never tell them what he had proposed.

"Always rude." Pel picked up my scarf and handed it to me with a polite bow.

"I will bring you wine," Shanika said. The two of them raced to the kitchen together, bumping into each other and giggling. They were precious. I wondered now how I would deal with the officer who had presented such an unthinkable thing. Could he harm us? I feared he could.

Mary and the Messiah were far from me, and I longed for an easier time.

CHAPTER EIGHTEEN

Meli had taken to sleeping next to Shanika. One morning I awakened to hear her sobbing because her faithful companion had died in his sleep. We all missed him. I felt farther and farther away from my mission to see Mary and Jesus. No day went by without my thinking of Ramen, hoping he was alive.

While the inn still lacked business, it did have a certain clientele who remembered it from earlier days. We were ready for night visitors. Bins and shelves of food were set to prepare for more guests. Word had gotten around the Hawara Inn was open, and Hannah, the midwife was available. I became very busy. I received messengers who asked me to attend a birth, and then another and another. Simon came to buy herb sacks for all his nieces and nephews to help them ward off their nose and chest ailments. One day rolled into the next.

Seasons and then years went by. I worried Father Moshe and Mother Lydia might have died of old age and I, at times, felt guilty for my neglecting the kind people who had raised me.

I had the distinction of being a healer as well as an innkeeper. A new loom I found at the market gave me a quiet pastime weaving in the evenings. I worked on a garment with my thoughts dreaming of bygone days. Shanika came in, wiping her hands on her apron. Pel was right behind her.

They approached me shyly and I wondered at the brightness on their faces what they were up to. Pel said, "I…I want to m…marry Shanika." While he tried to be grown up and serious, he had a silly grin on his face. To me, they seemed far too young to be marrying. The announcement took me by surprise as I had always thought of the two as brother and sister even though they were not related. As an adopted person myself, and wanting the best life for them, I had treated them with love and care as I would have my own children. Both were of slight stature and I had never learned their true ages.

"Are you ready to commit to a lifelong relationship? Shanika, what do you want?" Many times after her ordeal with the soldiers, I wondered if it had scarred her spirits to the extent that she would never be able to think about marriage and family.

"I do want to be his wife." She shyly twisted a corner of her apron in her hand. Love glowed in her eyes and lit her sweet face.

"What a wonderful surprise." I opened my arms and I hugged them together. Still struggling with a bit of disbelief, my tongue failed me. They waited quietly.

"Are you unhappy with me?" His pleading eyes asked me.

"No. You surprised me." Since I would have to pay for it, I wanted to keep the wedding ceremony simple. "I am happy for both of you. We will have to plan your wedding. What do you want?" I smiled at them.

"I want it here," Shanika said.

"Not a lot of people." Pel scuffed his toes against the floor.

We had a quiet ceremony. The rabbi refused to officiate at first because Pel had been a slave. When I offered more money, he finally agreed. A few friends attended the wedding in our central courtyard by the inn. Shanika wore a plain white linen tunic with a red scarf tied about her waist. Pel wore white trousers with a long striped tunic over all. He had new thong sandals, the first shoes he had ever worn. Our tables had been polished to a shine and were festive with candles. I served the best wine. Roast lamb was hand turned by young Simon. I had made sweet date and honey cakes. All ten guests drank to their health and long life. "Shalom." We were at peace. I could not have been more proud if they were my offspring. For a bed, I gave them a woolen woven cloth I had made from my own carded, spun, and dyed yarn. What had promised to be a perfect day became shattered when our front door suddenly swung open wide.

"Pel, what do you think you are doing?" Pel's former owner shouted. We sat in shocked silence.

"I am a married man," Pel shouted back. "You set me free long ago, and I am never coming back."

"You think so?"

"Yes, I think so," I said. I stood between the officer and Pel. "You cannot come into my inn and take a hireling from me. If you wanted him, you should have come for him long ago. Now, get out of my inn." Hands on my hips, I felt ready to fight this abusive man if necessary. I would not back away. Simon and the rabbi stood on either side of me, supportive. Suddenly a woman burst into the room. I recognized her, as I had attended the birth of her son a year ago.

"What do you think you are doing?" A roundish, short woman walked up to him, shaking her finger at his blotchy face. "I forbid you to come here and ruin their wedding day. If you lay a hand on any one of them, I will go to the authorities and tell them all about you."

"Enough." Red faced, the officer turned on his heel, stormed out, and muttered under his breath about marrying a scolding woman.

"I am sorry, Hannah, I tried to stop my husband before he left. He gets mean when he drinks too much. Now, please go on with your celebration." She smiled grimly and left.

The day after the excitement of the wedding settled,

I began weaving a sun-bleached flaxen robe I challenged myself to create as a one-piece garment without seams. The fibers had been a gift from Zeke the rug man and I smiled thinking of him. My shuttle dipped and wove evenly now as I had years of practice. I wanted to give the robe to Mary for Jesus when I saw her again. I wove it with the utmost care. Up in the corner of my room, I saw a spider web. I thought how both of us were weavers. Then I shuddered. Was the weaving an omen?

A vision crossed my mind. Had it now been twelve years after the birth of Messiah as well as the Iscariot baby? Had baby Judas survived when the boy babies were all killed? I hoped his parents had returned to Iscariot before then. I imagined Mary, Joseph, and family would be making the trip to the temple in Jerusalem for Passover. It would be soon. I might go to Jerusalem myself and mingle with the crowds. I could possibly leave Pel and Shanika to keep the inn while I was away.

I found Shanika in the midst of draping a bright colored bed cover across a braided line and asked her what she thought. "Shall I go to Jerusalem at Passover? Do you think you could manage here?"

"You must go. Pel and I can take care of everything here." It was true. They knew all about running the inn and they worked well together. Pel took one corner of the freshly washed cloth as Shanika took the opposite and together they draped it to dry.

For the first time in awhile I had an urgency to travel with the hope of seeing Mary and the Messiah. Of course,

I wanted to go on the religious journey to the temple for its own purpose. Simply being in Jerusalem would be enough.

I saved money and traded for a donkey for the trip. I washed and mended my clothing, and I finished weaving a precious seamless garment. I fondled the sturdy material I had woven and wrapped it carefully in a length of cloth to protect it. I wanted it to be in good condition when I gave it to Mary for her Son to wear. I thought it would probably be too large for Him now. He could grow into it.

One last time I checked my supplies of dried fruit, barley flat bread, cheese, and skins of water and wine. I packed herbs in small sacks I tied about my waist and sewed coins inside my garments. Two bed rugs were strapped to my donkey to even out the load.

Finally I felt ready. Simon casually announced he and some of his family would be going to Jerusalem. Although I had grown up as a nomadic girl, I had not ventured very far from Bethlehem for years. It would be comforting to go with a group from the village. Simon and two young nephews were going. Since I had taken over the inn, I was considered to be Ramen's widow, and respected as I traveled with friends.

We began our journey early, before the sun rose. The measured clop of the donkey's hooves on the packed road echoed in the still morning air. Simon's two nephews, young Simon and Peter, took turns riding on his donkey. While Peter, a gangly youth, rode on the donkey half asleep, his brother strode along sullenly. I remembered fondly young Simon, the child I had treated for a dripping nose about twelve years ago in his uncle's inn. I wondered if he recalled the incident at all, or if he had been too young. Excitement put a smile on my lips and I hummed as I walked beside the little gray donkey. He looked back at me with soulful eyes and bobbed his head comically.

"I am glad you are making the journey, and coming with us," Big Simon said.

"I have always wanted to go for the Passover Celebration in Jerusalem, and this will be a wonderful trek."

"You will be handy to have around for any nicks and scrapes, as these boys are prone to."

"Oh, I hoped to get away from all that for a few days." I laughed. Life was good at the moment, with the weather promising to be sunny, and a light breeze keeping things cooler. We walked along, chanting simple psalms as more people joined us on the trail.

Young Simon, thin and gawky, walked with his eyes cast on the horizon, unmindful of where his sandals trod. He tripped on a rock. As he went down, I saw it and rushed to him. I noted, while no bones were broken, he had a nasty gash on his right knee and both his hands had tiny red scrapes. As I cleaned the wounds with strong wine, he complained, "Ouch, it hurts."

"Simon, be strong. If this is the worst you ever feel you are fortunate." I applied an ointment made of goat fat and herbs.

"Could you please call me Sim? I am not my uncle."

"Yes, for me your name has now been changed to

Sim." I smiled. When I was through applying the soothing balm, I stood and helped him up. The rest of the party had stopped momentarily, but except for his uncle, they were continuing on the trail.

"I am weak." Sim sat down in the sand.

"Is he all right? Will the boy live?" His uncle, Big Simon, had a twinkle in his eyes.

"He will barely make it." I laughed. "But you can go on. We will catch up."

"Stop, please." Sim glared at us.

"Here." I gave him water from his flask. I wondered how far the others had gone down the trail. Big Simon turned, waved to us. "Sit for a moment, and then try to stand again," I said. Sim continued to loll on the warm sand, rolling his eyes. I wondered if he exaggerated soreness, or if he truly hurt. No murmur of air visited to lift our spirits.

"I am sorry." He looked at me with pleading eyes.

"They are going on ahead, and we will have to go fast to catch up. Are you sure you cannot walk?"

"I cannot." He shook his head.

"Simon." I yelled as loud as I could, but my voice was lost in the vastness of the surroundings. Of course I had to stay with the boy. My donkey was too burdened for me to add Sim to the load. The forms of Simon, Peter, and the donkeys were tiny dark shadow shapes now. Others trekked on the trail, but they also went on.

"When we fail to make a timely arrival at the spring, they will come back for us." I sat next to the boy and tried to shade him from the sun as best I could by spreading a cloak over the donkey and us. I offered him dates and wine mixed with water. It felt good to rest my feet, so I was temporarily content. Sim soon dozed off to sleep. The wind started again and cooled my face. Lulled by the warmth and quietly swishing breeze, I fell asleep.

A sound awakened me. My life pulse raced madly. I had a momentary disorientation, not knowing where I was. I stood up to gain a clearer view of the trail. Scrub brush and rock terrain prevailed as far as my eye could see. Our group had disappeared from my sight. When I gazed back down the trail, a stranger and his donkey were coming toward us. I stiffened. My heart pounded in my ears, and the hair on my arms prickled.

CHAPTER NINETEEN

he man walked with a limp, almost dragging one leg. His face was nearly covered completely by an oversized linen headdress, secured by a brown braided tie. He appeared to be a tradesman, as his donkey was laden with baskets of colorful wares hanging from either side.

"Good day." I wanted to be friendly, but felt cautious. My inner being had not stilled its alarm.

The man grunted back, nodding his head as he approached. One of his legs was a half-stick, and he used a staff with each step.

"On your way to Jerusalem?" I decided to make friendly conversation.

The man did not answer, but stopped his donkey, and stood beside it.

"My boy took a fall and is trying to recover before we

continue our trip to Jerusalem. I would ask if we could let him ride your donkey, but I see the beast is already burdened."

The man stood quietly. Perhaps he was either deaf, or unfamiliar with my language. I then repeated the same thing, using three different common dialects. I almost tried a fourth dialect when the stranger shook violently beneath his head covering, finally laughed out loud.

"Come, he makes fools of us. You are fully recovered," I said. I was afraid the stranger's mind had taken leave of him. I pulled Sim up and walked with him down the trail. Sim grinned, but did not laugh, as he feared I would thrash him royally if he did.

The man followed, and when he continued to chuckle I feared he had been seized by a demon.

"You have a lot of gall." I faced him, wondering what caused his merriment. In a moment of anger, I wheeled around, stepped toward him, reached up and yanked the cover from his head. I gaped at what I saw. One half of a face, none other than Ramen, shocked me to my core. I would have fainted, but he caught me with a strong arm.

"Oh, Hannah, Hannah, I did not want you to see me. I was afraid." His eyes were sad. "I have much to tell you." We were both astounded for a few moments. He pulled off my head covering and spoke into my hair, kissing my head all over. "I am sorry I laughed, but I could not help it. Your sincerity appealed to my humor as you tried earnestly in three different languages to have me understand what you were saying." Sim stood watching us, unsure, arms dangling like empty sleeves at his sides.

"Sim, this is Ramen." I pulled back from Ramen.

"You must know the man, but what is wrong with him?" Sim was wide-eyed.

"That is what we will find out." I turned my attention back to Ramen. I reached up to trace the angry red and pink scar on his cheek. " Where have you been? Have you been to Bethlehem?"

"Yes, and no." Ramen still stared at me, the way he would at a mirage.

"Have you a new woman?" I eyed him sharply.

"Hah! No. No woman would look twice at this old wreck. Besides…"

"Are you very sure?" I still felt the strength of his arm he now wrapped around my shoulders. He had a lot of explaining to do, but I felt so relieved to see him I wanted to pinch myself to know I did not dream. I had almost given up hope he was alive.

"So much time has passed. I let you down, I failed to protect you and Medina, I stayed with the Romans after they captured me…"

"Be quiet." I put my finger to his lips. I felt tears stinging my eyes. We would sort everything out later.

Sim, apparently fully recovered and embarrassed, walked ahead of us down the trail. Ramen and I went slowly.

"Walk carefully now and lead his donkey," I called to Sim. He came back, shrugged his shoulders, rolled his eyes at us, and took the reins as we continued on. Ramen and I walked side by side and I held his arm. We said nothing to each other, as we had far too much to talk about, and anything else would not matter. The sun began to create deep shadows of any hillock or bush. I wondered whether Simon and Peter would be backtracking soon, or if they would set up camp and wait. After a time we saw a tent in the distance. Sim took off in a run.

"The boy looks well now. I think I see the camp up ahead. Simon will be happy to see you."

"He has seen me. I went to see him a few days ago while I sold my wares in Bethlehem."

"You were selling in the market place? You did not come see me." Confused and angry, I let go his arm and faced him.

"I was afraid for you to look at my ugly scars. Can't you see? The man I used to be has fled."

I said nothing as we were near the others now, but I felt hurt he had not sought me while he was in Bethlehem. Simon and Ramen greeted each other with affection, and Simon introduced his nephews.

"You boys have grown too tall." Ramen cuffed their arms good-naturedly. They responded with mock jabs back at him.

I laid out a cold meal of bread, wine and dried fruits for everyone. At first they discussed the weather, but soon their conversation turned to politics. "Herod is going to kill us all with his taxes."

"When will the tyranny end? Soldiers are brutal and

show no mercy."

"We need a savior. Isn't a Messiah foretold?" Simon asked.

I sat quietly, wanting to blurt out He had already been born and I wanted to see His mother in Jerusalem, and hopefully Him as well. In all things there is a time to keep quiet and a time to speak, and this was not the time for me to talk.

No one mentioned years had passed or what had transpired personally during the time Ramen had been gone. When the moon and stars were well lighted in the heavens, Simon said to his nephews, "Time to sleep, boys." Simon's tent was large enough for a family. He took the spot by the opening, and next to him were his nephews, then Ramen and me. I had planned to sleep out under my cloak, but the men wanted me to be protected inside. All of us were fully clothed and on our sleeping mats. Mine was the farthest from the opening. I hoped I would not have to make an urgent exit during the night and disturb four sleeping men. I was sleepless for a long while as I tried to comprehend how my life would be now.

A whole lot of unanswered questions disquieted me. Had his injured appearance prevented him from coming to me sooner? Would he stay? I wanted to awaken him and insist we take a walk. I wanted to tell him about my life these past years, and also desired to know about him. My back was against the wall of the tent and I curled next to snoring Ramen. I tried to remember him when we were first together. Now I would have to become acquainted with this man all over again, if he still wanted me. Perhaps he did, but his hardened emotions about his lame leg and physical appearance stood in the way.

The next morning, Simon and his nephews broke camp early to continue on the trail to Jerusalem. I went away from the men to do my morning ablutions. I thought about what I must do now. Thoughts of the Messiah, and the hope of seeing Mary again, were very strong. I had counted on this trip to be special. I had been set on my adventure for weeks. I had no thought at the time I would see Ramen. I doubted he planned to go to celebrate Passover in Jerusalem, because I knew we did not have the same religion.

Ramen came near as I swished my feet in the cool water of the spring. I felt his presence before I turned to see him. He stooped and put his arms around me loosely. I drew away from him, dried my feet, and stood. I was still hurt and angry he had chosen to distance himself from me for so long a time.

"Are you terribly repulsed? Who am I to blame you?" He sounded defeated. "I slept next to you all night and wanted you, but I dared not touch you." He looked at me tenderly with his good eye. "I will leave now and you never have to worry about my coming into your life again. I will set you free, my love. You may marry another, if you want."

"No." The word came out flat. I had to think. "How can I be free? I still care for you. You are underneath all the scars. Are you going on to Jerusalem?"

"Yes, to sell my wares. I knew you were going, so it was a selfish trip for me." He sighed and leaned more heavily on his walking staff. "I still love you, but…"

"Where do I begin?" I looked down at the brown stubble which had once been green grass. I too, had been eager to make the trip for selfish reasons.

"As my healer."

"What do you mean?"

"My leg. It pains me greatly. I thought I could make the trip, but it gets more difficult with each step. Thank you for your assistance yesterday helping me walk."

"Could you ride? We can shift your load to other donkeys and yours can be free to carry you. But here, sit down and let me have a look at your leg. I will do my best." I pulled herbs from my pack and set out my flasks.

Ramen sat obediently and pulled back his garments allowing me to see the area where the leg had been removed right below the knee. I was horrified at what I saw. A crudely fashioned stick stuck to his flesh with what had the color and consistency of pitch. His stump appeared puffy and red streaks mottled his thigh. Greenish looking sores seeped where the stick met his flesh. I marveled he could stand to hobble on this mass of disease. Perhaps he might lose even more of his leg. I set about cleaning and prodding. He winced occasionally. When I finished with the examination, I put my hand to my head and closed my eyes. I had never seen such miserable sores before.

I prayed, hoping a caring Yahweh would hear me, asking Him to heal Ramen. He ought to be off his feet as soon as possible. We needed a physician who knew more than I did about severed limbs and this kind of putridness. I had to make a difficult decision. Shall I try to heal Ramen, or shall I go on to Jerusalem to seek Mary? I was torn between what I wanted to do and what I knew I must do. I wrung my hands and walked a ways from the group to think.

I feared it would be unwise to continue on to Jerusalem with Ramen in need of greater care. I knew an experienced and respected physician, Mark, in Bethlehem. The journey would be about a day away if we rode the donkey. Hannah the healer won the argument I had with Hannah the adventurer. I went to Ramen and the group.

"Ramen and I are going back to Bethlehem." I stood by Ramen.

"Hannah..." Simon started to speak, but Ramen interrupted.

"You cannot do this thing. You had your mind set on going to Jerusalem." Ramen stood bravely. "I never intended for you to sacrifice your trip when I asked you to look at my leg. I can make it. Jerusalem is not much farther away."

"We can take turns helping him," Simon said.

"No." I had made up my mind, and I planted my feet stubbornly. I had seen putrid tissue affect the whole body and kill people. I feared it could take his life, and I had to help heal him if possible. "We must find Ramen a more knowledgeable healer than me. I know and trust Mark, a physician in Bethlehem, and I want to take him there. I do not know any healers in Jerusalem."

The men looked at each other and threw up their hands. The nephews were having a rock-throwing contest to see who could toss the farthest. I shifted donkey loads. My donkey had a light load on its back. I placed my bedroll on Ramen's donkey and left the extra food for the boys who were always hungry. I gave Simon a skin of the ointment I had used on Sim and told him how to use it. In a way, it was difficult to change my plans, and disappointment grieved my mind, but I would not tell Ramen. He had both a wounded body and a broken spirit. Was I up to the challenge? I vowed I would do my best. I lifted the bundle that contained the perfectly seamless garment I had woven and gave it to Simon. "Please give this to Joseph and Mary of Nazareth as a gift for Jesus. Tell them it is for Him to grow into." I thought how, once again, I healed others and failed to pursue my search for Mary and the Messiah.

"How will I know them?" Simon frowned

"You will probably be able to recognize the couple who had the baby in the stable about twelve years ago."

"I will try." He put the bundle in a sack with his things. "But there are always throngs of people."

"Do your best," I said. "Yahweh be with you."

Simon took the belts, pottery, and mats to sell for Ramen. He helped Ramen onto his donkey, cuffed him on the shoulder and smiled. "Good blessings to you as you face the wind."

"Go with your God." Ramen waved to Simon and the boys who continued on the trail to Jerusalem with the wind at their back. We went the opposite direction. I trembled.

CHAPTER TWENTY

amen rode on his donkey and I walked. At first we traveled in silence, each waiting for the other to speak. Finally, I said, "I will tell my story first, if you want, but then you must tell me what happened to you."

"You don't want to know."

I did not know how to respond to his words. I waited and then spoke. "Do you remember Pel?"

"Oh, yes, and he is at the inn with you?"

"Yes, he is. Have you any idea what happened at Hawara in Egypt after you were taken to parts unknown?"

Ramen stopped the donkey. I watched his arms handle the reins. He was well muscled in spite of the thinness of his body. Perhaps he could overcome this putrefaction in his leg. When he turned toward me, my eyes beheld his uncovered face. His left side presented a grotesque, blotchy mass of red, pink and white scars, and his eye was barely visible in the crease of a hairless eyelid that would not close. On the right side of his face, he looked handsome to me, save for a white line spanning from his lip to his ear.

"What terrible accident happened to you to make you lame?"

"Where shall I begin?" He looked at me evenly with his good eye.

"Why did you come back to Bethlehem?"

"To see you." His voice was husky. "Hannah, I saw you at a distance at the rug man's market stall. God knows I thought I would be a stranger to you, so I ducked inside a shop until you were gone. I thought I would want to come back to you and dreamed you might love me again, but you looked happy and content. I felt so grateful and very proud of you. You were taking care of the inn and running it quite well. I...I was, and still am, afraid I might ruin your life."

"The Roman soldiers who captured you ransacked Hawara, nearly killed Orem, killed your aunt, raped the slave girl, and left her almost dead."

"I learned of all that happened and I am sorely ashamed at not being able to protect Aunt Medina and you. I tried to fight them with my fists as I had no weapon, but they outnumbered me. They grabbed me and pounded me into the rocky ground. They took me forcibly, tied me up, and threw me over the back of a pack horse. I heard Orem yelling, dogs barking ferociously, and then nothing. I thought I would die of thirst or bleed to death from my wounds. One of them cut me here." He pointed to the scar on the right side of his face. "It was open and flies buzzed around it, and crawled into the gaping slice." He shuddered. "In my delirium I kept hoping you would come and heal my wound. Can you imagine that? I passed out completely, hating to think of what they might be doing to you and my aunt. I felt helpless and I wanted to die."

"Oh, Ramen." I came closer to comfort him.

"When I awakened, many days unknown to me had passed. One of the soldiers told me it had been several days. One of them was a physician of sorts and had put a salve on my face wound to help it heal while I had been unconscious. We were far from Hawara's land, and we still traveled in a band on horseback, with one open cart for arms and supplies. They offered me a skin of wine and water mixture. It tasted of salty seawater. Next they gave me a thin gruel to eat. I slept deeply the way one would when given a strong herbal wine. As days passed I grew a bit stronger. They did not untie my hands, and never let my legs free except when I needed to relieve myself. Two strong men relentlessly guarded me." He looked toward the horizon.

"I went through hell, and feared for my life, afraid you were dead, but what you endured sounds even worse."

Reluctant to tell my tale of woe, I waited to hear more of his story. "Please go on if you can."

"We came to a stream of water and everyone bathed, including me. It was the first time they untied me, but I was naked. I wondered how far away I would escape were I to run away. I decided I would be unable to break free in daylight. It would be too dangerous. That night, I tried in vain to remove the rope ties on my ankles by biting with my teeth. Finally a guard heard me and beat me across the legs sharply with a whip. They gave me enough food to stay alive, and they joked with me as we traveled. When I asked what they wanted of me, they all laughed. It finally dawned on me I had been conscripted into the Roman military by force. All too soon they gave me a spear and lance, and I practiced how to use them to kill. We clashed with a marauding band of ragtag soldiers who said they were rising up against the government. It was kill or be killed, so I chose to fight alongside my captors. I cannot defend my actions now, but I justified it as the only thing I could choose to do at the time."

He stopped talking and wiped his eye. Stunned by his words, I said nothing, and he continued.

"At the time, I grieved as from the tales the solders told, I was sure you and Medina had died at their hands. I thought it would have been far worse for you if they had brought you with them. As far as I knew I had no family, nothing else mattered, and I continued to fight beside them. One night when I was on watch, a fellow soldier told me in great detail how they had raped a young slave girl, a Moor, and left her for dead. When I realized the man told me about Shanika, I became extremely enraged, beat the man, and almost killed him with my bare hands. They put me in chains."

"Ramen." I wanted to say more, but words failed me.

"You told me Pel married Shanika. I am glad the girl lived."

"Scarred emotionally, but alive."

"The captain from the Bethlehem regiment came to confer with ours, and I saw it was Pel's master. I wanted to have a word with him, but being of a rank inferior to him, I paid a servant to tell him I had an urgent requirement to speak with him about matters in Bethlehem. The servant came back, and surprised me with the word that the captain would speak with me. He remembered me as an innkeeper, in fact, the one where the boy had been born in the stable during the tax enrollment. I asked if Pel was still his servant, and he told me he was. He said you were managing the inn and had a black servant girl. I felt elated. I immediately wanted to break away and go home, but this captain's knowledge of me made it a futile effort. It had been more than two years, maybe three, since I had been captured. Then the captain said you had turned my inn into a brothel. He said it pained him to give me the news about my woman, but all women were alike. I knew he was lying. I felt so frustrated and enraged I wanted to kill him."

Ramen stopped talking and had a faraway look on his face for a while. He continued with a sigh, " The scrap of good news in this story is what I am about to relate. When the captain started to leave me, I stopped him. I gave him a sack of coins and asked him to free Pel. Of course, I had no way of knowing if he kept his word or simply took my money. From gossip I recently heard in town, Pel is free from his master, but as you said earlier, has entered into another kind of happy bondage."

"They are happy."

"I am glad to hear. I suppose I ought to tell you about these burn scars."

"I have wondered." The air had stilled as though it too waited to hear.

"Some time ago, I have lost track of the years, our regiment torched a village. It was horrible. Women and children were running and screaming pitifully, men dashing at flames with inadequate skins of water. I had no stomach to be assigned as a fire carrier. I acted as a lookout, and I heard below me a woman's shriek like I had never heard before. I charged toward the unholy sound, and found the young woman engulfed in an inferno, trying to reach two babies to save them from the wreckage of her home. Intense heat pushed her back. She was terrified. I threw myself into the fire and tried to move the heavy beam which had fallen between her and her babies. I crawled through the fire. Flames licked at my clothing, and my hair singed and burned. I was afraid to pull the babies up to my own burning body and stood dumbly, awaiting my fate. I remembered your God. I called on Yahweh and every god I have ever heard speak of to save the babies. And that is all I can recall of the fire." He sighed, shaking his head.

"I awakened in camp, in horrible searing pain, with one side of my face burned beyond recognition. I asked how I had gotten there, and the men told me a pretty half-naked, doe-eyed woman in burnt garments and an old man had dragged me to camp on a rug. They questioned them, then gave them wine and let them go. I asked if she had babies with her and they laughed and told me I might work fast, but not that fast. 'It usually takes about nine moons,' they joked. They didn't know what I talked about, of course. They thought I was having my way with a village woman and had gotten caught in the flames. My flesh took forever to heal, especially traveling day after day as we did. Would I live or die? I thought a lot about you, and hoped to escape and go back to Bethlehem. In time I healed enough to again join the others in fighting. Over a year ago, my leg was slashed badly in a battle and the butcher cut it off. Nobody wants a one-legged soldier. They were through with me, and discharged me from service." Ramen sighed.

"But you did not come back? Why?"

"Look at me. I have tried to find within myself enough courage to see you. Years ago I would have run to you if I had a chance. I do not know why I allowed so much time to pass. Even though I abhorred the Roman soldiers, I became one of them. I don't know if you can forgive me for all these years. Now I am of scant use to you."

I went to Ramen then, and kissed his scarred face. My anger had melted during his story. We wept together.

"You are a good man. Let me judge for myself. Now I will tell you what occurred when the soldiers invaded." I gave him a brief story of what happened. As I told of finding Medina he wiped his face with his sleeve, and then put his hands up to hide his tears. "Hannah, I am very sorry for what you had to go through, but I cannot go back and change anything."

"No, we only have today, because we do not know what tomorrow will bring. Yahweh alone knows."

"Thank you is such a feeble comment for all you have endured and all you have done. I truly appreciate you for keeping the inn open. I can never repay you. Now I have to rest." His voice fell to a whisper.

I looked at his wound and applied more ointment. The festering had worsened and his brow felt hotter than the sun. My own spent arms and legs felt numb and my tongue dallied like a dry twig in my mouth. Would we be blessed with healing for Ramen? We resumed our slow trek.

CHAPTER TWENTY-ONE

I felt helpless, overwhelmed. While I was relieved Ramen was here, our future appeared to be bleak and fraught with misery.

"We went through ten years of life in a matter of minutes," Ramen said.

"You wanted every mundane detail, I suppose. Every wine skin emptied, every loaf of bread taken from the oven, every skinned knee anointed, every baby birthed, every…"

"Stop, Hannah. I did not mean to mock you. I am sorry."

"It is all right. Mark must see you and help you heal or I may lose you." And never be allowed to fill in the missing years. I stopped the donkey, stood by his side, and lifted his garment to check on the leg stump again. His thigh was swollen and streaked red.

A light breeze wafted across us, and I grabbed the reins of the donkey. "Let us be on our way." We rode thus for awhile. Ramen slept and I was left alone with my thoughts. I daydreamed about the Messiah and my girlhood friendship with Mary, my desire then to become known among people. My grand ideas had changed as life happened. I thought we were less than a day journey to Bethlehem, but as the evening sun was well on its way to the horizon, I found no sign of it. I wondered if continuing on to Jerusalem would have been a wiser choice. I saw what appeared to be a green area with a spring ahead. People and animals were near. Strangely, this place had eluded my vision journeying my way on what I thought was the same trail. People were resting and getting water as we soon would. Perhaps they could tell me where I had gone wrong on the trail.

"Halloo," called a friendly voice. As we drew nearer I saw they were shepherds, and sheep rested in the nearby grassy knoll.

"Good day," I answered. Ramen stirred and opened his one good eye. I continued on toward the trees. As I drew near, I believed my eyes deceived me. The men wore familiar robes with the red stripes of my family. I wondered if the nearest man could possibly be Benjamin, grown older and a bit rounder. Could his boyish face be under the bushy dark beard? I smiled at the coincidence, wondering at Yahweh's plan. I felt tears stinging my eyes and kept my head and most of my face covered. Often, I thought about Father Moshe and Mother Lydia, and wondered how everyone was doing. About to find out, I wanted to tease Benjamin a bit first, not tell him right away who he saw and spoke with.

Benjamin approached. "Can I help you?" He offered his hand to Ramen and helped him dismount from the donkey. He supported Ramen until he steadied himself upright.

"Thank you," Ramen said in a quiet voice. His good eye grew wide when he saw it was Benjamin. "I believe I met you before. It was a long time ago."

"Is that right?" Benjamin raised an eyebrow. "I am a poor shepherd, and I have roamed around a bit, but I am sure not as much as you. You are, or perhaps were, a soldier?"

"Yes." The blood left his face except for the angry scar. Benjamin held his arm securely as we approached the grassy area.

I unrolled a rug and spread it out on the grass to make a place for Ramen to lie down. We helped him to the makeshift bed. I shielded us from view as best I could with my cloak and pulled back his robe to look at his infected stump. It oozed blood and putrid matter. I removed salves and herbs from my pack on the donkey and tended Ramen, cleaning his wound and applying ointment.

Benjamin stayed a respectful distance, and looked on with interest. He approached after I finished. "My name is Benjamin. I went looking for new grazing as the season has been late, producing a scarcity of grass where we have been camped."

"Ramen of Hawara." Ramen lay on the rug where I

covered him with a cloak. Benjamin opened his mouth to speak, but did not.

"I can contain myself no longer. I am Hannah." I brushed aside my scarf, and went to Benjamin. We kissed cheeks, and I held him in the arm embrace of relatives. "How are Father Moshe and Mother Lydia? Are they still alive? And Naliah? And Serena?"

"Slow down, Hannah. You have not changed a bit, asking too many questions at once. When I saw you applying the medicine, I knew." He chuckled. He stood back to look at me again. "First of all, I am sad to say both Moshe and my mother have passed away. They died of natural causes due to age. People say Lydia's mourning is taking its toll on her. Serena left our encampment and went with another branch of our tribe. It was rumored she found a husband among them. I married Esther who died in childbirth along with our firstborn." His voice was controlled. "And what have you been doing all these years? I see you are still a healer."

"I am saddened to hear of your loss, and I will miss Father Moshe." I sobbed, thinking of Father Moshe. When I composed myself, I was reluctant to reveal more at this time. " Yes, I am a healer, but there is far too much to tell about what I have been doing all these years."

"Laban, come and see our old play friend, Hannah. Remember how she used to beat you at footraces?"

"What? How can it be?" Laban came forward, and shook his head in disbelief, recovered, and nodded to Ramen, then to me. "It is good to see you, Hannah.

Benjamin, she beat you at races too, as I recall. You are still healing people, I see." His hand was raised to his face, still trying to come to grips with seeing us. "We could use a healer in our community, as we no longer have Serena. Everyone tries to remember how to treat ailments themselves with whatever herbs we find." He gazed away from me as he spoke.

"Her man needs her much worse than the whole lot of us." Benjamin scoffed, and turned to me. "The sons of Laban are with us. See those boys over there?" Twin boys, about age ten, stirred the water with sticks, and played on the grassy bank by the water. While they were ordinary playful boys, they already were well schooled in how to take care of a flock of sheep. I looked at the familiar men and young boys, and the sight of them brought back memories of childhood. Of course, I pondered long about the good times.

"Will you stay and visit tonight?" Benjamin looked at me directly.

"We will be here until morning, because it would be best for Ramen."

The men set up a makeshift tent of skins to keep the sun and wind off Ramen.

I set out dried fruits and bread. Benjamin brought stew in an earthen bowl. We sat on our rugs under the stars and ate while we reminisced. "Was your mother terribly angry when I left?"

"Yes, she was. You were the talk of the whole encampment. She wanted me to go after you and drag you back to camp, but I refused to do it. After a while she got over it."

"I am sad to have neglected Father Moshe and Mother Lydia. I regret I have not come home to visit. Of course, I would not have known where to look for all of you."

"You would know. You could simply follow the green grass as we have always done."

"True. I have no good excuse." I paused, wanting to talk of something else. "Have some more dates. I have plenty."

"You haven't forgotten my favorite sweet food." Benjamin reached for a handful.

"When you return home, please give Mother Lydia my warmest greetings. Also, I hoped you could point me in the right direction tomorrow. I had thought I was on the trail which would lead directly to Bethlehem, but I arrived here instead."

"You came to a split in the trail and took the one to the spring instead of going straight on. It will be no problem. If you wish, I can go with you tomorrow to help you."

I looked anxiously at Ramen who had eaten no food. As I bathed his feverish brow, I hoped he would make it through the night.

CHAPTER TWENTY-TWO

Benjamin built a fire to ward off the cool night air, and then we talked long after sunset. Ramen was nearby, asleep. The others listened for a time and then retired. As best I could, I related my recent life to Benjamin. He interrupted me now and then to offer me figs or more wine and to shake his head in sympathy or even disbelief. When I finished my saga, he spoke.

"After Esther died I grew very lonely, but did not marry again. The women who are eligible are far too young for me."

"Too young for you?" Years had gone by, but he was still little Benjamin to me.

"No, might be all right, but I want a woman who can take care of me." He chuckled, ever the selfish boy. He quieted for a moment. I heard night birds calling and the hum of insects. "What will you do if Ramen dies?" He asked, looking at me with his calm brown eyes. According to custom, as his brother's widow, I continued to be his responsibility.

"I have told you, I reunited with him after a long absence. I suppose I will go on as before. I want to see Mary and her Son again and I was hopeful I would at Passover. As I traveled on my way to Jerusalem Ramen showed up on the trail." The night breezes gusted, stirring up winking coals of the dying fire. I gratefully absorbed the silence.

Benjamin spoke quietly. "You still believe the Baby you delivered in the stable is the Messiah? People in the village say He is quite regular boy. He learns quickly and keeps the elders on their toes with His questions. I have heard tell He is pretty headstrong, too."

"Jesus…His name is common. But if He is ordinary, then why do the villagers speak of Him at all?"

"Hmm." Benjamin scratched his chin thoughtfully. "I had not thought of that. It could be because His birth caused such a stir years ago. He is sort of a legend. You know how people are."

"It is with a troubled conscience I confide this to you. After the horrible experience at Hawara in Egypt, I lost my faith for a time. Now I pray to the Messiah and Yahweh, and I hope they listen. My desires are mostly unmet, but I sense He is with me. At times I have a reassurance, a sort of peacefulness. Even when I hid from the Roman soldiers I felt His presence. I do not think Yahweh would prevent anything bad from happening… either the death of Judah bar Cleodan or Medina, and Ramen's ordeal…but either

He or His Son helped me through what happened. It is difficult to explain." As the embers died out leaving a scent of smoke, a vision of Ramen facing flames which almost killed him, flooded my being. Prickles stood out on my arms.

"You have to deal with things however you can, I suppose. And you have had a lot of trouble." He rose and stretched. "Now I must sleep so I can have an early start tomorrow."

"It has been wonderful getting caught up on the years."

We each went to our tents. Ramen slept, albeit restlessly from the look of twisted bedding. The wind picked up and flapped at our tent as I tried to curl up on the wrinkled bedding and sleep.

When I awoke, the sun was already on the horizon, and the first shafts of light illumined the water. The lush greenery and reeds framed the pool and were mirrored there. Benjamin and his companions were packed and ready for the trail. "I am glad you are finally up. Thanks to you, dear princess, I am getting a rather late start," Benjamin teased. "But I wanted to make sure you got Ramen back onto the donkey."

Ramen barely roused. We walked him to the donkey and lifted him onto it, but he was too weak to sit up straight. I dreaded if he were to fall. The men went off briefly, and then Benjamin and Laban came back. "Two of us will see you all the way back to Bethlehem. The rest will go on with the sheep."

"I would not want to delay you further. We will manage. How far are we from Bethlehem?"

"Carrying this one, we may take a day or more, I think," said Laban. They made a makeshift cot with rope handles at each end, tied to the donkey, and two men and I took turns carrying the back end. Indeed, it took the entire day before we could smell the smoke from Bethlehem's ovens and see the town silhouetted against the setting sun. Exhausted, we made it to the Hawara Inn after dark.

"Pel! Shanika. See who is here. It is Ramen." They roused from bed at the sound of my voice. I tried to sound excited, but my tired voice came out flat. I quickly motioned the two of them to ready a bedroom for him.

"And more guests." Pel looked aghast for a moment because of the lateness of the hour. He wrapped his outer garment more securely and greeted everyone. After Pel kissed Ramen's exposed cheek, he went to fetch fresh water. Shanika put clean linens on the mat atop a layer of fresh straw. Soon Ramen was in his bed.

"Come sup wine and refreshments, Benjamin. You know where the well is located. Help yourselves."

"We did wash, thanks. Where are you off to? It is too late for you to go out." Benjamin saw I had directed everyone else, neglected to refresh myself, and went toward the front door.

"I am getting Mark. This physician is across the village from here. No matter the time, I know he will come when I tell him about Ramen."

Mark roused and came immediately. "I cannot heal

him, and it will be a miracle if he lives." He shook his head sadly, and held the oil lamp. "The redness has traveled up his leg. His belly is distended, his life pulse is faint, and his good eye has yellowed." He touched Raman with experienced hands. "I have this potent new herb which will keep him more comfortable."

"We tried to encourage him to drink, but his lips are slack." I was as one who has been beaten. In my heart and mind I wanted to ask for strength, but failed in my attempts to pray to Messiah or Yahweh.

"I thirst." Ramen's voice was barely audible. I smiled and offered him the liquid sedative Mark had put in a cup, mixed with wine. Thankfully, Ramen sipped it, and soon his head slumped. At first I feared he had died, but I felt light breath coming from one of his nostrils. He slept.

Benjamin grasped both my hands the next morning before he left. "If you have want of me for anything, please send Pel to let me know, and I will be here as quickly as I can. We are moving our flocks south of where we were camped." We kissed cheeks and he went on his way.

My days were filled caring for Ramen. He talked some and sat up occasionally. On an especially good day for him he said, "Do you remember the shepherd Orem hit with his stone slinger?"

"Yes." I was startled to hear Ramen say anything about Ham. I had never found out what happened.

"Orem thought he killed him." Ramen coughed, gasping for breath. "The man fainted away in a deep slumber, but did not die. The Romans took him, and put him in chains to control him after he went to the house and took Popo. An officer took the dog to give to his new wife."

"Oh, poor Popo." I was near tears remembering.

"The man, who called himself Ham, fought beside the Roman soldiers as I did. He died in the first battle." Ramen's voice slowed as he spoke and came out as a mere whisper.

"Rest now. Thank you for telling me." I was glad to hear what he told me, but I did not want to burden him with my history of fearing Ham.

My faith wavered. I began thinking about the Messiah in the midst of my scattered thoughts. Thoughts of Mary and her Son had once brought hope and comfort whenever I had a problem or felt distressed. I longed for the Voice I used to hear in the wind, but it was elusive and then I doubted if it had ever been there.

Ramen took the herbal medicine Mark had brought. While his demeanor was one of being comfortable enough, he stopped uttering words as time went on. We placed Ramen in the courtyard where he had plenty of fresh air and sunshine. Alone with my thoughts, I waited for the inevitable. Memories flooded back of the good, as well as horrible, times. As I sat resting, I glanced at him and saw he had stirred. A bird made twittering noises.

"I wish to return to Egypt." Ramen's strength had waned to the point where he stayed on his sleeping mat, barely raising his head.

"But you are too weak." I kneeled at his side bathing his swollen body. My mind raced through the details of how I could possibly grant what could surely be his last wish. I decided it was impossible, and patted his shoulder without saying anything. I believe he must have returned in his own mind to his home in Egypt, because later that day he asked a simple question.

"Hawara?" Ramen asked, raising his head and opening his good eye.

"Yes," I went to him and put my arm around his bony shoulders.

"Home." He lay peacefully for a long time and then death came in such a subtle way I almost did not sense it. His breath became quiet and light, and finally ended in a last weak gasp. His life here was gone.

While I had already grieved deeply knowing he would be gone, now that it had happened, I wept. When I could clear my head, I sent Pel to Simon to inquire about the burial cave where the body of Hawara had been placed. I prayed to Yahweh and Messiah, and felt a sense of peace. Afterwards, Pel and neighbors sealed the tomb with large stones.

"He died happy, I think," Pel said.

With Ramen gone, a chasm had broken open before me and my faith plummeted into the bowels of the earth. Burdened with grief and emptiness, I returned to Hawara Inn.

CHAPTER TWENTY-THREE

I awakened with a start. Sunlight streamed in on me, fresh air teased my white curtain, and I pinched myself to see if it was real. Brown and green hand woven rugs lay on the floor next to me. Nearby shelves held my scarves, garments, and shawls. At home in Bethlehem at Hawara's Inn, I wondered with amusement how long I had slept. Most days were the same as the one before. It was as though I had been in this place for years, and I had.

Shanika tiptoed in bringing me a cool cup of water. "I think a new life comes." Shanika said, glowing, and patting the front of her tunic.

"What good news." I sat up suddenly, feeling alive. "Are you sure you are with child?"

"Yes, as you told me I would know if my time of the moon cycle did not happen for two moons, and my taste might sour in the mornings. To smell food cooking was unpleasant, and I took to my bed two days. You will be with me at this birth?"

"I wondered if you were ill. I hope you are right and you have no other problem. Of course I will be delighted and honored to be your midwife." I got up and put a motherly arm around Shanika.

We had seven moons of happy preparation as I threw myself into the shopping, making swaddling cloths, preparing a cozy area in their room for the child.

It was a difficult birth lasting from before sunrise until after sunset. Shanika lost much blood, and the bleeding continued. I finished cleaning and swaddling the newborn. I handed the healthy, dark-eyed baby to Pel, who lingered near with tears on his cheeks. "You are a father," I said. When it appeared Pel would drop the little bundle, I took the baby from him, and I put it on Shanika's breast. She lifted her hand to his precious head, and smiled weakly.

"Pel, please hurry to alert Mark, and tell him her bleeding will not be stanched."

He left quickly and returned with Mark, who examined Shanika and the child. "He is a healthy boy." The baby let out a lusty cry.

"His name is Ramen, but we will call him Ram." Pel held his swaddled son. His brow furrowed with worry. "Shanika?" Pel asked with a quavering voice.

"We must wait and see. She has lost too much blood." Mark's voice was deep and unemotional. He applied cool cloths to her body and put a rolled rug beneath her legs to elevate them. Tiny Ram soon slept on her breast. His dark bristly round head looked like a little ball of black goat hair in the midst of the white swaddling cloth and coverings.

Pel and I stayed with Shanika for a day and night, barely eating. She died in spite of our best efforts. I felt devastated with grief, but I had to go on.

We found a wet nurse for Ram. He brought joy to the inn and thrived under my care. As time went on, I kept up with Ram, a healthy toddler who was playful and curious about his surroundings. Pel tried hard to be a good father, and had achieved a reputation as an excellent baker. We managed the inn, serving meals regularly, but had few overnight visitors.

My life was full, and I continued to help many people. But at night when all became quiet, I still had a restless desire to see Jesus and Mary. Was it mere curiosity, or did my faith, however skeptical, once more knock on the door of my soul? I tried to imagine how the Baby Jesus had turned out as a young man. When would He make himself known to the whole world?

During the ensuing years, I often went at night to a quiet place in the courtyard where I gazed in awe at the star-filled skies and felt the peace and comfort of the Messiah. I heard rumors Jesus associated with a man who lived in the wild and dressed in rough skins. We had heard of such a man from travelers. I wondered if it was the same John they had talked about. A band of rowdy fishermen followed Jesus the Teacher everywhere. Perhaps it could be another man. I thought Jesus would have grown up in a more mannerly way. Joseph and Mary were respectable, upstanding people. No, it must be another person with the same name. He would most likely be helping Joseph in the carpentry shop, and be learning to take over his father's business.

One day as I was mending linens, I heard a knock at the back door. Supposing it to be a neighbor, I did not rise to answer it, but called out, "Door is open. Please come in."

I looked up from my work to see Benjamin standing there. I squinted at him in disbelief. His face looked round beneath the full gray-streaked beard, but he appeared to stand more erect and more mature in his goat hair cloak than I remembered. I had recently finished my morning hair combing ritual, and my dark hair, with beginning streaks of white, was shining uncovered. We stared at each other for a time before either of us spoke.

"Good day, Hannah." Benjamin reached down to help me up from my floor mat.

"You are strong as an ox, you." I laughed as he pulled me into an embrace. "What brings you here?"

"I wanted to see you." He looked earnestly into my eyes.

"Benjamin, welcome. I am glad you are here." I kept looking at him and casually draped my tan linen scarf over my head. "Come to the table and I will bring you wine. I have much to tell you. And I want to hear about you and everyone. Is Mother Lydia well?"

"Yes, she is still with us, yet takes to her bed now and

then. As for me, I have little to tell. My life has been much the same. Day after day, year after year, I mind the flocks. I go where food and water is available for them and when it has dwindled, or weather changes, I wander to grassier places. You know the story. You were with us once."

Benjamin followed me as I went to the kitchen for wine and flatbread. I placed the items on a wood table and I motioned for him to sit. Then young Ram burst into the room excitedly, blurting, "Someone is here. A flock of sheep is in the stable and a brown herding dog is minding them."

"Truly? Ram, come and meet my brother-in-law, Benjamin bar Cleodan. I told you about him, but now I shall tell him of you." Ram stared warily at him, while Benjamin checked a bemused smile.

"Ram is Pel's son. His mother became ill during his birth and passed away." I lowered my voice. "My Ramen died years ago, a few moons after you accompanied us here. I meant to come back to see all of you, but many things happened in between. I am raising Ram."

"It was nice to meet you. May I please leave now?" Ram tapped his bare foot. "There are jugglers and dancers in town. Josh and Matt are going to see them and I want to go too, please."

"You may go, but first put on your sandals and wash your face."

"I cannot find my sandals."

"They are right where you left them." I took Ram's

hand and pulled him to the back doorway. "You are fortunate I allow you go out at all, as dense as you are."

I sighed and plopped down on the bench, taking a big gulp of wine from my cup.

Benjamin chuckled. "For one who was barren, you are quite a mother. I understand at this age boys give nothing but trouble unless you keep them busy working from sunup to sundown."

"He is spoiled. His father tries, but remembers nothing but enslavement from his youth, and wants an easier life for his son than he had. Therefore, I have to be careful how much work I ask the boy to do."

"Work would be good for the boy. Remember young Benjamin, the spoiled one? Now, one could say I have been a slave to sheep most of my life." We sat quietly drinking wine and finally he cleared his throat. "I have not married."

"Oh, well, what shall I say? Were there no girls?" I continued to gaze into my wine cup as though an interesting morsel floated inside of it. I was certain he had not come here to pay a casual visit.

"No, I want none of them. I need you." Benjamin rose from the bench, stood behind me, and put his hands on my shoulders. "In my old age, I came here to ask you to come with me and be my wife. I have been to Bethlehem two times in the past twelve years. I listened to people in the village talking and I heard Ramen died. I thought the child was yours at first as I heard him call to you on market day once. And I saw you with him. My courage failed as I have feared you would reject me. We know each other, Hannah, in spite of the years we have been apart. We grew up together, and now more than ever I need you, and I think you need me." He stood gently holding my shoulders.

"I have to think." His proposal surprised me. Many years had passed. My face flushed with excitement at the thought of comfortable companionship, but more people must be considered. I looked up at him. "At almost ten, Ram is not old enough to be on his own, in spite of his wanting freedom at every turn. He began his lessons with the local rabbi, but no bar mitzvah will be celebrated on his birthday. The rabbi insisted the boy is smart enough, but slow to learn. While I protested, Pel allowed Ram to stop his lessons."

"I wonder how well he would do herding sheep." Benjamin laughed. "Remember what a lazy lad I was?" He walked around the table and sat across from me. "If the boy is the only thing standing in your way, would Pel let us have him for a time?"

Pel cleared his throat loudly and we both looked up. "Did I hear my name?"

"Yes," Benjamin said firmly. "Please pour more wine and come sit here."

Pel did as he was told and sat stiffly at the table.

"You were listening to our conversation?" I felt flushed beneath my scarf. The scent of browned meat, bread, and ripe fruit emanated from the kitchen and curled around my nose.

Pel looked away, embarrassed. "I meant no harm. Can you forgive me?" He stood.

"Sit down," Benjamin commanded. "Now, listen to me. I want to marry Hannah, and I do not require your permission. Hannah became rightfully mine when my brother died many years ago. Yet in all that time, I have never forced her to be with me as I have great respect for her. And I have tried to think of those she loves. At our advanced age, both of us have to consider comfort and companionship."

After a long silence Pel looked at me. "Hannah, I am your servant. I know you say Ram and I are free, but I know nothing except service. Wherever you wish to go, we will go with you."

I composed myself and sipped the dark purple wine thoughtfully. "How well do you think you could handle a herd of sheep?"

"I could try." He was wide-eyed, grinning a lopsided smile.

A broad smile filled Benjamin's face. "You may leave now, Pel. Please go to the stable and check on my dog and sheep."

When we were alone, I looked at Benjamin. "If I go with you, many details must be worked out. What shall we do with the inn? Ramen had no heirs or relatives. The Roman government thinks I make more money than I do and regularly harasses me about taxes. Were I to leave, they would simply confiscate it, the community oven, and the well. That would be bad for the neighbors."

"Umm." Benjamin rubbed his beard thoughtfully.

"Simon, my old neighbor, is a good man. He almost never takes guests unless they are traveling relatives. Perhaps he would be happy to oversee the public oven and the well and use the inn as an overflow during festivals."

"You have changed, Hannah. Always the impulsive one before, now you must work out all the details."

"Years of responsibility tend to have such an effect. How can you come here and ask me to change my life?" I had not yet agreed to go home with him.

"Think about the rest of your life." He rose and walked toward the doorway. "Speaking of forcing a woman…many years back, Ham was caught with a young girl. Her father, along with a council of men, drove him into the desert and came back without him. He has never returned."

"Oh. Thank you for telling me." I was glad Ham had finally received full measure of the pain he had inflicted on my husband Judah and me. "Ham managed to wander off to Egypt. He died fighting for the Romans who had captured him."

"Oh, I suppose you hear a lot of stories here from travelers." He paused, and turned to face me again. "I care for you deeply, Hannah."

"I must think, please excuse me as I have much to do." I avoided the issue, of course. I rose, brushed crumbs from the table, gathered our goblets, and took them to the kitchen. I continued outside to the oven, toting bread loaves ready to be baked. The day was glorious with warm earth at my feet and gentle breezes kissing my scarf and face. It was such a routine. I felt torn. I loved this place, yet hated the thought of the emptiness I would have when young Ram would be old enough to leave. While men rarely went to the wife's family at marriage, I hoped he would break tradition, and bring a bride and run the inn when he grew old enough.

Benjamin would provide for me in my old age. I knew I could count on him. While the older generation I had known was mostly gone, many of the people I had been raised with were still with the encampment. I would also be going home to care for Mother Lydia. In recent years, I had at times regretted leaving Father Moshe and Mother Lydia to pursue my life of searching for the Messiah and all that had happened as a result. Much of my life had been spent caring for others. I regretted I had not seen the Messiah after swaddling Him at His birth. Now He would be a grown Man. What would He be like, I wondered? Was He still wearing the seamless cloak I had woven and sent to Mary for Him? Had the gossip been true He had become an outspoken young Man with a rough band of fishermen following Him? Poor Mary. If Jesus had turned out thus, had she been deluded thinking He was God's son? Had I believed in a mirage?

I removed a batch of nicely browned flat bread from the oven. The aroma floated through the air. I slid Pel's loaves into the oven to bake and stood up. Simon came and I greeted him.

"Good day. I came to take those out, thank you. Sim

was too busy and I feared the bread would burn." His hair had become white and Simon walked with a limp. It was difficult for him to bend over the oven, as his back was painful from years of hard work. Sim had married, moved in with Simon, and was learning to be an innkeeper.

"I had to put the bread Pel had made in to bake. I would have carried your loaves to you." I wondered how to begin the conversation about the possibility of leaving. "How is young Sim these days?"

"Ah, his wife is with child. They are fortunate to have a neighbor such as you."

"How wonderful." I wondered if now would be a good time to mention I might leave this place. "I am getting up in years. There are other midwives."

"Nonsense. You are the best and we will insist on the best." He loaded his bread loaves onto a woven willow tray. A sheep bleated from the stable. "Your shepherd brother has returned, I see."

"Yes, he is here." I nodded.

"Has he finally come to claim you?" I could rely on Simon to be insightful. Perhaps Pel or young Ram had been speaking with him.

"Yes, but I am undecided what to do." I looked down, avoiding his eyes.

"How does your heart direct you?"

"I…I am not sure." The breeze halted, and the warm air caused me to perspire.

"What would you do about the inn?"

"The inn? Close it, I suppose, or if Pel stayed he could

turn it into a bakery." I spoke hesitantly at first, and then my words tumbled out in a rush. "But I would want you and your family to manage the oven and the well."

"I am getting up in years." He smiled.

"Nonsense. You are my best choice and I insist on the best."

Simon chuckled at my mimicking him, and then sobered. "I do not want you to leave, but you must do whatever is right for you. Each of us has a number of days on this earth. I grieved far too long over the death of my wife and never married again. Perhaps I should have. Yet, I have young Sim, my nephew, and his wife Kalah to keep me company in my old age. What more could I want?"

"You have family. That is the most important thing."

I walked to the stable and found Benjamin with his sheep. His back was to me, and he reminded me of a boulder in his tan robe. His dog rose as I approached and then settled back down with a hand signal from Benjamin, who had turned to see who came. "Hannah, have you thought about…?"

"As I said earlier, I must have time to sort everything out in my mind. People need me here. A neighbor is expecting a child and requests my attendance to midwife soon. Right now I simply cannot go. Can you understand?"

"Yes, I suppose." Benjamin sounded dejected. "These sheep have to be grazed. Otherwise I would stay on until I could convince you to travel with me. I will come again."

Heat penetrated my entire body as we stood ceremoniously kissing cheeks and holding each other at arm's length. "Go with Yahweh, Benjamin." My life seemed like a weaving. Choosing the colors for the weft had to be done carefully for the fabric of my life to turn out in the best possible way. I wondered what choices I had.

"Hannah, we have a guest," Pel called to me. "He looks like a rabbi."

CHAPTER TWENTY-FOUR

bram sat at a table when I hurried in. I stopped, surprised and in awe of his almost regal appearance. His blue talit was loosely draped about his shoulders as though it was a natural part of him. *Tefilin* dangled from its edges. He wore a *yarmulke* on his head, and curled sidelocks framed his face. The last time I had seen him was the day on the trail long ago when I was intent on finding Mary after she had fled to Egypt.

When he saw me, he stood and we kissed cheeks and embraced as old friends. I wondered at his sudden appearance at the inn. "Abram." I felt almost overwhelmed by his spicy scent. "Welcome to Hawara Inn. Please sit, I will pour you a drink."

"Thank you." Abram nodded and sat on a bench by a table. Pel brought wine and fresh bread, bowed slightly, and rushed off.

"What brings you to Bethlehem? Have you time to visit?"

"I traveled in the near area and I heard you were here. I remembered the night long ago when we looked at stars with Mary. Do you?"

"I have never forgotten. Another star appeared the night I was at Mary's side when she had the Baby. But surely you did not come here to reminisce. Please enjoy the wine." Even though social custom would frown upon my sitting alone and talking with a man, I felt at ease with Abram, as a rabbi and friend.

He tipped the wine cup to his lips. "I believe the young man is in danger."

"Mary's son Jesus?"

"Yes. The Pharisees and others say He blasphemes. They say He set Himself up practically as God. I fear unless He stops speaking and behaving that way He will be arrested." Abram's brow creased.

"So the rumors are true?" The stale air lay heavily around me despite an open door and window.

"Truth can be elusive. Yet time will reveal it. He has done miraculous things. He heals people with a touch of His hand, they say. Food for a multitude of people showed up when He blessed a few fish and loaves of bread. Talk about the area is He fed thousands who had come to hear Him. They say He even raised his friend Lazarus from the dead. Only God knows how or if He accomplished a resurrrection."

"Raised from the dead? Have you seen any of these

miracles? That is even more than I have heard." I nervously smoothed my tunic.

"No, I personally did not see any of those miracles, but my friend Joshua saw Him heal a young girl, actually bring her back to life."

"Oh, my. How is Mary taking all this?" Being a healer, I felt skeptical. People did faint away and then recover. I remembered Mary's words from years ago as she said she would give birth to the Messiah, and I knew she must be anxious for her Son's safety. I wondered if His mystical powers indeed proved He was the Son of God.

"She is worried about the threats against Him. In Nazareth, they led Him to a cliff and would have shoved Him off and stoned Him, but He disappeared into the throng unharmed."

"I am glad He endured no stone injuries. Does He have brothers or sisters?" Of course God's Son would not be slain.

"Oh, that is another story. Joseph has died and Jesus's place is rightfully at home taking over the carpentry shop, but His bench sits idle while He roams about. You can imagine what His brother James must think about being abandoned in favor of a bunch of fisherman. Mary is at peace about the carpentry even if James is not."

"What can I do?" I wondered.

"Who knows? His ears are deaf to the family and the Pharisees."

"Excuse me, Abram, I must see to the kitchen." Confused, I leaned on the counter and closed my eyes to think. I felt troubled and disturbed hearing Jesus disrespected the wishes of His father and mother. Yet Mary knew her Son would grow up to be so much more than a carpenter. The miracles showed, perhaps proved He was the Messiah, or at least a very special person. I came back to sit with Abram. Deep inside I felt bad for neglecting to look for Mary all these years. "I am sorry, please forgive me for the interruption." I sat once more.

"That is all right. I am truly unsure what we are to do." He looked directly at me. "He is headstrong, He is very kind to everyone, yet He has neglected His family. Mary said you were the first hands to touch Him, and you swaddled Him in a cloth you had made. You have been quite an influence."

"Me important to Jesus? I am sure not." I sat there humbled, and truly unworthy. A light air freshened my surroundings. I gulped the purple liquid and fidgeted with my scarf. "Way back when I was a girl Mary told me she would bear the Messiah. At that time, I thought both of us would enjoy being greatly reknown all over Judea. People for all time would remember me, the lowly shepherd girl, midwife who touched him first. To even be there, much less be rewarded for what I did, is an unbidden thought to me. I cannot begin to tell you how many times I let other things hinder me in heeding the Voice in the wind as it persisted through the years, and told me to go seek Mary."

"I think you could help my cousin Mary." Abram looked directly at me with eyes that attempted to penetrate into my soul. I said nothing at first, and he looked away.

"It has been such a long time. What could I do for her?"

"She needs a friend who will listen to her and understand her worries and fears as well as her joys."

"I wonder if she still remembers me."

"She does. You are a blessing, Hannah, a healer of many and a weaver of life. When Jesus was twelve, I believe you managed to send Him a seamless robe you had woven. He still wears it proudly. While you may not have been aware of it, your life has been interwoven with Mary and her Son, the weft and warp bound together to create a wonderful tapestry."

"You are wrong. I am a poor weed, grown in the desert among people who herd flocks of sheep and goats. While I am honored by it, I cannot believe you would even think to visit me."

"Hannah, I am no better than you. We are all equal in God's sight. Please think about what I said. Mary needs you." He stood. "I must be going now."

"Thank you for coming." I pondered on the thought. How might I help Mary and what must I do?

After we kissed cheeks and he left, I went back to the kitchen. Pel should have begun making the food for the evening meal. I stoked the fire and put on a kettle of salted water for fish, and then I went to my room and stared at my weaving loom. I vowed to finish setting the warp threads the next morning light. The spun balls of flaxen thread waited in my reed basket. Dust motes stirred as I handled them.

The day had been too full. First Benjamin had come and proposed, then gone on his way. Now Abram had arrived to request I go befriend Mary. My head reeled. I was at a split in the road as I had been the day on the trail when I brought Ramen home and had stopped where Benjamin camped. I had two different courses to take. Unlike the message delivered by a Voice in the wind, this time it had been delivered by Abram, a human being. What did the heavens have in store for me now?

Pel rushed in, rubbing his face on his sleeve. "Ram got in a fight." Pel worried about anything where his son was involved.

I went to him, and held his shaking shoulders in a side embrace. At first he could not speak, so I waited. "Is he hurt?"

"A few scrapes, but mostly his pride." Ram came limping in as Pel spoke. He had an angry furrow on his brow.

"Who did this?" I motioned for Ram to sit on a bench and left the room to find cleaning cloths and an herbal salve.

"Peter and I got in a huge squabble about who was the strongest, and we wrestled to find out," Ram yelled to me from the next room.

"So?" I asked.

"He did not fight fair."

"So Peter got the best of you. I will speak to him about fighting fairly," Pel said.

"He called Amos to fight with him, and then they defeated me."

"I will talk with the fathers." Pel frowned, and kept his own anger under control.

"What now?" I asked the heavens, as I felt myself being tugged in yet another direction raising this active boy who would soon become a man.

CHAPTER TWENTY-FIVE

I sat at the loom continuing to weave the linen cloth. I looked at my work from time to time and admired the evenness of the yarns I had spun and was now weaving into a plain length of cloth. The flax had come from a traveling tradesman who had bartered for food and lodging. It felt good to be sitting in the warm sunlight of the morning doing what had come natural to me through the years. I smiled, remembering how as a young girl my first efforts had yielded tangled, and broken threads and tears. In my imagination I saw Mother Lydia who cared for me, often saying, "My girl, it is no matter. You are learning and soon you will be proud of your work." I must go to her. She had been a good mother and I hoped I did as well for Ram.

Sometimes I still experienced the abiding presence of purity and goodness I had known the night the

Messiah was born. Abram had brought me troubling and conflicting news of Mary and Jesus. The day he came I had felt an urge to make the long journey to Nazareth, but had not acted on it as it had been the day Pel and Ram truly needed me.

The incident with Ram and his friends had been settled amicably. Pel spoke with the boys' fathers. One of the fathers told Pel that boys always fight no matter what, and fathers ought to refrain from getting in the middle. I suggested the boys and fathers meet together. The result was the boys were admonished not to put two against one, and to settle quarrels without resorting to rough fights.

Not long afterward, Benjamin came back to see me. Without any fanfare except to let me know he had come into the room he said, "Hannah, you look well."

"I am happy to see you." We kissed cheeks. I walked with him to a bench where he sat. I went to the kitchen for wine, poured our cups and sat with him.

"I want to see you every day." Benjamin looked up at me with pleading eyes. "I have come to claim you as my wife."

"Benjamin." I could not rebuff him yet again. "Is Mother Lydia well?"

"Lydia is still alive, but now hardly moves from her bed."

"Oh, I feel badly for her. Does anyone look after her?"

"The women try, but they have their own home concerns."

"Then I must go to Mother Lydia." I thought carefully

before making my decision. I had been thinking about it for a while. I immediately made ready to leave. Mother Lydia needed me to take care of her. Sometimes the right thing to do is presented at the right time. It was time for me to become Benjamin's wife.

Pel and Benjamin helped me close the inn, and we placed it under the care of Simon and his family. Pel and Ram came with us, and Ram was eagerly looking forward to an adventure-filled life as a nomad. My sadness about leaving the inn was buried in preparation for the journey and my sense of duty to my mother. Much to Ram's disappointment, nothing much happened on the trip.

Young Ram had rebelled when we first got to the shepherd encampment, sulking belligerently when asked to mind the sheep with Benjamin and Pel. One day he simply quit complaining and rose up with the dawn to help. I saw him carrying a new lamb. It was one he had watched being born. New life had a way of inspiring people. "Ram." I waved to him. He was becoming a handsome youth, with a high forehead and jet-black hair he drew into a band at the nape of his neck. He grinned with his whole face and freed his left hand to wave back. When he did, the lamb leaped to the ground. He scooped it up in a cuddle, laughing.

I took care of Mother Lydia who was filled with joy at my return, saying, "My girl, you are a good daughter." I rearranged the covers around her to make her comfortable thinking I should have come sooner to care for her after Father Moshe had died. Her mind often wandered into the past, and she looked for Father Moshe. I patted her hand and listened to her, as it did no good to correct her illusion.

Back in my element, I tended the sick and assisted mothers as they gave birth. I once again had popularity and respect among my people. Abram's words still haunted me, and I heard those words in the night wind, "Mary needs you."

Benjamin sat and sipped wine with me one evening. "You are doing well here, and I think your mother is getting healthier having you care for her."

"Mother Lydia is doing better than I expected. The simple life suits me well, yet I do miss the activity and social life of the inn."

"Would you want to come along next time I go to Jerusalem to trade goods? Several of us are going and I thought you might enjoy visiting the marketplace." Jerusalem was the nearest city and the place Benjamin would go to trade, bringing wool, woven materials, rugs, pelts, and goat cheese. It would be near Passover when many travelers would be there.

"I would love to go. Meda, who abides right next to Mother Lydia's tent, has been helping me with her. She will do well as she was taking care of her before I came home." My excitement rose at having an opportunity to be among more people. I wondered if Mary would be there, because I still wanted to see my friend after all these years.

Donkeys were laden with all manner of items to be traded or sold. Our jugs of drinking water and wine were secured on either side. I folded and packed a length of fine woven cloth to trade. I felt peaceful walking next to Benjamin. He carried a pack on his back filled with cheese. I had small flasks of herbal oils and wine tied to my waist. Pel trailed behind with the others who were minding the donkeys. Shepherds were chanting in unison as they walked. It was a joyful sound and a lovely bright, breezy day. We camped at night, and continued on the trail for many more days.

CHAPTER TWENTY-SIX

As we neared Jerusalem, the pleasant atmosphere changed suddenly when we heard a terrible din in the distance. We wondered fearfully what was happening in the city. We all slowed our pace. A group of men turned back and were shaking their heads, and some wandered aimlessly, unsure of what to do. One said, "We picked the wrong time to come here."

"Should we stop and wait until we know what is going on?" I looked at Benjamin.

"How would one understand it, Hannah? What do you think?"

I merely nodded, because I had no knowledge of what was happening. I kept walking slowly, reluctant to stop when we were so near. Our natural curiosity moved us forward despite our misgivings about what might be ahead. When we entered the city gates many soldiers marched the streets, and roughly pushed people with menacing clubs.

"Move, get out of the way." A soldier threatened to shove Benjamin and others who led donkeys. One prodded me with a light tap of his club, and gave me a leering smile. I looked away and shrugged it off, because a few shepherds were no match for the Roman soldiers. People were milling around, speaking in high spirits. "He incited people to rebel against Herod," a man yelled. "He blasphemes."

"Make way!" The soldiers shouted. The air, which had been beautiful and sunny, became stifling and still as we walked into the town. Clouds festered overhead. It was spring, yet the heat was intense like a blast coming out of an opened oven. People were tense and angry. Mothers called children to come inside. Men carried on rumbling arguments. I wondered what happened in the city to create such chaos. The mood seemed ominous, and I looked to the heavens to see if a storm hovered on the horizon. A noisy mob roared down the main thoroughfare. The temple stood majestically, a silent sintinel watching everything.

"He would overthrow the government," a white bearded man said.

"The man has a lot of gall. He thinks he's God." A young man laughed derisively. "One of His own followers told the authorities where He stayed."

I wondered who the hated man could be. Benjamin grabbed my hand and led me and our donkey down a side lane. "We do not want to be in the middle of this." I realized while I had been mesmerized by the scene, Pel and the others had fled down side streets and had disappeared from view.

Men told us they could see in the distance three prisoners being led to Golgotha outside of the city. The convicted men wore nothing but loincloths, and were being goaded with whips as they stumbled. Benjamin tugged at my arm, but I froze, shocked by the words I heard.

I had a deep foreboding and sadness. My chest was constrained as if a tight band encircled it. I flashed back to Bethlehem where I had first gone at an angel's bidding. Suddenly I had a vision, which brought chills to my being and the hair on my arms prickled. I looked at Benjamin. "I must go there. Mary needs me."

"Why would Mary be there? I don't understand what you mean. Why would you want to be nearby and watch the gory crucifixion of these criminals? I have heard they are thieves and murderers. One is the despised despot who planned to overthrow the government. What if one were to break away and take people with him? The soldiers could kill without hesitation. No, Hannah, please stay by my side for protection." He held firmly onto my arm.

"What are their names?"

"Barabbas is one, but I think they have decided to let him go. And the political criminal is being taunted as King of the Jews."

"Oh, no." I barely breathed, hoping this man was not Mary's son. I thought of Abram's words. I pulled free of

Benjamin's grasp, leaving him to call after me as I took off running with the crowd toward the outskirts of town. I saw a young man walking hurriedly. He appeared as one I remembered. All at once I thought of the other baby I had delivered the day before the Messiah. This young man looked much the same as the father Iscariot. He staggered the way one would when drunk. "Pilate should have freed Him," he screeched in a high pitched voice.

I was jostled and shoved, but I pushed back and finally one criminal who carried His wooden cross piece came into closer view. People were jeering and hissing, and rowdy boys threw dried dung. His back bled where He had been striped unmercifully by a murderously pronged whip. On His head He wore a mean crown of thorns. Blood trickling down His face added to the red stripes as they meanly cursed His back. Blood drips that had the appearance of rose petals marked where He walked. Weakened, He stumbed as He carried the weight alone. Then He fell to His knees on the stone walk and the guards yelled at Him to stand up, with clubs raised, menacing.

Out of the crowd came a well-dressed man whom they asked to lift the cross piece and help the Man to His feet. He continued carrying it on the ascent to Golgotha, the hill where executions would take place. I heard a woman say, "He is Simon of Cyrene." I had been bound up by the scene, and I had not noticed him before.

Women were wailing and beating their breasts in agony as they walked along, following the procession. At first I thought my eyes were playing tricks on me, but then I knew. My attention was drawn to a woman overcome with weeping. A thin man dressed in a plain torn robe helped her along the road. I elbowed my way through the crowd to where she walked, being held up by friends. I kept going until I stood next to her.

"Mary?" I truly hoped I was wrong. Although her face was almost covered by a scarf, I recognized her. "I am Hannah."

"Hannah, my friend," Mary sobbed, bent over with grief. "Oh, Hannah, see what they have done to Him." We embraced quickly, and then were shoved forward by throngs of people. "When He grew tall enough for it to fit, He proudly wore the garment you made. Now it is in the hands of the soldiers who will no doubt rip it to pieces."

"Or cast lots for it." The young man beside Mary nodded gravely. I thought perhaps he was another son as he treated Mary as his mother, guiding her expertly through the crowd.

Mary quietly said, "Hannah, this is John, a follower and best friend of Jesus. And, John, this is Hannah, my friend and my midwife at the birth of Jesus."

John nodded. Grief creased his brow.

A dark blue-gray cloud hung ominously overhead. The whole world was weighed down. We were silent while I held her icy hand as we walked. With a heavy heart, I experienced the pain Mary endured at the torture her son had suffered and the agony he would continue to undergo until he died on the cross. Some devotees threw themselves to the dust and tore their tunics, wailing. We had made it to the summit, and now stood in the inner circle as the soldiers nailed the three prisoners to crosses. Upright posts stood waiting ominously. Mary the wife of Cleopas, and Mary Magdalene came and stood with us. I supposed they were relatives or close friends of Mary. The crowd quieted to a murmur as people held their breath as one and watched the gruesome scene. I felt ill, a burning sensation in my throat and stomach. I could not bear to look up.

Then all three crosses were erect, and prisoners moaned and cried out for mercy, but Jesus suffered in silence at first. I hoped He was truly God's Son, and He would not die. Perhaps Jesus would disappear as Abram had said He had done the time He had been driven to a cliff to be stoned. They now put a banner above His head, "Jesus of Nazareth, the King of the Jews." A man yelled out, "He saved others. He is unable to save Himself." They derided Him, "If you are the Son of God, come down from the cross." A din of human voices sounding like a bee swarm filled the air.

He looked with pity on the people around Him. His eyes locked upon His mother and disciple John. I stood behind them, but I could see the kind eyes of the Baby I had held who was now a grown Man nailed to a cross. He bore His punishment with dignity. Jesus looked down at Mary, "Woman, John will see to you the way he would his own mother." Then He looked at John. "Here is your mother." If she had other sons, I wondered where they were. Perhaps they stayed away out of fear for their lives.

Mary looked up to her Son and smiled even with tears in her eyes. Then she bent in uncontrollable sobbing. John tightened his arm around her shoulders for support. "He is such a good Son. Even as He is dying He is looking after my care. Now His Father is calling Him home."

"What do you mean?" I felt exhausted, and wondered how Mary could talk calmly.

"He was only given to me for a short time to raise, not to keep for myself. When He was twelve He told Joseph and me that He had to be doing his Father's business." She stood straighter and dried her tears on a cloth. John released his hold, but stayed next to her.

I looked up, mesmerized. He had become all I had hoped for Him, a strong, kind, and impressive man who had performed miracles. Now He was dying. I had known at His birth and all these years He was truly God's Son, even though I had doubted it at times. His spirit had always been my guide. I felt perplexed. It made no sense to me. Why would He allow himself to stay on a cross?

He spoke again. "I thirst." The guard took a sponge full of wine vinegar, attached it to a branch of hyssop, and pressed it to His lips.

My thoughts were reflected when John intoned, "His kingdom is not of this world."

I wondered why I had been denied seeing Jesus all these years. Obstacles had gotten in my way. It seemed I was always caring for other people. When I looked at Him

Jesus spoke to me without words. In my spirit, I heard Him say as I had done it for the least of these people I had done it for Him. Weeping now, almost uncontrollably as I watched the suffering, I put my arm around Mary's waist to support her, and she did the same for me. We grieved together. Jesus ministered to the bandits who were taunting Him as they hung on crosses on either side of him. It was difficult to hear above the murmur of the crowd. In a brief lull of quiet Jesus said, "Today you will be with Me in Paradise." He was on the center cross looking at a fellow who hung on a cross next to His. Pain filled his countenance and dried blood made reddish brown tears line his cheeks. I wondered why Yahweh would allow His Son to be put through this torture. Then I heard Jesus again.

"My God, my God, why have you forsaken me?" He cried out in a voice strong enough for the stunned throng of people to hear. And then His head relaxed. The earth beneath our feet shook with a violent quake. A deathly silence occurred for a few moments. Then people scurried away, leaving only the most devout lingering near the crosses. I stayed for a long while near Mary. We both kept looking up in disbelief, hoping we would see Him move or hear Him speak.

As Mary wept silently beside me, I remembered the precious linen cloth I had woven and carried in my pack. Wordlessly, I handed the length of white cloth to Mary. We embraced, and she said, "Thank you Hannah. We will wrap Him in this."

"I have no myrrh for His body. Shall I go buy the burial spices?" I prepared to search in all the shops until I found them if necessary.

"No, I have taken care of everything to do with His burial. We only lacked the shroud you made," said a richly dressed gentleman. He took the cloth Mary handed to him, and pressed a money bag into my hand. "Please accept payment for your excellent work. Her family is hidden away as they may be in danger, and they did not want to watch Jesus's crucifixion." I tried to put the sack of money back into his hand, but he turned and hurried away, disappearing into the crowd.

I stood alone as they ushered Mary off to wait with her close friends, and I looked with deep sorrow on Jesus. When I turned to walk back toward the streets to look for Benjamin, I saw the young man I had recognized as possibly Judas of Iscariot. He was running toward the guards who were at the foot of the cross playing some sort of game. Then I saw the garment stretched on the ground before them as they were casting lots for it. Judas slowed as he ran past, and our eyes locked as I saw his deep distress. I remembered the strange dream I had the night he was born and wondered if the son of Iscariot had betrayed Jesus. He stepped up to the guards, threw money at them and charged away. I wondered why Judas ran in a circle back toward where I was walking and I heard him mutter, "I cannot live! Why did I heed those guards who offered me blood money to deceive Him?" I looked out among the people, anxiously searching for Benjamin.

He finally came to me from the thinning crowd. "There you are, and not trampled by the hordes. I had hoped you did not go to Golgotha." He looked at my tear-stained face. "Oh, Hannah, I am so sorry. Pel watched you from afar and told me you were with a woman who may have been related to one of the men being executed."

"All too tragic and horrible, but I did what I was destined to do." I collapsed against Benjamin, sobbing. To comfort me, he gently stroked my head for a short while. The air had become fogged and dark and I tried to make sense of the day, to return to what I could comprehend. "Did you sell the woolens and cheese?"

"People in the street bought them, and I traded with merchants in the marketplace who were anxious to finish before the Sabbath." Our donkey was laden with a fresh supply of wheat grains and other household goods. Benjamin put his arm around me and guided me away. "Let us go back to the hillsides to attend our flocks."

As we walked on the rutted street dejected, and saddened beyond grief, I failed to be mindful of where I put my feet. Suddenly, I tripped on a stone and fell to the rough earth. Benjamin helped me stand, but my ankle swelled in pain. He helped me sit down next to a post.

"Rest here for awhile." He reached for his flask to offer me wine.

"My ankle is strained." I felt foolish for stumbling. I drank the wine and breathed in the dusty air in the gloom that settled around us.

"People are leaving and I have no more wares to sell. So if you cannot walk I could unload the things I have bought for our use, sell them, and you can ride home."

"No, Benjamin, I am sorry. Please do not make such a sacrifice. We need those supplies."

"Then we will pitch a tent and stay on the outskirts of town until you can travel," he said.

We stayed for three days near a garden outside of Jerusalem. Early on the third day I heard women coming down the road. Hushed chatter lingered in the air and then wafted off into the distance. A while later I heard excited voices. "He is not in his tomb. The stone has been rolled aside."

Could they be talking about the Messiah's tomb? Was I near there? I rose from my rug, listening. Compelled by something unseen, I followed the pathway to the garden. A pleasant Man of about thirty, dressed in a plain white robe stood before me. He appeared to be infinitely kind and His dark eyes looked into my soul. "Even as your woven cloth has been a part of My life, I have always been with you, Hannah. Does your ankle feel better?"

"Yes, I can walk without discomfort. Did You...?

"Be well, Hannah. I am going to my Father, but I will always be with you and those I love."

I was too awestricken to speak at first when He had addressed me by name. I had seen Him dead, hanging on a cross. Who else would know what I had done for Him? It must be Jesus alive, risen from his death.

"Jesus." I reached out to Him, but He backed

away and disappeared, leaving my hand to feel the air. Why could I not touch Him? I felt awed, excited, and peaceful all at once. I had seen the Messiah, the Son of my friend and Son of God all grown up. While beyond my perception of how it could be, the Messiah was alive, visible fleetingly to me. Though deeply saddened, I felt a tranquility which permeated my entire being and made my whole life worthwhile. Through the miracle of His spirit, I understood I had always been where I belonged helping others. I thought about poor Mary, but I knew that if He had shown me He had risen, surely she had been comforted with his presence too.

"Benjamin, I saw Jesus. He is alive!" I had hurried back to our makeshift skin tent where Benjamin was awake.

"Hannah, you must sup and have a morsel to eat if you are seeing such visions." He eyed me skeptically. "Your halting steps have left you?"

"Truly, Jesus is alive, and He healed me. He disappeared before I could touch Him." I wanted to insist that Benjamin believe me, yet I could tell he simply meant to humor me.

"Since you can now walk, we will eat, then go home to tend our flocks."

"All right." Another day I might convince him to believe I had been divinely healed by the Messiah.

EPILOGUE

While my name is unlisted in any historical or scriptural book, my purpose was fulfilled as a weaver of life. The first to touch Jesus, my hands wove His swaddling wrap at birth, His seamless garment for travel, and provided the cloth for His burial. I did not become famous for being the first to touch the Messiah, as I had desired when I was a young woman, but my life has been meaningful and complete. I have lived to an advanced age giving myself to a life of healing as well as proclaiming the Messiah lived, died, and rose to give new life for all of us.

GLOSSARY

Bar mitzvah: A Jewish boy who has reached his thirteenth birthday and attained the age of religious duty. It is the ceremony to recognize the boy as coming of age.

Brit: The word for circumcision in Hebrew is brit, which means "covenant." It is done the eighth day after the boy is born.

Comfrey: From the Latin conferva, meaning to heal; a plant of the genus Symphytum.

Festival of Booths (Sukkot): An agricultural holiday. "You shall live in booths seven days in order that future generations may know that I made the Israelite people live in booths when I brought them out of the land of the Egypt." (Leviticus 23:42-43)

Gilead: The balm of Gilead is a medicine made from the buds of a tree that Americans call the poplar. The region east of the Jordan River was home to Elijah the Prophet as well as the battle scene between Gideon and the Midianites. (Gen.37:25: Jer. 8:22)

Golgatha: Also known by the Latin name Calvarius, which means bald skull. It was the hill outside of Jerusalem on which Jesus was crucified.

Isis: Isis was one of the most important goddesses of ancient Egypt.

Mancala: Any of various games played in Egypt, Africa, and other countries involving competition between two players in the distribution of pebbles or beans into rows of holes or indentations under various rules that permit accumulation of pieces by capture.

Messiah: An expected deliverer or savior of the Jews.

Mikva: The mikva (sometimes pronounced mikveh) is a body of natural water in which a person who has become ritually impure purifies himself or herself by immersion.

Mite: Lepton, the smallest coin, of the least value. Even the metal deteriorated easily.

Orem: Yiddish word for arm.

Passover: Feast of unleavened bread, beginning on the fourteenth day of Nissan and continuing for a week. It was established before the giving of the Law to celebrate the Exodus from Egypt.

Ptolomie: A dynasty of Macedonian kings that ruled Egypt from 323 to 30 BC.

Rabbi: Teacher.

Sabbath: Saturday, the Jewish day of rest.

Shalom: Sometimes sholem. It means peace.

Shomer: Until burial, someone must stand guard beside the deceased. The individual is a shomer or a shomeret if a woman.

Sitar: A guitar with a long neck and varying number of strings.

Slinger: An instrument for throwing stones usually consisting of a short leather strap with two strings fastened to its ends or a string fastened to one end and a light stick to the other that is used by whirling round until on loosing one end the missile is let fly with centrifugal force.

Synagogue: A local assembly for Jewish worship.

Talit: A covering worn by those going to prayer, a fringed shawl.

Tefilin: Phylacteries are leather boxes containing parchment on which there are selections from the books of Exodus and Deuteronomy. "And thou shalt bind them for a sign upon thy hand." (Deut. 6:8)

Torah: The law, or the entire Pentateuch (first five books of the Old Testament) became known as the Torah.

Warp: A series of parallel yarns or threads set up in a loom for weaving or textile processing.

Weft: The weft is the thread or yarn that is carried by a shuttle and is interwoven from selvedge to selvedge with the threads (warp) that have been set up in a loom.

Yahweh: The Hebrew name for God.

Yarmulke: Skullcap.

Sources:

Kolatch, Alfred J. The Jewish Book of Why. New York: Penguin, 2003

The Holy Bible, Authorized King James Version. Charlotte: Bible House, 1961

The New Compact Bible Dictionary. Special Crusade ed., Minneapolis: Bryant, T. Alton

Webster's Third New International Dictionary of the English Language. Chicago: G. C. Merriam Co., 1981

ABOUT THE AUTHOR

E. Ruth Harder

Elsie Ruth Dornbusch grew up on a farm in Uvalde County, Texas. In 1957 she married Charles Harder (deceased 2003). She was a Technical Information Specialist at Lawrence Livermore National Laboratory until retirement. She achieved a Masters in Library Science from San Jose State University in San Jose, California. She says, "Critique groups and workshops of the California Writers Club, Tri-Valley Branch help keep me motivated as I pursue my passion for writing."

Advances in Library Administration and Organization, Vol. 13, 1995, published her work, "Library Automation's Effect on the Interior Design of California Public Libraries." She has written scripture–based puppet scripts performed for children at Sunday morning worship at Holy Cross Lutheran Church in Livermore. Her poem "Widow's Window," is published in the *Voices of the Valley: Encore*, the 2013 California Writers Club Tri-Valley Branch Anthology. "A Light in Every Corner" is in *2014 Word Movers, An Anthology of Creative Writings by Seniors.*

"Daily prayer and Bible studies, my Holy Cross Lutheran Church family, and those at Faith Lutheran Church in Kamiah, Idaho, keep me focused on what is most important in my life, the eternal blessings of the Lord and Savior, Jesus Christ."

CPSIA information can be obtained
at www.ICGtesting.com
Printed in the USA
FSOW01n0748030516
19963FS